MEOW!

by

Jeffrey Plough

DEDICATION

I dedicate this book to my lovely wife, Susi. For the past 25 years, she has tolerated my whims and endeavors, my ups and my downs, and my hobbies. I love her more than ever for just being the beautiful person she is, for being willing to share her life with me. Thank you for being my wife for the past 25+ years.

PROLOGUE

Cameron Robert was a young man from the typical rural Indiana farm family. Since he was very little, the adults around him noted that he was bright and energetic. He was a pleaser and as he grew, could be counted on to do what was right and to always help whenever and wherever needed. He developed an obvious passion for animals and could be counted on to take care of them as though they were his children, his two closest pets was Max, a domestic cat and his dog Ellie, a Norwegian Elkhound. Even as a young man, his desire to assist his family and to nurture the animals at the family farm would become the building blocks for his future. Responsible young men like Cameron eventually become the backbone of our society and he was well on his way toward fulfilling his destiny. As he progressed through his public school years, Cameron's abilities shined and he always performed at the top of his class. As any young man in a rural setting, he developed close friendships, friendships that would come in handy in years to come. Those around him projected a successful future for this young man and eventually his teachers began to notice that his strengths in Chemistry and Biology, along with the known interest in animals, all made for someone destined to become a Veterinarian. Upon graduating from high school, his undergraduate degree, and ultimately his degree in Veterinary Sciences, he became a valued advocate for animals and was prepared to engage in a successful practice and build a life for himself. Everything was on track until one day when he made a revolutionary discovery, one that would change his and the lives of those around him forever. Join Cameron and his family and friends as they travel down the road of intrigue and danger as they combat officials that take advantage of his efforts from his research in treating a feline illness, as they work toward addressing the unanticipated use of his development.

1

HOME

To some, he was an odd young man. To others, he was a young man with a dream. To those who knew him, Cameron Robert was a young man that that cared about animals and his family. Cam, as most everyone close to him called him, had always been drawn to animals for as long as those close to him remember. Growing up on an Indiana farm, his family raised cattle, and of course they had the family dog and the cats that roamed the farm to keep the rodents at bay; something every farm needed. He kept track of the cats particularly and had a name for them all. He loved his dog, Ellie, a Norwegian Elkhound. Such a bright and active dog she was. She always was with someone and was protective but mischievous. You would swear she was a retriever because she loved to go after anything thrown. But it was the cats that he watched over the closest. Max, Sam, Dearfoot, Mouser, and all the four cats would come to Cameron. Most were skidderish of everyone else, avoiding them as though they were out to get them. Everyday Cameron would make sure they all had plenty of water and food. The cats would crawl on him, rub on him to the point where sometimes it looked like he had on a fur coat. Max was the one cat that seemed to always be wherever Cameron was. Although he liked all of the cats, Cameron enjoyed Max's company while doing his chores. The cat would hop up on the railing in the barn and watch him as he cleaned out the stalls; he would sit on the picnic table and watch Cameron has he mowed the lawn, and every morning he would be sitting by the door, waiting for Cameron to come out. The two were buddies and the affection was mutual. Ellie would also accompany him around like Max however she was easily distracted, chasing birds and butterflies. The two animals remarkably were accepting on one another and could be found lying together often. As he grew older, his ability to spend time with them would lessen, but he would make time for them every day. Cats were his true love and everyone knew it. He just seemed the most comfortable around cats. He was like most of the other boys in a number of ways; he grew up playing little league baseball and with the farm, he had a great place to practice, but baseball was not his passion. He did it to just be one of the guys and to also please his father who really liked baseball. As is known around the country, basketball is king in Indiana and was one sport that Cameron liked; you just can't be from Indiana and not like basketball. He found that playing team sports was not something he appreciated. Seeing the pressure that some parents put upon their children to excel, that some of the kids used their talents as a pass toward being treated better or more special, these things were a turn-off to Cameron. Again, to some he was a bit odd, but to more people he was definitely more mature for his age than most of his peers.

He was a curious young boy, always following his father on the farm, asking questions all of the time. Some said he was his father's shadow, but to Cameron, he wanted to be just like his daddy. Orville would get up early every day, like the normal life of a farmer, and Cameron would bounce out of bed right along with him. Cameron wanted to help wherever he could and could be counted on to do whatever his father told him. But just like all young boys, his eagerness sometimes got him into trouble. There was the one occasion where he had become comfortable with feeding the livestock and through this familiarity, had become too comfortable around them. His father would set the cows loose into the field each day for them to graze, after they had been fed in the feedlot with a mixture of range meal and the corn he raised specifically for this purpose. When he was eight, there was one particular cow he had named Elsie. Cam gained a unique interest in her and made certain that she was the first to be fed and that she had plenty to eat. He would talk to her each day and although she was not for show, he would brush her and treat her more like a show animal. Although being raised on a cattle farm, Cameron had never any desire to try and enter competitions showing cattle. He didn't appreciate the process and his father never pushed him into this activity. His comfort in being around these large animals became apparent one day when while brushing her, she inadvertently stepped on his left foot, breaking a couple of his foot. His father, although he loved his son, was frustrated at this mistake and scolded him for his lack of carefulness. Of course Cameron's mother Marjorie had a little discussion with her husband when out of eye shot of Cameron. Later, his father shared with him about a story of him being knocked backwards through a stall by a turning cow one day and upon tripping over some equipment, banging his head on a beam in their barn. The accident left him with a concussion and a chewing out by his dad as well. The two laughed about his mistake and a mutual agreement that things just happen. By the end of the six weeks, his cast looked like something of a big brown sock since he continued to work with the animals.

By the time Cam was ten, he had gained his father's trust in working with some of the farm implements. Orville started by allowing Cameron to ride with him on the tractor and gradually let him drive the tractor. Due to his lack of height, Orville needed to attach a block of wood to each pedal so Cameron could easily depress them as needed. When his father finally allowed him to operate the tractor on his own, it wasn't possible for the boy to have any bigger smile than he displayed. The life of a farmer also required becoming familiar with the repair of equipment and Cameron also was deep into this responsibility. Marjorie's men would come in from working on one of the pieces of equipment and it was not uncommon for Orville to come in relatively clean, but to her dismay, Cameron would come in looking like the had crawled through so much oil, grease and muck that she cringed at how hard it would be to clean his clothes. But ultimately the bond between the two was as close as it ever could be between a father and his son and so Marjorie never said anything about it.

Growing up on a farm was hard work and as he grew, Cameron continued to be there for his father. Up at five AM every morning to make sure the cows and chickens were fed; Cameron would help his father prepare for his day. The chickens that they kept were just to have fresh eggs and so they only had eight or ten chickens at a time. One of the things that Cameron liked to do was to assume the responsibility of selling any of the extra eggs from the chickens and would set up a table by the side of the road. The money he would earn from this typically wound up in his pocket for gums and candy at the grocery store. From an early age, the traits of working hard, doing the right thing, and helping others were values that had become instilled into the young man and he could be counted on to do his share of the work with never a complaint.

Orville, Cameron's father was a kind man, one that most everyone found easy to talk to. He was always the first up and the last to bed; the life of a farmer. The farm had been started by Orville's grandfather and he held it as an honor to be responsible for caring on the family business. He did well in providing for his family and helped his family however he could. He fit the mold of an Indiana farmer; strong, loyal, reverent, and hard-working. Running a farm was hard work but something he loved just as his father before him had. He had been in the Vietnam War and completed two tours, but didn't talk about it. Maybe that Purple Heart he had won was part of the reason; maybe it was the horrors of war, no one really knows and they respected his privacy on the matter. He was a quiet man, but his family meant the world to him; values instilled in him by his parents. He did his best to instill in his children the importance of working hard and in doing a job well as his father had done with him. "If you do it right the first time, you get more done," he was well-known to say. He was a God-fearing man and he and his wife Marjorie would attend church every Sunday. Orville had finished high school before going off to war and one of his goals in life was to see that his children had it better; from an early age, the expectation of a college degree was not a topic of debate and Cameron and his sister Emily knew it.

Cameron's mother, Marjorie was a school teacher and also believed that hard work paid off well in the end as well. She and Orville met when they were young one summer up at Lake Maxinkuckee. Orville's family lived in Culver, Indiana and Marjorie's family would come up there for the summer. Their chance meeting eventually blossomed and upon Orville's return from the war, they married. Marjorie had received her teaching degree from Jones University and was teaching English in one of the local area schools. Her background was one reason why she expected Cameron to do well in this area; maybe that's why Cameron didn't like English class. Boys are kind of that way, you know, sometimes they are a little rebellious and this was Cameron's one area. Boys have to find their own way at times and besides, English was boring and was the one subject he would pass on if he had his choice. Mrs. Robert shared her frustration with Cameron sometimes but she saw that his focus was way was different than hers and began to accept this. Together, both Orville and Marjorie came from close-knit families, which is probably why they expected the same of their family.

Then there was Emily. Emily was Cameron's younger sister, 3 years younger than he. She was bright as well, but being the little sister, she was at times a thorn in his side; she would always want to know what he was doing. When they were young, the two played together frequently, but as they became older; well, Cameron's friends had interests that were more attractively appealing than playing with his little sister. She eventually became a nuisance in his eyes, as she followed him around like a little puppy asking what Cameron thought or what he was doing which was annoying to him. He would try and ditch her, but if either of his parents saw this, he was quickly reminded that this was not acceptable. However he loved her like a big brother should and would do anything for her as he aged; just not as much when his friends were around. He just needed some alone time to work on his projects and spend time with this friends. But as a family, the Midwestern values kicked in and each loved one another.

Cameron had demonstrated that he was a bright young man in elementary school. He was very well mannered and always completed his work on time. He did seem to find math as a relatively easy subject for him and would commonly help some of the others in his class whenever allowed. That was where he began to develop friendships with a couple of other boys in his class, particularly Brian Morgan and Andrew Michael. Brian was a more mischievous than Cameron and he at times would pull him into the fringe of trouble. There was the time when Brian thought it would be neat to shoot paper wads at one of the girls in their class. He would shoot one and then quickly put the straw in his desk, the recipient then being unable to tell who had assaulted her. She would of course report it to the teacher who would scold the whole class and expect the culprit to come forward, but this never happened. Without Cameron knowing it, Brian had placed a straw in his desk and after about a week of this foray, their teacher took it upon herself to inspect the desks one day after class. When Cameron came in the next day, he was called to the Principal's office to explain. Cameron was flabbergasted by this accusation and denied any wrongdoing, but the proof was in the hand of the Principal. Cameron did not want to give his friend up, so he took the punishment for the deed he had not done. Brian took great joy in this; Cameron however took great exception to his on the recess playground while the teacher was not looking by punched Brian in the arm. An unusual thing for Cameron to do, but Brian deserved something for his exploits. His teacher had her belief that Cameron was not guilty, and sometime later, the true perpetrator was discovered, clearing Cameron's name. Considering the additional circumstances to these actions of Brian's his parents were brought into the picture and let's say, upon getting home, it took a little time before Brian could comfortably sit down.

As the years went by, he still had a close-knit group of friends, Brian being the closest. Their parents were friends and farming families as well, so the two grew up together they remained friends through high school. Cameron's family would almost every Friday or Saturday night head down to the Morgan's and play cards until the wee hours of the morning. Cameron and Brian would stay up late and watch the horror movies that played on Sammy Scary's show on Channel four. Sometimes it would scare the liver out of them both and when this happened; they seemed to enjoy watching their parents play cards! Brian was just a couple of months older and less directed that Cameron. Brian, being a farmer's son too, helped with the chores as Cam, living about one-quarter of a mile down the road; his father growing corn and soybeans. This made it easy for the boys to play together and they were commonly found playing Indiana's sport, basketball, out together at one of their barns, but sometimes the two did manage to get into trouble. Nothing really terrible but as boys will be boys, there was a few things that happened that were not forgotten; let's just say memories were made.

There was the time when they were nine where the fascination with fire and gasoline occurred over at the Morgan's. Brian had seen how flammable gasoline was as his father used it routinely to help burn some brush from the farm. Cameron and he was playing one afternoon when it came upon Brian to use the old ketchup bottle his dad kept gasoline in to start fires, to use it for a new purpose. After getting the bottle, Brian thought it would be cool to write his name on the ground with the bottle and then catch it on fire. Brian would spray and Cameron would light the fire with the stick match once the deed was done. Sounded easy enough and it should be safe enough, the two young boys thought. Once sprayed, Cameron quickly lit the match, tossing it on the cement pad next to the barn.

Whoosh! Brian's name lit up like a light switch had been turned on. The two boys laughed and beamed as their experiment continued to burn, the flames flickering in the wind. Something that they had not taken into account however was the wind and the dry grass located nearby their creation. As the wind picked up the flames, a small patch of dry grass began to burn and as it burnt, it began to creep rather quickly toward the barn, fanned by the wind. Both boys watched in horror as the flames kept moving closer and closer to the barn. Brian, stunned, just stood there and looked, kind of frozen for a time. Cameron however, realized that he needed to do something and ran for the garden hose. Turning on the water, he ran toward the flames now advancing dangerously close to the barn, only to find that he could not get completely close enough to easily spray the flames, ending their dash toward the barn. He arched the water stream as high as he could and could not completely cover the burning area. The flames now were reaching the barn and with the yelling and fear emanating from them both, it got the attention on Brian's father who came running over to see what was wrong. Quickly sizing up the situation, Mr. Morgan grabbed a five-gallon bucket, filled it with water from the near trough, and came running over through the stream of water that

Cameron was aiming toward the flames, dousing him thoroughly and then poured it on the grass at the base of the barn. Mr. Morgan was able to effectively control the fire with one more bucket of hastily procured supply of water, to put an end to the inferno with the continued aid of Cameron. Needless to say, Mr. Morgan was not impressed! He surveyed the damage; about a forty foot area of grass that had been burnt toward the barn and a blackened area about one to one and a half feet up from the bottom of the barn. "What were you thinking?" yelled the elder Morgan, looking at the boys angrily as he retrieved another bucket of water to pour at the base of the barn. "What are you standing there for? Grab another bucket and douse the other side of the wall, Brian!" he said. Cameron kept spraying the grass, accomplishing little at this point. "Cameron!" Mr. Morgan said, "Grab a bucket too and get busy! Good Lord!" Finally realizing that he was not accomplishing much of anything, Cameron dropped the hose and ran to the barn for another bucket. "Pour it all around the grass and especially down where the flames we hitting the barn," said Mr. Morgan pointing to where he meant. Once their firefighting efforts were believed to finally be effective, Mr. Morgan said, "Cameron, I'm certain that this was not your idea, am I right Brian," while looking at his son.

Brian, glancing down toward the burnt grass said, "Yes, Dad, this was my idea. Please don't get after Cameron Dad," he said. "I kind of thought so," said Mr. Morgan. "I will decide you punishment once I settle down a bit." "Mr. Morgan," said Cameron. "Yes Cameron?" said Mr. Morgan gruffly. "Brian wasn't alone in this. I lit the gas and am just as much to blame. I'm really sorry!" said Cameron with tears beginning to well up on his eyes. "Me too, Dad!" said Brian. Still with a disgusted look on his face, Mr. Morgan said, "I know boys; I certainly hope you learned something from this." "We did!" both boys chimed in almost simultaneously. In years to come, this story will probably be shared with others, as well as the punishment they received; part of this being the prepping and re-painting of the affected area on the barn. This and many other adventures Brian and Cameron experienced through their childhood, but as time passed, grew somewhat apart due to their different paths. Although this isn't uncommon in life with friends, there remained a connection that if either needed help, the other was there.

Andrew was another of Cam's close friends. These two boys had a little more in common that Brian and Cam did, and so there also was a special connection between the two. Andrew grew up a few miles from the Robert farm;

his father was an engineer with a local corporation and his mother was a nurse who worked in one of the local hospitals. Andrew's father Ron had an observatory at his house; something that he had built himself. The two boys from a relatively early age had learned and listened from Andrew's father about Astronomy. Cameron and Andrew on the other hand did not get into trouble together. Andrew's father was someone that you just did not want to disappoint. His father was well-respected in the community, taught at the local university on the side and was active in their church. Rather than utilize corporal punishment, Ron would let you know he was disappointed and would send Andrew to his room to think about his actions. He would expect that after a time of reflection, that Andrew would come down and explain his error, what it could lead to, and why he would not do it again. There were times where Andrew would have preferred a spanking over the silence of his father. So, not only did Cameron learn the rules of life at home, these were reinforced through Andrew's house as well.

Over time and through the watching of television, the boys played space travelers, heading off to some of the distant planets his father had shown the through the telescope. They enjoyed these activities and unknown to them both; this was the beginning of their interest in science. They also were at times able to assist Andrew's father in some of the work he would perform in his workshop. Andrew's father, being a mechanical engineer, would design and build things in his workshop and would include the two boys. He would further their curiosity and deductive reasoning skills by giving the boys a scenario or two and give them the latitude to work out a solution. Not too involved at first; but he would make these exercises more difficult as they gained more experience and knowledge.

Andrew, like Cameron, did not have much of an interest in sports. They did play on little league teams together while growing up; to be like the other boys their age, but they were not the best players. About the only sport the two played on a somewhat regular basis was basketball. Each boy's ability mirrored the others and they presented each other as worthy opponents. One time at Cameron's house, Cameron was driving to the basket and on the way up, he accidently hit Andrew in the nose with his elbow. Blood began gushing from Andrew's nose and he bent over in pain from the innocent attack. Cameron laughed as he finished the lay-up, knowing that he beat his friend soundly, but he did not realize until he turned around that he had done this in two ways. He rushed over to help him bleeding friend and not knowing what to do, called to his mom for help. Marjorie came out from their back door and on sizing up the situation, grabbed a kitchen towel and ran over to help the injured lad. With a little pinching of the nose and through rubbing some ice over his nose, the bleeding stopped fairly quickly. Cameron was apologizing repeatedly throughout the process of treating his injury and Andrew eventually looked up and said, "Knock it off, Cam. I know you didn't do it on purpose. By the way, nice lay-up!" This was how good friends deal with accidents.

Cameron's time in middle school provided a better understanding of this young man and his abilities. As he progressed through this learning period, Cameron became one of the students that the school faculty used to their benefit. His grades were commonly the highest in his classes, with the exception of English in which he was an average student to the chagrin of his mother. He and Andrew became involved as tutors to assist other students that were experiencing challenges. They would meet with other students during study hall and help with whatever they needed. Each was particularly good at math and science courses, each of these being strong interests for them. These activities helped to cement their relationship and they started working together as a team, using each other's talents to help their classmates.

It was during this time of life; around thirteen was when Orville began to incorporate Cameron more directly into the operation of the farm. "Cam," his father said, "by the time I was your age, I was helping your grandfather with the tilling, planting, and almost everything else. Cam's grandparents had both passed on many years ago and Cameron did not recall them. Lloyd Robert had passed on when Cam was three years old from a heart attack. He like Orville had carried on the family tradition of running the farm. Things were much more manual and self-reliant then than at this time, but the same basic principles of hard work, long hours, and devotion to the needs of the farm will forever remain as the stalwarts farming. Cameron's grandmother, had passed on a couple of years before, right after his birth. She was the devoted farmer's wife and worked as many or more hours than Lloyd to keep the other side of the farming responsibilities running smoothly. As Cameron grew up, he saw the other kids in school being able to experience their grandparents and at times longed for that too. On grandparent's day, Orville would make certain he was there for Cameron.

While in middle school, Cameron became greater exposed to the sciences and particularly found an interest in chemistry. Although the experiments that they performed in class were very basic and rudimentary, Cameron was fascinated at the opportunities this area provided. Whenever he was not tutoring another student, he would be allowed to come up to Mr. Donavan's class to just sit in, and on some occasions, be allowed to help some of the other students struggling. It was amazing to him that so many common everyday things were easily explained through chemistry. This new fascination almost became an infatuation for Cameron. There were a few times where Orville had to get after him to get his chores done. Cameron had always been responsible but this change of direction was frustrating to Orville. "I swear, that if that boy doesn't get his nose out of that chemistry book or quit with his experiments in the barn, for once I might have to tell him to not work as hard at his studies!" he exclaimed to Marjorie. "Now Dad," she said consolingly, "who knows where this will take him. Give him time. Cam has always been a good boy; he'll come back to earth soon." Shrugging his shoulders and shaking his head as he walked away, he said, "I know. You're right, but darn!" The only thing that Cameron wanted for Christmas that year was a chemistry set. And somehow Santa came through.

In high school, Cameron really excelled. With the expanded range of classes and a higher level of challenge, this was welcomed by Cameron. He was getting bored in middle school because things seem to come pretty easily for him while there. Of all the classes he had taken to date, science classes were still his favorite, English his least. His friendship with Brian and Andrew had continued through high school and Brian was one of the students that he helped in chemistry. Brian was doing fairly well, but needed to try and bring his score up a bit. Andrew was doing fine with this course and in no way needed any assistance. He too seemed to enjoy this area. Andrew was involved with helping other students in this area as Cameron was. With their interests, it was not uncommon for Mr. Neuhauser, the chemistry teacher, to provide the young chemists a challenging assignment, something different than the remainder of the class was expected to complete. Cam and Andrew would stay late to work on these assignments and would ultimately, to the surprise of Mr. Neuhauser, figure out the answer to the given problem. Cameron seemed almost driven to solve the problem. He would also stay after school and help Mr. Neuhauser with

any experiments he was working on and to help clean to
room at the end of the day. He helped Cameron learn how
to perform research and to better work through challenges
he would encounter; something that should benefit him
greatly in the future. Mr. Neuhauser was a kind and caring
man who truly wanted his students to succeed. He would
make himself available to help students having trouble and
was the advisor for the science club at the school. High
school was good for Cameron.

Although Andrew and Cameron considered each
other good friends, over the years they were not as able to
get together on as frequently as with Brian. Andrew lived
about six miles away from Cameron's farm, too far from
his parent's perspective for Cameron to ride his bike over
there. Andrew's family, although not in farming, had a
connection with the other families due to their boys'
friendship. Andrew and Cameron's parents became friends
and they occasionally would help each other out as
possible, but they were not quite as close as Cameron and
Brian's parents were. Andrew and Cameron had developed
their friendship mainly at school, with a rare situation
where they were able to play together at their respective
homes when their fathers got together to help one another.
Andrew was a better student than Brian and was known to

help him as Cameron did. The three young men played well together over the years and supported each other as needed; the things that good friends do for one another.

Science by far still remained Cameron's most favorite subjects and he had endeared himself to all of the teachers. This interest in science was one of the primary reasons why he did not participate in sports while in high school. Mr. Neuhauser was by far his favorite teacher and he has taken a genuine interest in Cameron. Along with his interest in animals, Cameron's great appreciation for chemistry eventually blossomed out into biology as well. It was Mr. Neuhauser that, through his knowing Cameron, suggested he consider becoming a Veterinarian. In his discussion with Mrs. Johnson, the Biology teacher, Mr. Neuhauser came to realize that Cameron's strong interest in both of these areas and the possibilities for Cameron. He could meld the two areas he enjoyed along with his love of animals, to be able to make a nice living after college. Along with Orville and Marjorie, Mr. Neuhauser would talk about his ideas with Cameron during experiment sessions and at their parent teacher conferences each year. This effort on Mr. Neuhauser's part planted the seed for what was to become a reality in years to come. His father had hoped Cameron would take over the farm from him one day, but down deep he knew this was not Cameron's passion. Being the kind of man he was, he was able to understand how important this was to Cameron and to allow him the freedom to choose his own path. Marjorie was proud of her husband for him not forcing or cajoling Cameron into choosing the farm over his desires.

With the input from those around him that he trusted and valued their opinions, Cameron ultimately decided to become a Veterinarian. With this fateful decision being made, as he progressed through high school, his teachers, parents, and school counselors helped him decide on where he would go to college. His other friend, Andrew, who was also contemplating college and veterinary medicine as well, was dealing with the same issues. In some ways this was a tough decision for Cameron. Cameron had not been away from home much but was lured to consider some of the more prestigious schools; Cornwell, Smith's State and James A&M were schools he and Andrew considered. He and his parents visited Smith's State since it was relatively close to home and one of the schools with an excellent reputation. Cameron liked the campus but was not completely sold on the idea. On the car ride over, the reality of the hours it would take to go back and forth combined other factors, made Smith's State not as enticing as he had originally thought. There was no doubt that Cornwell and James A&M was out of the question; they were much too far away. His other college of interest, Knight University, was the closest to home, a little over an hour away. Although not as prestigious as the other schools, it was ranked 14th in the nation. His parents and counselor offered advice but the decision would have to be Cameron's. By their junior year, Andrew had decided; he was going to Smith's State. Cameron vacillated, weighing all his options.

Early in his junior year of high school he had landed a job with Doc Hughes, the local veterinarian. Doc Hughes was a Veterinarian that was about ten years younger than Orville. He had been in practice for about twenty years and was doing well for himself. Cameron has known Doc for most of his life it seemed. Doc had been working with the farm for the past 15 years and would come out about at least yearly to give a Brucellosis vaccination to the cattle and for any issues that might surface. Sometimes he would stop by the just say high when in the area and see if Orville had any questions or concerns that had popped up. Doc felt committed toward helping his customers succeed and he believed that part of his responsibility was to be considered an asset and a friend, not just someone looking for another buck from the area farmers. His efforts paid off as the area farmers looked forward to his impromptu visits and he quickly earned their trust. He helped with some of the difficult calf births over the years at the farm which was something that Cameron did not particularly appreciate.

Cameron would help his mother when taking the dog and cats into the office which was his probably the beginning of his interest in veterinarian medicine. Cameron would watch with an eager eye as Doc worked with each one and would gladly help as needed. He looked forward to these times and on one occasion, while examining Ellie, Doc mentioned that he was having trouble keeping up with things at the clinic and that he needed some extra help. Cameron jumped on the comment, asking what kind of help he needed. "Well," said the vet in his typical slow, down-home drawl, "I really need someone to help me tidy up the office a bit and to clean out the cages. Ali has been bogged down with the paperwork in the office it's been hard for us to keep up. She's here too late too often for my liking." "Do you have anyone in mind?" asked Cameron eagerly. "Oh, I don't know…" as Doc paused a bit. Cameron quickly piped in, "Doc, with you only being a mile or so down the road, I mean, maybe I could help you." "Now that's an idea," said the vet as he looked over his glasses at

Cameron. "Cam, I think this is something that you and your parents should discuss. I would be fine with you helping us, but what about your chores at home? How can you do this, your homework and help your Dad?" the Vet asked him. Cameron looked quickly over at his mother with the eager look like that a six-year old has when talking about opening Christmas presents. "Mom, what do you think? I'm sure I can do it." There was a slight pause and then a tiny smile forming in the corner of her mouth. "Cam, we probably should talk this over with your father before making any commitment. This is kind of a big decision." "I know," he said, "but I'm certain I can do it." As he glanced over toward Doc, Doc smiled a bit too saying, "Cam, your Mom's right. Go home; talk it over with your Dad. This should be a family decision and something that can wait for a little while. Home, school and God should be your priorities." After finishing with Ellie, they left and all the way home, Cameron couldn't stop talking about the possibility. What could he learn? How this would help him in Vet school; how this might help improve his chances in getting accepted to Vet school. Later that evening after supper, Cameron brought up the idea to his father. Orville was always the type that rarely made a snap decision. After an idea was suggested, he would mull it over for a while, like a cow chews its cud; rushing this man for an answer was futile. Cameron sat on the edge of his chair, eagerly awaiting a response from his father that did not come. "Dad, what do you think? Did you hear me?" asked Cam impatiently. After a moment, his father looked up at him, "We'll see," he said as he stood up. "I'll think on it. It's nearly time for bed son. We gotta get up early in the morning. Chores to do you know." Cam was disappointed, and a little angry due to his eagerness and impatience. His mother, putting away the dishes in the kitchen, came out, looked at her slightly dejected son and said, "Cam, don't worry. Your father will think it through; just give him a little time. You know how he is. However, I would suggest you hit the homework for a little bit and get to bed. Tomorrow would not be the day to be late with getting your chores done," she said, smiling as she patted him on the shoulder, leaning over to give him a kiss. Reluctantly, Cam headed off to bed after helping her in the kitchen. He spent the next hour going over his homework like his mother suggested and then he went to bed. He didn't sleep very well that night.

2

LEARNING

Working at Doc's clinic was harder than he had thought it would be. He found out very quickly that this additional responsibility did require that he use his time wisely. He could not afford to let his parents down either from the perspective of the farm or in his grades. He knew his parents expected these be maintained. But his parents were confident that his need to juggle these responsibilities would pay off in the end for Cameron. His father knew the importance of learning time management skills which was one of the primary reasons he consented to Cam's working at the clinic. Getting back and forth to work sometime required he ride his bicycle since he did not have a driver's license yet; sometimes he needed to walk because it occasionally was too late to safely ride his bike home after dark. Cleaning out the cages, making sure all the animals were fed and had water, and helping hold the animals while Doc examined them were some of his main responsibilities at the clinic. All of this and more occurred during his time at the office. It really wasn't hard, but it was fast-paced. Cam and Ali quickly became friends. Ali was a few years older than Cam, graduated from Western High School about four years ago. She was Doc's granddaughter and had grown up around the office. When time allowed, Cam would help Ali with her work and sometimes would help with the phone. Occasionally he also would bring his homework which was something that Doc insisted upon; keeping his grades up was a condition for continued employment. Cameron still had not decided on which college to attend and one day while helping Ali in the office, he glanced into Doc's office and saw his diplomas hanging up on the wall. He looked around; no one was near to ask if he could check them out, so he stepped in to get a closer look. There were three of them, the largest at the top. It was Doc's diploma from Knight University, graduating class of 1975. Below his vet diploma was a diploma from Knight, a Bachelor's in Biology. The last one was from DeKalb High School, graduating in 1965. "Those were from a long time ago," Doc said, which startled Cam who was deep in contemplation. "Sorry, Doc for coming in here, your diplomas caught my attention." "No harm done, fella. I figured you'd wander in here some time or the other," he said. "Your parents said you hadn't made a decision on which college to attend. I figured we might talk about it one day when you were ready. This is a big decision and something that took me a couple of years after being at college before I decided to enter into this field. At first I considered being a Medical Doctor, but I realized that people gripe too much. Animals are nicer and easier to work with overall," Doc said as he slid around Cam to sit in his chair. "Sit down for a bit, if you want Cam." Cam's thoughts were swimming around in his head; he wasn't sure what to ask. This encounter took him off guard. He had kind of pushed the thought of college out of his mind for a time. "This has been a tough decision, Doc," said the young man as he glanced up to look at the diplomas. "How did you decide to go to Knight?" he asked, looking back over at Doc. "Well," said the kind-hearted Vet, "there were a variety of reasons, probably the most was money. My family was not well off. My parents worked hard, but neither was lucky enough to go to college. The world was much different in their time as well. My dad was a laborer at a casting plant in Waterloo and my mother worked as a waitress. Now mind you, we weren't poor, but with my other three brothers and sisters, things were thin at times," he said as he looked out the front window and then panned over the pictures of his family on the wall. "I'm proud of who I am and where I came from," he said. "Knight is still is a good vet school, there are only twenty-eight in the nation, you know." "Yes," said Cam as he watched the Vet shuffle some papers on his desk. "Knight did me well. Now I did not get all tied up in the frat scene, didn't party like most of the others did. I just kept my nose to the grindstone. Oh, I had fun, but saw a dang too many kids disappear; partying, you know." The phone rang and Doc answered it while Cam sat there and looked around the office. He saw all of the pictures, the large number of books in the office, and the small, but fairly neatly piles of papers on Doc's desk. The clock on the wall kept clicking as the seconds passed, which seemed to annoy Cam slightly, like a reminder that time was slipping away from him. As Doc hung up the phone, he looked at Cam and said, "It's a big decision and anything you want or need from me, just ask. From my point of view, and not just because I went there, you can't go wrong by going to Knight." As he began to straighten up, he said, "Come on, we'd better get back to work before that granddaughter of mine reminds us were slackers, she's a slave driver, she is." For the remainder of the day, Cam was quiet, busily getting his work done while thinking about what Doc said, mulling over his options.

A couple of days after their conversation, and while they were out at the Dunn farm checking on a sick calf, Cam said to Doc, "Hey Doc, do you know anyone at Knight that I could talk to?" "Well, I think so. I can make a call and see if the guy I know is still there. I'll do it when we get back to the office. You talking to any other schools?" asked the Vet while he worked. "No, but I've got to make a decision I know and I need to do it soon. Time's working against me," said the young man as he struggled with the calf he was hanging on to. On the ride back to the clinic, Doc asked Cam some probing questions. Why was he interested in becoming a Vet? Had he considered whether he wanted to specialize or be a general practitioner? Did he realize that he would need to complete an internship to become board certified? To each of these questions, Cam answered each without much effort and at times would provide additional information which covered some of the other questions that Doc was prepared to ask. Cam had done his homework and it showed in his answers. He had shown a desire to become a Vet a while back and had surfed the Internet often to have a greater enlightenment into the profession he planned to train in. Doc's raised his eyebrows to some of Cam's answers as they were an indication of Cam's preparedness and he was pleased. "Cam," Doc said as he pulled into the parking space at the clinic, and after being back for a short time said, "I just called your parents about touching bases with the person I know at Knight while you were putting things back in from the truck and they were fine with me touching bases with my friend. I've set and appointment for you with my friend Dr. Gill, an old classmate of mine at the university next Tuesday at two o'clock. He'll be able to answer any questions you might have." "Really...Thank you so much, Doc!" said Cameron as he cleaned out the last cage. "I have the address and everything you need to find him. Joe's a good guy and I know he can help you with your decision. Make certain that you take your high school transcript with you, a resume, and the letter of introduction which I have drafted for you to give him. It's all on my desk; make a couple of copies for future needs." Doc said as they walked into his office to sit for a minute to continue talking. He stopped and turned to Cam. "Cam, from the time I have known you and the time you have worked here, I am certain you will be a great Vet. Come on, let's get a soft drink." As they were sitting there enjoying their soft drink, Doc's wife, Susi walked in. "Hi there!" she said as she came in carrying a bag. "I knew you had to go out for a call and thought you might like a little surprise. You must be Cameron," she said as she put the bag down. "Yes Ma'am, I am," said Cam. "Where are my manners?" said Doc as he stood up. "Susi, this is Cameron Robert. Cam, this is my wife, Susi," he said as he opened the bag to see what she had bought. "Oh my," said Doc. "Apple turnovers! My favorite! And Cam, there is enough for all of us. She takes such great care of me. Love you Hon!" he said, reaching in to grab one of the luscious delights. "Love you too honey. Enjoy." she said as she waved, heading out of the clinic door.

3

THE BEGINNING

In some ways his decision for Knight was tough, in other ways easy. He wanted to remain close to home which was a definite plus for choosing Knight. But he also knew that some of the other, more prestigious schools might offer more opportunities to him in the future. When finally weighing all of the options, Cameron eventually settled on Knight and he enrolled in early January. It helped for Doc to arrange the meeting with Dr. Gill, the dean of the Vet College. This encounter helped Cam become more comfortable with his decision. Yes, the other schools could offer the *potential* of a better position, but the costs, combined with the distance away were strong factors against these universities. "You get out of it what you put into it." This was the final driving point that resonated in his mind; something that Dr. Gill had said to him in their discussions. Dr. Gill and his father seemed to hit it off as

well when they all met; something that was not an easy
thing from someone to do with his father. The connection
between Dr. Gill and Doc Hughes was another important
point in Cameron's mind. The two Vets were roommates in
college. Although they did not take the same paths, Dr. Gill
specialized in veterinary pathology while Doc Hughes in
canine and feline and beef cattle practice, they both
remained the best of friends. Following the guidance from
Dr. Gill, Cameron had taken note of the need to take the
GRE exam prior to applying for admission to Vet school.
In his application to the college for his undergraduate
degree, he had to provide three personal references and all
the other various information requested by the university.
Cam listed Mr. Neuhauser, Doc Hughes, and Mr. Morgan
as his references. Everything required was submitted well
within the university's application submission
requirements. He also knew it would be important down the
road to note his work at Doc's clinic when applying for Vet
school. Now was the hard part, it was time to wait.

A couple of months passed since the application
submission and Ali and Cam had just run to the store to
pick up a couple of things that Cam's mother needed for
dinner. The two pulled into the drive at the Robert's home,
passing his mother with the mail in her hand. As she sorted

through the mail, she came across a particular envelope, and upon seeing it, she stared heading toward the car. "Cam!" she shouts. "This is for you!" As Ali and Cam are coming out of the car, her arm outstretched with the envelope in hand, she approached. As she comes to him, she handed him the envelope, the return address showing it is from Knight University. His father and Ellie come up after hearing Marjorie and they all stop and look at each other for a moment. Cam looks down on the envelope, paused for a moment and then looks up at them all. "I can't imagine that this is anything else other than there decision about my admission. I'm nervous." he said. "I'm sure," said both parents also simultaneously. Taking a deep breath, Cam turns the envelope over and begins to peel away the flap which closes it. He pauses, takes a deep breath and then pulls the letter from the envelope. Opening it up, he scans the letter quietly while the others anxiously await his response. Cam smiles and begins to read aloud, "Mr. Cameron Robert, it is with the upmost pleasure that we inform you of your acceptance to the Knight University. Your achievements fall well within the bounds of our university for admission and we look forward to assisting you in meeting your academic goals." Yahoo!!" shouts Cam as he jumps up, waving the letter in the air. His parents and Ali all share their excitement with Cam and hugs and congratulations go out all around. "Great job, son, we're very proud of you! This sounds like a great reason to have a celebration dinner. Where would you like to go, son?" asked Orville. "I don't know. I'm kind of a little numb at the moment. Ali, where would you like to go?" he said looking over at her. "How about Joe's Steak House? They always have the best steaks in the area and prices are right," she said. "Joe's it is," said Orville. "By the way son, I think you have to make a stop somewhere before we go out; Doc Hughes." "You know, you're right, dad. Ali, would you come with me?" "Sure!" she said. "You take care of that letter," said Marjorie. "We need to frame that!" as the kids climbed back into the car to head to the clinic. As they pull out from the driveway, Orville says to Marjorie, "With his grades, I couldn't imagine they would have turned him down for admission." Marjorie nods, looking up at him as he reaches around her to give her a hug.

Both of the young people arrive at the clinic a few minutes later, seeing Doc heading toward his car. "Doc!" yells Cameron as he waves the acceptance letter out of the car window. Doc stops for a moment, smiling as the two leapt from the stopping car. "Doc, they accepted me at

Knight!" Cam said as they raced to Doc's side. "I'm not surprised one bit," said the seasoned Vet as he was leaning against his car with his legs crossed. "We did it! Thank you for everything you did to help me," said Cam as he vigorously began to shake Doc's hand. "Cam, we didn't do anything; you did this; nobody else. Congratulations my boy!" "Doc, I'll always consider everything that you have done for me as leading to today and I will be forever grateful to you," said Cam. "However there is one thing that I would ask of you Doc. Please call Susi and join us all at Joe's Steak House for a celebratory dinner. My parents are getting ready for us to go there as we speak. It would not be the same if you were not there. Please come," asked Cam of his mentor and friend. "Please Grandpa; we're all going," said Ali. "Ok," Doc said as he raised his hands as though he were giving up. "I'll call her and have her meet us there. Besides, we were having tuna noodle surprise. I'll be glad to pass that up for a steak at Joe's!"

The end of Cameron's senior year of high school ended all too quickly. As time passed, through his hard work, Cameron became the salutatorian of his graduating class from Western High School in 1993. Cam had enjoyed his senior year and looked forward to moving on. His graduation was the typical Indiana high school graduation with Cameron needing to deliver a speech at commencement. He had worked on writing his speech over the final six weeks of school and after many drafts; he finally was satisfied with his work. To be sure it was correctly written; he had his mother review it. She felt it was fine, which was a definite relief to Cameron. Cameron was nervous as he approached the microphone on the stage, but as he looked out toward the crowd, upon finding his parents, once he had seen them a feeling of calmness came over him as he prepared to speak. Both were sitting in their chairs with the biggest grins that anyone could ever have. He challenged his fellow classmates to realize that once each day passed, that they would never live that day again. His challenge to his classmates was for each of them to work toward their full potential, to be a positive role model, and to not waste their lives focusing on the enticements of life that are short-lived infatuations; don't waste a day was his message. A great future medical researcher, physician, politician, Supreme Court Justice, or an astronaut may be sitting there in their cap and gown right now; they just needed to make it happen for the betterment of themselves and all. He wished them all good luck.

The summer before a young man starts college is one that many consider as their last opportunity to hang with their friends before going off in the big, big world. Cam was no exception to this as he spent a significantly more time with his friends. Of course he still helped his father with the farm and Doc at the clinic, but there were many more basketball games at his and other friends' homes. An occasional trip to a couple of the amusement parks in the area also helped complete what most would consider as their last summer of freedom. Then there were those times where he needed to give attention to those motherly instincts regarding the preparation for the coming fall. The buying of clothes, supplies, and the other necessary items he would need to have in his dorm room, were his mother's responsibilities, along with the advanced consideration toward the things he would want to have at Knight to provide a little touch of home. Even Emily became involved in this endeavor; after all, being a teenager now, she had a lock on the fashion world now and would be mortified if Cam were seen in just plain jeans and a t shirt. Cam would roll his eyes at his mother concerning his sister's antics while participating in the dreaded clothes shopping trips; but he would be careful to not let Emily see his response. The summer clicked away, faster than most want, but their preparations had him as ready as possible for college.

Cameron had not in the past, other than a sleep over here and there at a friend's some nights, really not been away from home. This new facet was something that he did not relish to dwell upon but that he knew was coming. Cameron tried not to dwell upon the thought of leaving his home which was probably one of the subconscious reasons why young men and women try to be so busy in their summer following high school. His parents as well were experiencing the reality that their oldest child's bedroom will shortly becoming empty. This time of life is a bitter sweet time for all; parents are proud of their child's accomplishments, but it is hard to let go. Children as well look forward to becoming more independent and successful, but the fear of the unknown and the missing of times past is a hard reality to accept. It is equally hard for them to accept that many of those friends from school, definitely the ones that have known for most of their lives, wouldn't be there; that they may not ever see them again. It's hard for all of us to leave comfortable times in our lives. The desire and attempts from all were to remain upbeat and positive; even though this was the plan, as the time to move into the dorm approached, there were the occasional tears that flowed, more on the side of the parents, who did their best to keep this from their son, but

Cameron had his somber times as well. As time neared, it became harder for his parents to look forward to Cameron's move date to college. It's tough to let go; but it's a little, but not much, easier when you know they are heading down the right path in life. Cam too had his reservations and questions regarding the future, but he did his best to hide these from his parents. Emily was in her own world, enjoying her summer as young teenagers do, but as the time for Cameron's departure approached, she too came to realize that a change of life was coming and she leaned on her parents, doing her best to not worry or upset Cameron.

With everything packed in the truck, Cam and his parents reluctantly prepared to head toward Knight University. It was amazing how much there was to take and along with this, there was the fear that something would be forgotten. Orville, the man of reason and common sense that he was, reminded the others that he was not leaving the planet and if some had been forgotten, it would be easy enough to correct the oversight. After loading, Cam stopped for a minute to look around and take in the moment. He saw Ellie lying over close to the barn. It was like she understood something significant was going down and she just looked at him. Cam went over this his dog and sat down next to her to pet her. "It's OK girl, I'm not going far and I'll be back soon. You keep an eye out for everyone." As he did this for a few minutes, his old friend Max, trotted over, coming up to him and began rubbing against his leg. Looking downward and seeing him, Cam put his hand under him and picked him up and started petting him. "Max, old fella, I'm gonna miss you too. You gotta keep an eye out for everybody too, you hear?" A tear started to form in his eye as he thought about the time growing up on the farm and how he would miss everything. The other cats stayed in the barn, all perched in different locations, sat there looking out at him as well. This was his farewell audience. Before his parents came out, he wiped the tears from his eyes and jumped up, grabbing a stick and threw it for Ellie to go after. She quickly ran after it and brought it back to Cameron who threw it again. Shortly, his parents came out indicating to Cameron that it was time to leave. Cam kneeled down to Max and Ellie and patted them on their heads before getting in the truck, telling both of them a final see you later, not a goodbye. As they pulled away, Cameron looked back and there sat Max on the picnic table, erect as though he was at attention, giving his friend a proper send-off. Ellie had sat up and started to bark with a little break between each bark, as though she were telling him goodbye. A few more tears formed.

It seemed like a long drive today, there was some conversation going over, the kind of superficial conversation that happens when people a going through a transition. They arrived at the university which took longer than usual due to the traffic, and it was a flurry of activity as most of the students were moving in. The move into his dorm, the meeting of new acquaintances and the new surroundings; this all went well for the most part. As long as everyone stayed busy, it helped. The time was exciting on one hand, but solemn and unknown on the other. The tearful goodbyes happened, most of them happening privately, but Cam was on his way. The drive home for Orville and Marjorie were quiet for the majority of the trip home; occasional surface comments were made to help work through what felt like the loss of their son, a few more tears, but they supported each other as best they could. Once home, both parents, each in their own time would occasionally stop at the door of Cam's room and look in. It was quieter at home now, and the emptiness of the room matched the feeling of emptiness in their hearts as they missed their son. Most every parent goes through the emptiness at this time of life, regardless of why their children have left, but like most things in life, we begin to cherish the things of the past when reality strikes us with the realization we are forced to face; our children grow up. They say that time heals which is true, but acceptance is the primary healing that occurs. Thank goodness for the blessings of pictures, home videos, and the best thing of all, the personal memories of good times past.

Once his parents had gone, Cam was faced with the reality of the situation; he felt alone and a little lost. He had lived in a fairly comfortable circle of family and friends and this was his first taste of being on his own. He knew that a couple of his friends were also on campus, so he had planned on searching them out sometime soon. But for now, without knowing anyone, he tried to keep his mind off of this. Cam was starting to put some of his things away when his roommate abruptly pushed open the dorm room door. "Hi, I'm Jim Thomas," said the boisterous young man that had entered. This abrupt entry had taken Cam off guard especially due to his nervousness at the time. "Ah, I am, I mean, I'm Cameron Robert, nice to meet you, as he extended his hand to shake. "So this is our digs," said Jim as he threw his bag of clothes on the bed. "Yes, this is it," said Cam. "Where are you from Jim?" he asked. "I'm from Nashville, Tennessee. A Titans fan through and through! Who's your favorite team?" he asked. "I really don't have a favorite team. I don't follow football much." "Come on, you gotta be kidding!" responded Jim. "No, I'm not much into sports. With all of the responsibilities that I've had growing up, I usually don't have the time to check it out. Now, don't get me wrong, I don't see anything wrong with football or anything like that." "Well, just be prepared. We will have the games on all weekend. Missing a game to me is like losing an arm!" Jim said loudly. "That's fine with me. If I have studying to do, I'll find some place to hide," said Cam with a smirk on his face. "Great," he said to himself, I get stuck with some goof that lives and dies for football." Cam finished putting his things away and took a walk around the campus.

Cam called his parents every day for the first week to let them know how he was doing. The first calls were tough since he missed them terribly, but he did his best to not let them onto this. They too did their best as well. He would call them every night before bedtime to tell them good night as well. In the following days, less and less students were seen with their campus maps out as they had pretty much figured out where their classes were and the offices that they needed to access. Cam's roommate remained a less than anticipated pleasure, but he was tolerable. He was a little slovenly and didn't shower much; both of which irritated Cam but he worked through it.

Each of the six classes that Cam had this semester were the typical freshman classes, Psychology, Sociology, freshman literature, chemistry, calculus, and the other course, the dreaded English composition. Cam had taken AP classes in high school and was able to start with nine credit hours already. Most of his professors seemed pretty reasonable, but there would be quite a bit of work. A bunch of reading and writing lie ahead for the future veterinarian; four books to read in the literature class, eight papers to write in English comp, and various other assignments in the other classes. Carrying eighteen credit hours would keep Cam busy, which is how he liked things anyway. One thing that he liked was that his dorm was fairly close to most of his classes, something he would definitely appreciate, especially during the long, cold winter months. He really was happy that his dorm had a cafeteria on the first level.

All in all, as the first few weeks passed, Cam became more comfortable with his roommate and his professors. He particularly liked Professor James in his Sociology class. Professor James was probably in his mid-twenties who seemed to have a closer connection to the majority of the students in the class, many that were fairly close to his age. Instead of the dry lecture class, he provided real-life examples and reflections on the events of the past decade. Cameron liked the idea of picking apart recent happenings. Cameron could see that Professor James also injected his own thoughts and beliefs into the discussion which further added flavor to the class by provoking some students to challenge his perspective; another positive of the class. Another class that he surprisingly found somewhat enjoyable was English composition. Unlike the high school English courses he was required to take, this professor allowed the students to choose the topics they were interested to write about which was a point that Cameron did not like about previous classes; required topics from the instructor. Cam overall was pleased at how things had progressed with his courses in this initial time period. He did however still have the emptiness from the missing of his family. But by keeping busy, this hole was pushed back away from his direct thought which was good. Cam and his parents had agreed that Cam should stay there at Knight for the first few weeks to get his feet wet; to build some relationships and to get established better. The one saving grace for him was the ability to see a couple of his friends, Tom Jensen and Jeff Henry, from the past which helped tremendously. They did not have any classes together this semester, but they all got together, usually a least once a day to compare notes on their day and to just hang out together.

Cameron had finally come home for the weekend, in the third week of classes. His parents couldn't possibly have been more excited to see him. They picked him up late Friday afternoon for the little over an hour drive home. Unknown to Cam, his parents were on campus about three hours early for them to walk around more on campus, hoping to catch Cam before their agreed upon time. This visit gave them all a chance to catch up on Cam's first few weeks without any interruption. And being a guy, he of course had a yeoman's load of laundry to wash before he returned Sunday evening. For probably the first time in her life, this laundry was something that Marjorie looked forward to doing. Upon getting home, Max and Ellie both greeted him at the truck. Ellie jumped and barked upon seeing him and Max came running to him. Cam stopped to pet them and spend a little time with them before unloading the truck. He then went into the house and started to unpack when Emily came rushing in to see him. She gave him a great big hug and wanted him to share what it was like. She'd be heading that way in a few years and she wanted the full scoop. They talked for about forty-five minutes up in Cam's room; he didn't get much unpacked but he didn't mind. It felt good to be back home as he missed his room, but he missed his family and pets more. Marjorie happily fixed Cam one of his favorite meals, sloppy joes and macaroni and cheese and everyone sat down for a long desired family dinner.

The next morning, Cam had gotten up early, just like in the past and helped his father with the chores; something his father had been looking forward to. "Cam, I'm glad you like it at school, but I really look forward to your coming home on weekends. Do you have any plans for the weekend?" his father asked. "No, Dad. I thought that I would just hang out with you and Mom. I've got a little homework to work on, otherwise nothing in particular. Probably should start back after supper on Sunday however," said Cam. "Well, how able Ali? I thought the two of you were hitting things off pretty well over the summer. "Yah, we did, but she's been seeing someone else a little older than her and school has kept me kind of busy, so we've drifted apart some. You and Mom are the only people I called while away at school," said Cam. "Well, son, your Mom and I will be here. Maybe after these chores you should run into town and say hi," said the elder Robert, with a little elbow to the side and wink of the eye. "We'll see," said Cam with a smile. The Robert men jumped into the chores as Marjorie was diligently working on preparing breakfast, one of the largest breakfasts that they have had in quite some time.

After the chores, Cam decided his father was right; he'd run into town and see Doc Hughes; maybe Ali would be there as well. Walking into the clinic, Ali had her back to the door and was on the phone. "I'll be right with you," she said without turning to see who was there. Cam looked around; the reception area had not changed, just as he expected. A couple of dogs were barking in the back room. He could hear someone moving around in the back but couldn't tell who it was but assumed it was Doc. There were a couple of cars in the parking lot, so Doc had a couple of patients he was seeing. Ali hung up the phone and continued writing something down, Cam did not pay any attention to her conversation. "How can I help…" Ali started to say as she turned, seeing Cam. "Cam!" she shouted as she glanced up at him. Opening the gate quickly, she quickly came up to him and threw her arms around him saying, "It's so great to see you! How's school? Did you just get back? How are your Mom and Dad?" all before he could think to answer. "Hi, it's great to see you too!" he said, returning the hug. He was a little surprised by the response from Ali. "I got in last night, school's going well,

and my parents are fine," he said. About that time, Doc
came out from the back and said, "Hey, what's all the
commotion?" Seeing Cam, he smiled and extended his
hand to shake saying, "Well, Cam my boy, how are you
doing? Long time no see!" "I know, Doc," he said.
"They've been keeping me very busy and I've not been
able to get home as much as I would like." "Things OK?"
Doc asked. "Yes, things are going very well. Dr. Harness
has been piling it on us, so not a lot of free time," said
Cam. "I'm not surprised," said Doc. "He is pretty thorough
and expects quite a bit from you guys, but when you're
done, you'll know you stuff!" "How's the advising going
toward admission to Vet school coming? I know they start
pretty early to make sure you are on the right track," said
Doc. "They seem to be on top of things. I have met with the
advisor once already in preparation for beginning the
application process," said Cam. "I imagine they told you
this by now, but your first year grades are a critical piece in
the application process. You're also probably already
experiencing the difference between high school and
college; something that is a real challenge for many new
college students," said Doc. "Man, you're right. Even
though these are freshman level courses, it definitely is
tougher than high school!" said Cam. "Keep your nose

down and keep plugging away; you'll do fine," said Doc in a fatherly manner as he placed his hand upon his shoulder. "OK, enough of this for now. I think that I've got everything under control around here," looking over at his granddaughter who just walked into the room, "So Ali, why don't take the rest of the day off. You two kids go and have some fun" "Really? Thanks Grandpa!" she said excitedly. "Cam, would you mind if I come with you?" "Of course not," said Cam, blushing slightly at her response. "That'd be great!" he said. "See you kids later," Doc says as they are leaving. He stood by the door, watching them pull out thinking, "She'll do right by herself with that boy." He then returned to the exam room to treat Mrs. Bolke's cat.

Cam and Ali finished their lunch at Louie's; a favorite place of Cam's, and then went for a drive down to Indianapolis. Cam wanted to pick up a couple more pair of shorts and he took advantage of the time that Doc had given the two. "So Cam," said Ali, "how are things at school?" "Not bad," responded Cam. "These first couple of weeks have been tough. I really miss everyone, which has been the toughest part, and if it were not for having my cell phone to talk with you all, it would have been unbearable. One thing that has helped is that I have a couple of friends over there at Knight with me, Tom and Jeff, which helps make this more tolerable. The food's not too bad, but not as good as my Mom's. My room's comfortable but I would prefer to have a different roommate. He's nuts about football," said Cam. "I'd imagine that's somewhat normal," said Ali. After arriving at the mall and about after roaming through three stores, Cam, or in reality, Ali, finally found some acceptable shorts and the two started back to Kokomo. "How about we go to a movie tonight?" asked Cam. "That doesn't sound bad Cam, but maybe we should you should head home and spend time with your parents. I know they miss you terribly. I would love to go to the movie tonight, but I think they need a Cam fix; if you know what I mean," said the wise young lady. "You're right Ali. Hey, how about we do this. Let's rent a movie, pop some popcorn and do an at home night? We can have dinner at home and all be together while watching the latest movie release. What do you think?" asked Cam eagerly. "Sounds like a compromise to me! Let's stop and pick something up on the way back to your parents," said Ali with a smile.

Sunday, Cam and his family went to church that morning after the chores were done and a quick breakfast. Cam was inundated upon entering church that morning. His old Sunday school teacher, Mr. Daniels came right up to him with a warm welcome and a desire to know how he was doing. The minister, Rev. Garr, excused himself from the line which was coming into the sanctuary to shake Cam's hand and welcome him home. Many other people did the same; his presence was appreciated by quite a number of the church. Rev. Garr made it a special point to note that Cam was back from church and for everyone to welcome him. The head's turned and the smiles formed on many a mouth. The church services lasted the usual fifty minutes and the congregation started to flow out. Mrs. Miller made it a special point to stop and say hi and to make sure he was getting his homework done. She always made it a point to let the young kids know that they get out of life what they put into it and that life won't give them anything for free. They headed home and for the remainder of the day, they spent working around the house, Cam helped his father with the tractor, and later spent time with his mother helping her fold his clothes. At lunch, Orville made hamburgers on the grill and they had a Robert family picnic at home for more family time together.

As his mother prepared dinner, Cam started to pack his things to return to Knight. He had spent most of the day catching up on what had not been shared on Saturday and as the day wore on, the reality of the need to prepare for his return left them all a little somber. His mother had placed his clothes up on his bed and Cam was carefully placing them in his bag. His mother had ironed everything, even his underwear, so it would be crisp and perfect; even after they had folded them together. As he packed, he stopped at times to look at some of the things in his room and to reflect. Cam was a bright young man, but he thought about younger days, days that had passed by. He stopped and thought about everything that his parents had done for him as he had grown up, the mistakes that he had made and the guidance and love they had given him during these times. He realized how blessed he was and how grateful he was for them. He thought about their growing up years and how Emily once was a thorn in his side and now how proud he was of her for becoming the beautiful person she was. He was a blessed individual and he knew it. He returned to packing and once done, he sat down in his desk chair and looked out the window that he had done so many times before and just looked out. He realized that the tree being bigger was the only change in that window and that he had grown as had the tree. His mother calling for dinner broke this rumination and he called down as he had done so many times before in his room, "I'll be right there, Mom!" He came down to his favorite, beef stroganoff.

Upon returning to school Cam transferred his clothes to his dresser and after studying a bit, called it a night. The next morning, after his first class of the day, Cam made it a point to seek out Dr. Gill. He had not seen him at Knight as of yet and he wanted to thank him for the encouragement and for his time and insight on Vet school. He had made a number of acquaintances while at working on his degree in Chemistry. Tom and Jeff were his closest friends of the past and all three desired entrance to Vet school. They had quickly become friends on the basketball court over the years and each had expressed their dismay with the college dorm scene. As luck would have it, the three young men found a house on the edge of campus and Cam and his friends moved into it about three months into the semester. Being on the fringe of campus allowed for there to be less distraction and noise, and even though it took longer to get to class, it was worth it. There were too many frat and sorority parties for their liking. These parties always seemed to get out of control and none were interested in being sanctioned by their school. The young men were pleased with their surroundings.

Tom was a little older than Cam and in being a little more mature, was more of a ladies man. With their house being off of the beaten track, they still could easily have people over for some late night fun without some of the oversight that occurred more on campus. Tom seemed to have his bedroom door closed a fair amount of the time and he was most often not alone. He was bright and did well in school, so the extracurricular activities of the night were not a distraction. Jeff was also a little more mature, although not as popular as Tom; he did have his conquests and friends. Being the usual of three young men, it was nice to have some of the girls around since they would help with keeping things cleaner and in better order. The laundry! Thank goodness that these ladies from heaven would often take it upon themselves to jump in there and help with this unpleasant task these three young men disliked. Since their help, the men seemed to have fewer pink and blue-tinted clothes. They all did let their hair down at times. Once there was the party where there was some alcohol involved and all were feeling good. Their house was built so there was a straight shot from the front to the back door. Once someone came up with the idea of parking the car in front of the porch and with the rounded roof on the car; everyone could get a running start at the back door, run down the hall, and jump from the porch onto the top of the car and use it as a slide of sorts. A few road rashes and a couple of bruises later revealed this was not their most stellar idea. Then there was the time where the group thought that an experiment with marijuana and a neighbor's cat that might be interesting. None of the young men had much experience with the evil weed, but being bored and having a couple of days free, young men sometimes come up with intriguing plans. Their plan was to try and get the cat loaded and see how she would respond. This was an experiment; after all, they were budding Veterinarians. So, as the night progressed, the three researchers shared their exhaled chemical with the cat they names Smoky, and somewhat kept track of the response. Along with their research, they gained great appreciation for the cat's responses. She seemed hungrier than in the past. They noted how the cat had difficulty walking down the hall without bumping into it. How big the cat's pupils became. All of these observations for veterinary medicine, you know. The next day, they reflected on the fun of the night and spied the notes from their experiment. Some of their writings were legible, some not. Oh well, maybe this research should be kept on a need to know basis. The Oreos, chips and milk glasses were still out from the night before. These and multiple other exploits of the "Knights of the Round Table" occurred; all in good fun and surprisingly to the three, done without the involvement of the campus constabulary. As time progressed however, this brief period of insanity, something that Cam had not expected, came to a close when Cam missed an assignment and received a zero for the paper. He had never obtained such a grade in his life and he wasn't about to continue this practice. This awakening brought Cam back to reality and the craziness ended right after this.

Food was another source of interesting stories. Each young man had their limitations of food preparation. If Jeff cooked, sloppy joes and macaroni and cheese were the typical meal prepared. If Tom cooked, well, grilled cheese and tomato soup was the order of the day. Cam, well his culinary skills did not fare much better either. Hamburger Helper and grilled chicken were his main offerings. Vegetables were a rare contribution toward their dietary needs, but they were young and their concerns toward a balanced diet did not hit the top of their list. They all finally figured out the spaghetti were something that they all liked and there was a phase where they had it every other day. Again, it was not uncommon for the young women that frequented their house to come to their rescue. Even and occasional desert would come their way! However, none of the young men starved nor looked to worse for their lack of culinary skills. Besides, from their point of view, almost anything that they would prepare was no worse than the food at the dorms.

The main drawback that each expressed about their house was the distance to travel to classes in the winter. Sometimes that Indiana winters were mild, but for the last two years of their undergraduate work, the snow and bitterly cold temperatures pointed out this main flaw to being away from the dorms. One positive was that their landlord did take care of making sure that that snow was cleared away from their porch and walks. Although the dorms were closer to many of their classes, the difference in distance was not significant enough. Nothing however would convince the young men that returning to the dorms was in their future. Each hurdle that they crossed made them better for the experience.

His freshman year passed fairly quickly from most everyone's perspective. Cam came back home about every other weekend and enjoyed the breaks. Overall, Cam had done well in his courses, the only exception being with the one paper that he received a zero score; otherwise he finished the year expecting a 3.90 GPA. Cam had found most of the courses interesting and although he kind of enjoyed it, he was finished with English composition! His favorite classes were chemistry, of course, and also the math classes he had taken. He found it ironic that the same book he used in Physics in high school was the exact same book he used at Knight. He had returned all of the books he had rented in the spring semester and was heading back to the house with Tom. "So, Cam," said Tom, "what are you planning to do this summer?" Well, I am going to work in the Vet clinic that I did earlier in the year to earn some money and to gain some more experience. Besides, the girl that I like works there and her grandfather is the Veterinarian that runs the clinic," said Cam confidently. "You dog!" said Tom. "I knew you had it in you!" "What do you mean," said Cam questioningly. "Smart man, going after the doctor's granddaughter!" he responded. This comment set Cam on edge as he snapped his head toward Tom and stopped in his tracks. "Tom, you're way off base on that! She's not another conquest to me like she might be to you! And by the way, I'm not looking for any handouts. I'll get where I do by my own hard work. Nothing's going to be handed to me!" said Cam in an aggravated manner. "Hey, I didn't mean anything by that old buddy. I was just kidding!" said Tom defensively. "OK," said Cam as he settled down a bit. "These people mean a lot to me and I don't want anyone thinking otherwise."

At the end of his freshman year, Cam's parents picked him up at the appointed time and once everything was packed and Cam had said his goodbyes to his friends, they headed back to Kokomo. They took this time to catch up on everything and to just enjoy their being together again. Only Orville and Marjorie came over to pick up Cam since they had felt that there might not be enough room for Emily was well. Orville made the right decision as Cam needed to sit on a bag of his dirty clothes to be able to make everything fit. He felt like he was sitting in a booster seat! The trip didn't seem as long as usual and they turned onto their road close to home. As their house came into distance, Cam could begin to make out that there were decorations on the porch, balloons, and table clothes on the picnic tables. There also were a number of cars parked by the barn; it looked like a party had been planned. As they pulled into the driveway, Cam began to see the people pouring from the house. There was Emily of course, but Andrew, Brian, Mr. Neuhauser, Reverend Garr, a number of people from church, Doc, Susi and Ali, and Mr. and Mrs. Morgan all piled outside. His return home had turned into a festival which was a surprise to him. Once stopped, he opened the truck door to a flood of people coming to greet him. Now he knows how it feels to be famous. Cam looked over and there sitting on the picnic table, just where and like he did on the day that he left for college, sat Max, patiently waiting for him. On seeing him, Cam worked his way over to him and picking him up and gave him a gentle hug. He was glad to be home. Ellie came running up to him and wouldn't stop jumping up to him until Cam bent down to pet her. He was home finally.

The summer plans were for Cam to help his father, to work with Doc again, and to spend some time with Ali. He also hoped to catch up with Andrew and Brian as well. He wanted to see how things were going for Andrew at Smith's State and to find out what Brian has been up to; he decided to not go to college and had been working for a local heating and cooling business in town along with helping his father at the farm. Being back was almost like he had not left. The routine around the house was the same and he got up early every morning to help his father with the chores. The one thing about being home that he appreciated was his bed. On his first night home, once he had lain down on his bed, he realized how much more comfortable it was than the bed at school and how the smells and sounds of the house were relaxing to him. It was much different than the music that was commonly playing in Jeff's room. There was not the slightly musty smell either. He was home and was glad to be back.

Ali greeted him at the clinic door on his first day back. "Morning, Cam," Ali says as she smiles, obviously happy that he is back. "Morning, Ali," said Cam as he gave her a hug upon coming in. "I'm glad to be back." "Cam, it looks like we have a busy day today. Doc has to run out to the Hanselman's to check on a horse he has been tending to and he said he'd like you to go with him." "What have I missed since I was gone?" asked Cam as he walked behind the counter. "Not too much. Just been the regular routine. About that time, Doc was coming back in at the same time that the first patient came and their day was off. Doc as well expressed his appreciation for Cam's return and welcomed him to join him on the trip out to the Hanselman's later that day. Later, as they were heading out to the Hanselman's Doc commented, "Cam, it sounds like things are going well at Knight. I hope you like it there." "Oh, yeah Doc, I like it. I'm glad to be out of the dorm and we were very lucky to find the house we have. Tom and Jeff are great friends, it may get a little crazy at times, but things have worked out pretty well and I would say that I'm blessed. I'm glad you're doing well." The two continued their conversation and upon finishing their work at the

Hanselman farm, they returned to the clinic to finish the rest of the day.

The remainder of the summer went well and Cam and Ali had taken some time to get better acquainted. With his work and Ali, Cam had not spent as much time with his family as he would have liked. Cam started to include his family more into the picture than earlier. He still had about half of the summer to go and would make the best of his time with them. Later in the week, he visited one of the local butcher shops in town and had purchased some steaks and arranged with Ali for them to plan on a nice dinner at his folk's house that evening. Cam mentioned to his Mom that he wanted to do have a cookout that evening which led to his mother getting excited and talking about the menu. "Mom," said Cam, "thanks for wanting to help with this, but Ali and I have got this covered." With this revelation, her mood dropped off a bit and upon seeing this, Cam quickly thought of a way to correct his error. "Hey Mom, come to think of it, there is one thing that I have been longing for. Would you mind making your sweet potato casserole?" Her face lit up and in an instant said, "Absolutely! We'll have sweet potato casserole for sure!" "I'll run into town and pick up everything and be right back. Thanks Mom," said Cam as he hurried out the door to pick up the rest of the night's menu. Later, they all had a wonderful evening, the steaks were great, the conversation better, and everyone, with the exception of Emily who was on a date, had a great time. After Cam left to take Ali home later that night, while cleaning up from the dinner, Marjorie said to Orville, "I'm glad that Cam's Back home. I really miss him." "Me too," said Orville as he was stacking the plates. "We've only got a few more weeks of this, so we better make the most of it."

The following morning, Cam joined his father out by the barn as he was working on the tractor, doing some preventative maintenance on it. "Morning, Dad," said Cam as he came up to him. "Morning, Cam. Missed you at breakfast this morning." "I know," said Cam. "I got in late last night after dropping Ali off and was kind of tired. "So how are things going with you and Ali," said the elder Robert. "Swell, Dad. She really is a wonderful woman. I really have grown quite fond of her." "We've noticed." About that time, Cam's two escorts, Max and Ellie both were trotting up from different directions toward him. He noticed their advance and bent down to greet them both. "Hey you guys!" said Cam as they came up to him. It was a competition to see who would get the most attention, at least from the animal's perspective. He rubbed and petted and played a little with them both before turning his attention back to his father's task. "I'm glad you're here this morning Cam. I could use your help in taking this alternator off of the tractor." Cam knew better. His father could easily handle this job, but in realizing that he had not spent much time with them, he knew this was a way for this father to ask for him to spend some time with him. Cam told his Dad that he would be glad to help and asked what he needed. The men finished their work on the tractor and Cam and his father ran into town to pick up some feed for the cattle. Cam enjoyed the opportunity to load up the truck with his father. He watched him as he almost effortlessly tossed the eighty pound bags into the back of the truck and compared this to his own abilities. "Wow! I forgot how heavy these bags really are!"

Cam didn't get to spend much time with Emily over the summer. She had entered the time of life where boys were noticed and she spent a fair amount of time with her boyfriend, Keith. This along with the job that she worked at a local clothing store significantly reduced the time they spent together. Of course this was not all Emily's fault; Cam worked too, spent time with Ali, and his friends which also led to this lack of time together. When they were able to connect, Emily initially wanted to continue to hear

Cam's stories about college, his apartment and the activities at the university. After all, she was now a sophomore in high school and in a couple of years she would be heading that way as well. On one hand, she was like most girls her age; she wanted to grow up faster to be able to experience the adult world and couldn't wait. On the other hand, she was a teenage girl and was in her boy crazy phase. Justin Bieber was the best vocal artist ever and she had become such as fashionista that her friends consulted her for advice. Regardless, during the time that they were able to get together, they both enjoyed talking with each other and Cam missed that little girl that used to bug him. He would occasionally take her to get a vanilla-flavored soft drink down at the convenience store just to be able to spend a little more time with her. Orville had confided in Cam that although he was very proud of her and that she was doing well in school, he too missed his little girl who would always be that to him. Cam was surprised that his stoic father would share this with him, but he speculated that has been a tough time for him.

The end of the summer came all too quickly from everyone's perspective. A similar ritual occurred as had last year when Cam headed back to school. It wasn't easy, but having the knowledge that through experience that Cam would come home and maintain contact with everyone made it a little easier. One of the things that Cam introduced his parents to over the summer was SkyCam, a program that allowed the users to have a video chat over the internet using the webcam he bought to put on their computer. Cam would arrange a time with them to contact them using the computer while he was at Doc's so they could practice this new method of maintaining contact. They practiced this until they were able to use it easily without concern. Orville had also finally came into the world of smart phones and now would be able to send and received texts. Cam was amazed at his father's transition to the world of technology and appreciated his efforts to maintain a connection with his children. Orville had said a number of times before that he did not see much use in these devices, that if anyone wanted to talk with him, they could call him on the home phone or come over; whichever was their choosing. Now, there he stood with the latest technology, working through the challenges of coming into the world of connecting.

Tom and Jeff both had moved into their house a couple of days before Cam arrived. It didn't take the three much time to catch up on the summer's events and to begin to get in the groove for the coming year. This year the young men would be taking some higher level courses and Cam continued on his track for the degree in Chemistry that he sought. Cameron found that starting this year was much easier and he fell into a routine fairly quickly with his classes. All of his professors seemed easy to work with and he welcomed the opportunity to learn. Again, Chemistry was his favorite subject and Professor Hughey had just started at the university after retiring from a pharmaceutical company. His life experience in this field was something that intrigued Cameron since his and other's efforts had led to many new medications and innovations that made a difference. "Dr. Hughey was a behind the scenes hero," thought Cameron, and he hoped to learn much from him this semester. His other classes took a back seat to Chemistry is Cam's mind, but not to the point where his grades suffered. One class that he was taking was professional speaking, something that Cam did not particularly relish. He attended and on finding out that he could choose the topics to present, this reduced his concern. It would be easier to speak about something I know or that is interesting to me than a foreign topic. He planned on talking about his pets, chemistry, and veterinary work.

The three men living in this house just off campus were a little more focused this year. There were no more experiments with a cat, or much of any other parties either. The female friends of Tom and Jeff continued which remained as blessing as in the previous year. One thing that did change for them this year was that they took a greater interest in the campus sports events. Cam had never been interested much in sports, but it became a nice distraction from the work they needed to perform. They would attend most home football and basketball games throughout the year. Cam found that being at these games was something neat to experience. The mass of people cheering on their team, the crazy students that painted themselves, and the community which developed at these events fascinated him. He spent as much or more time enjoying watching his fellow students and their actions as much as watching the game. There were some games that at the end, Cam could not tell you who won or lost. He had a unique admiration for those students that would do some of the crazy stunts and activities before, during, and after the games, but he could never bring himself to be so bold as to try them, at least early on.

There were a number of football games where Cam invited Ali over to watch the games with him and for them to spend more time together. He took her to some of the local hangouts for dinner and a couple of beers. He came home less this year and when he did, instead of both his parents, just Orville came to pick him up. He came home about every two to three weekends a month. This partially was due to homework and partially due to the home games. Cam felt it better to wait to buy a car until he graduated from school to reduce the overall expense; after all, there were the financial aid loans to consider upon graduation, so they economized to work toward paying this off while he was in school. Their time at home was more special and he tried to stay home more than in the past. Orville had hurt his hand while working on the tractor and if some mechanical work needed to be done, Orville would text him to let him know and Cam would definitely come home that weekend. When he couldn't get home, he was certain to connect with them on SkyCam and although some of these visits were short, they all appreciated the opportunity to see and hear each other. Orville shared with Cam that he had even gotten into the college football spirit and had watched a number of Knight's games on the television; another surprise. With this revelation, Cam was able to get a couple of tickets and Orville and he went to one of the home games; something that Orville had not ever given much thought to. They both enjoyed the opportunity.

Basketball season had started toward the beginning of November, but with the first semester coming to a close, Cam didn't attend any of these games. He concentrated on his studies and finished the semester strong. Once the second semester started, the three young men still continued to have a greater time at the games, but he asked Ali not to plan on coming over. With the unpredictable Indiana winters, he did not want her on the road if things changed and the roads got ugly. He planned on connecting with her on SkyCam as he had done with his parents. So, he attended the games with his friends and as a result, he started to come out of his shell and he wound up joining some of his painted classmates; he even wound up on ESPN in the broadcast of the game with Smith's State; Andrew's school. His picture was displayed on the arena screen and his father, who happened to be watching the game, caught a glimpse of his son as he had never seen him before. By the time Marjorie came into the living room, Cam's picture was off of the screen and the two shocked parents were amazed at his transition to being more outgoing. They both laughed and hoped that someone they knew had taped the game. The next day, they took advantage of SkyCam and contacted Cam with their computer. "Cameron that was you on TV last night, was it not?" said Orville in kind of a stern tone. Cam's facial expression changed, his father only used this tone when he disapproved of something and one of the last things on earth the Cam wanted to do was let his father down. "Well... yes Dad, it was me," Cam said sheepishly, expecting to receive some sort of an Orville the father response. To Cam's surprise, his father burst out laughing and talking quickly, trying to find out more about his antic. "WOW!" he said. "Cam, we've received more calls in the last eighteen hours from people that saw you last night than we have had in the past two months. You have become quite a celebrity here back home," said his father as he continued to laugh. Cam was relieved that his father appreciated his antics and that he was watching the games. Cam thought that it was time his dad slowed down a bit.

The life of a college undergraduate continued for Cam. His stories and experiences helped mold him; prepare him for his next endeavor, veterinary school. He still continued to be involved with some of the sports scene at Knight, but as he traveled down the road of college life, he found that the classes were becoming more difficult and this required more of his time. To compensate for this, the frequency of his coming home dropped off; he made it home an average of every three to four weeks now. The frequency of his involvement with activities across the campus fell off as well, as it did for Tom and Jeff. Ali would come over every once in a while to have dinner with him, but their time together had dropped off as well. As he rolled into his senior year, Cam had gained the respect of many of his professors. He had been able to maintain his grades and to have fun at the same time, but he realized that he did not want to place this at jeopardy, so he focused more. His friends, Tom and Jeff did well, but not as well as Cam, but this was not a competition, however Cam related this to their spending a little more time than he by being distracted by other pleasures of life. All in all, the three young men were progressing through their college well and were looking toward the next step in their career, gaining entrance into veterinary school. As time passed, eventually Tom and Jeff started to spend less of their time with the extracurricular activities as Cam had, because there was a point where their grades started going the wrong direction.

4

SUCCESS

Cam had done well in his undergraduate work. His overall Grade Point Average was 3.89 which should place him close to the top scholastically. The Bachelor degree in Chemistry with a minor in Biology that he had been working on would help him in his goal toward Veterinarian school admission. Mid way into his junior year, Cam completed the GRE test as was required for admission to Vet school. He scored quite well; a 560 in verbal reasoning, a 665 in quantitative reasoning and a 4.5 in analytical writing. His references remained as previously used but now he had his college transcript to assist him in gaining admission. He was well on his way and he believed that his chances were good for admission with his proven track record. He also felt it beneficial that Dr. Gill checked in on him occasionally too. Dr. Gill had noted that he would not be directly involved, but as Doc had noted before, he was on the fringe and knew about the other's applying, so overall having him demonstrating interest in Cam was a good sign. Cam was nervous about the process, not because of his performance, but the unknown of the other students that would be applying and whether they might be able to beat him out of a spot or not. Like his father said, he had done well; it was now in God's hands.

The exploits of the three budding veterinarians was growing within the college community. Although they desired a more relaxed atmosphere, some of their adventures reached the notice of a couple of the fraternities and the three were invited to join at the start of their junior year. Each of them was enticed with "special" activities, such as naked twister or guess whose chests. The three young men attended as an "opportunity to expand their horizons," as Tom said, but ultimately they declined, especially after the naked twister match as interrupted by the campus police who were responding to a call that scantily clad students were see frequenting the porch of the frat house in February. The color of skin contrasted greatly upon the snowy background. No one really knows who made the call, but the three young men left hastily from the back door of the frat house and over the fence into the alley where they quickly made their way back to their own house. Yes, this was an eye-opener for the young men, but as the close call brought them back to the reality that they couldn't afford to have to explain their actions to the dean of the school. With the end of their junior year of school coming, each felt it wiser to prepare for their final exams.

Cam completed all of the steps toward admission to Vet school and he waited. Knight, as the other universities also required an interview. Although a little nervous during the interview, he believed that he had completed this portion of the process well. Dr. Gill, who normally was a member of the interview committee, recused himself from the interview to eliminate any conflict. About mid-semester of his senior year, he was called to contact Dr. Gill's office at his earliest convenience to schedule an appointment with him. "Doc, what do you think this means," Cam asked his mentor on the phone. "It's hard to say Cam," he responded, not wanting to give away what he already knew. "It's been a while since I have seen him; maybe he wants to just check in and see how I'm doing. Or maybe… he's going to tell me that I got admitted to Vet school!" said the young man eagerly, trying to play Doc for some information which he might have to answer his speculation. "Maybe; I guess you need to ask him, not me," said Doc. "I hate it when he's right," thought Cam to himself. The following Tuesday, Cam arrived at Dr. Gill's office slightly before the appointed time. He had just seated himself when Dr. Gill came out from his office and greeted Cam. "Cam, I'm so good to see you. Won't you come in?" he asked as he extended his hand to shake Cam's. "Thank you sir," said

Cam upon returning the hand shake. They both entered the office where Cam was surprised to see his mother and father and Doc sitting in the office, smiles showing all around. "Cam," started Dr. Gill, "you really have done very well here at Knight and I wanted share with you your acceptance into the school of Veterinary Sciences. Good job young man!" as he handed him the formal acceptance letter which was housed inside of a padded portfolio. Cam was stunned but elated. Everyone rose and came around him to offer their congratulations, hugs, and other words of praise and encouragement. "Wow!" said Cam as he stood there still somewhat dumbfounded. "This is great! Thank you all for your help and your belief in me. I won't let you down!" "Cam, you have never let your mother or me down, son," a firm hand shake and hug coming from his father. They talked together for some time and eventually worked their way from Dr. Gill's office and down to one of the campus coffee shops. Everyone was proud of Cam's accomplishments and further was elated that they could participate in this event. Much laughter and happiness abounded throughout the remainder of the afternoon. Tom and Jeff both received their acknowledgement of their acceptance into the veterinary school as well a few days later and the celebration started all over again for the three future veterinarians. Cam graduated in the spring with an Honors diploma; a Bachelor's degree in Chemistry.

The summer prior to his entrance into Vet school was one that provided him with a greater insight into the field. Under the tutelage of Doc, he was exposed to more of the field of veterinary medicine. He continued to assist in the clinic, but now Doc allowed him to be much more involved. He became experienced in drawing blood samples from the patients. He also became proficient in administering intramuscular injections under Doc's watchful eyes. There even were the situations where he was able to scrub with Doc and assist in some of the surgeries that needed to be performed. Cam's first surgery was not one of his better days however. Doc needed to perform surgery on a golden doodle that was found to have an abdominal abscess. Being raised on a farm, Cam felt prepared to handle this event; after all, he had been around many unpleasant things with the cattle they raised. In this situation, the incision and the opening of the layers was taken in stride by the budding veterinarian. What really got to him in this procedure was that once Doc located the area of concern, the stench that pervaded the room was nearly more than Cam could handle. "How in the world could there ever be such an awful smell?" Cried out the young man as he stood back from the scene; covering his nose with his arm. The situation was then further aggravated by the suctioning of the abscess by Doc and the viewing of this vile substance and the resultant unpleasant slurping sounds coming from the belly of this poor animal. "You doing OK over there Cam?" asked the violator of this animal's abdomen, looking up at his young assistant's slightly pale face. "Yeah," said Cam quietly. "I'll be all right." "Well, if you need it, there is a chair over there," as Doc pointed to the desk in the corner of the room. "Make sure you sit down before you fall down," said the wise and observant veterinarian. Cam looked over at the chair and decided that this was probably a good idea and decided to take a seat. Doc continued with the procedure and after rinsing out the affected area, began to close the incision. Color and strength began to return to the young man as the procedure was ending and he was ultimately able to help Doc move the golden doodle off of the table and into his cage. "Man," said Cam. "I thought that I had experienced quite a bit out on the farm, but there was something about the smell that really got to me." "It's really tough to be human at times," said Doc consolingly. "I would imagine that each of us has something that can get us rolling! I personally don't like clearing out a dog's anal gland, but it comes with the territory." The following surgeries that Cam assisted with went much better than this initial event and Cam and Doc were grateful this happened. A Vet that could not perform surgery would not be a good thing.

Cam started his first year in veterinary school at Knight. With the undergraduate degree he had obtained, a few of the initial courses were relatively easy for him. Microbiology, cell physiology, and anatomy were areas in which he was well versed and he flew through these courses with ease. Of course there was the scientific writing course he needed to complete which must to his chagrin, he did not fare as well in as he would have preferred, but he did complete it. His GPA suffered that semester; he dropped to a 3.2 which was his lowest GPA ever. He was glad to have been able to work with Doc in performing surgery as this helped him with the gross anatomy courses. However, he completed the first year with relative ease and a GPA of 3.68. Cam had anticipated doing better than this, but as Doc shared with him, he was in an area of much more intense and specific training that it was not uncommon for this to occur. Doc was confident that Cam would continue to do well and that his grades would eventually improve. Cam listened to his mentor and tried a little harder. One thing for sure from Cam's point of view was, there was not much room for extracurricular activities, but he still worked in being able to go home occasionally.

The summer following his first year in veterinarian school left Cam busier than ever. He had decided to stay at Knight as he was one of the students chosen to help work in the veterinary hospital. There were limited opportunities available and when Cam heard of it, he was one of the first to step up. This endeavor required he work at the hospital forty hours a week. Most of his responsibilities were to perform many of the same functions as he had at Doc's, but he was more limited in his duties. Cleaning out stalls, brushing and washing animals, assisting the senior year veterinary students as needed were some of the primary duties he performed. This experience gave him an even greater awareness and exposure of some of the wide variety of duties the veterinarians must face at times. For his participation in this program, his housing and meals were provided and he was given a small stipend to help with some of his incidental expenses over the summer. He did not make a much monetarily as he would by working with Doc, but the experience would more than pay the difference in the future. Cam's parents would come over whenever possible, since Cam worked different days each week since he was in a rotation for weekends. They would spend as much of the day with him as possible, but mainly it was either to go out for lunch or dinner and touch bases for a few hours before heading back home. Ali came over occasionally was well, but most of their connecting was through SkyCam. Cam found this the best way to remain connected and to still keep touch with everyone. That is as long as the internet connection worked.

One of Cam's most memorable experiences of the summer was the time where he was involved with the care of an ostrich. The size of this bird was intimidating to Cam as it probably would be to most. He had not ever personally seen an ostrich before and although he knew they were large birds, he was not prepared for it to be slightly taller than seven feet. This particular bird also weighed three-hundred and twenty-two pounds. Prior to working with this massive bird, Cam spent some time with one of the senior vet students and they had become what Cam considered friends. Ostriches can be dangerous to work around as was described to Cam by George Mizsak. "Cam, this fella is here for some GI problems and has been diagnosed with Hexamitiasis and we are trying to correct his problem. He comes to us from an ostrich farm about sixty miles from us." "Really, I didn't know that there was one in our area," said Cam. "Now when working with these birds, you should always approach them slowly from the rear. Ostriches can only kick toward their front, so a frontal approach is not the best, as they can become temperamental easily. They mainly feed on seeds and other plant matter, and in the wild eat insects also; these amazing creatures do a good job of caring for themselves. Another important issue is that they will eat almost anything, even more so in captivity, so if you are working with them, take only the essential items in with you. They don't have teeth to chew as we do, so if you look around his stall, you will see that there are some small pebbles lying around. They will ingest them, their body using them as gastroliths to help grind the food in their stomachs. Their senses are quite acute and as such, any loud noises or fast movements catch their attention and could cause a defensive response." "I see," said Cam as he listened intently. "When we need to work with him, these birds can be cantankerous, but if you approach them from their blind side and are able to place a bag over their head, once this is done they are completely docile and much safer to work with. Your responsibilities will be to feed and groom him, and to assist me with examining him. Have any questions?" Cam thought for a moment and asked, "When do we feed him?" "Oscar is a grazer and as such will eat various times through the day.

So all you really need to do is to make certain that he has food around in his stall. He will take care of the rest." "OK, that sounds easy enough," said Cam. "Oh, yah, one of your pleasant responsibilities is to also clean out the excrement throughout the day. You will need to take a grain shovel and a five-gallon bucket with you for that chore," said George as he slapped lightly on Cam's back with a smile. "Don't worry though. For the first few times, we will have you working with someone to help you become better acquainted with Oscar." Cam survived this responsibility well, no major incidents occurred. He didn't expect to work with another Ostrich in the future, but one never knows.

The following year Cam gained knowledge over subjects like immunology, parasitology, bacteriology, and pharmacology in which he found each of these areas interesting. He found that these areas had a connection to other areas he enjoyed which made these classes even the more enjoyable. He spent a considerable amount of time in researching these areas and found great pleasure in being able to work with some of the senior veterinary students working on their research papers which further broadened his background. He found that he loved doing research and had to be careful as to not have this activity interfere with his other classes. He continued to work about six hours a week at the hospital in which he was able to expand his knowledge more through the interaction with the upper classmen. Tom and Jeff relied upon Cam to help them in some of the areas since they did not have as keen of an interest in them as Cam did. Cam would further help them in providing some of the research information when he knew it was germane to areas they were studying.

To fulfill the obligations to his classes and the hospital, he rarely went home during the year, the only exceptions being around birthdays and the various breaks or holidays given throughout the year. He did however use SkyCam at least every other day to maintain contact with his parents and Ali. Their conversations were short at times due to some of his deadlines, but he used the technology to fit his needs. "Yes Mom, I am eating well. If I do say for myself, I have become a fairly good cook since being over here. Of course, your recipes made a huge difference in my ability, but I put it together and watched over it, just as you showed me," said Cam as he sat in front of his computer. Marjorie sat up in her chair straight, being proud she had being able to help him. "Cam thanks for saying that. Sometimes I wonder whether your OK or not," said his mother as she made a special effort to look for any signs that her son did not feel well or that he looked stressed.

"Mom, you and Dad are my rocks. I really miss you guys and know you are there for me and Emily. I hope that I can do as good of a job with my kids one day as you guys have with us." Smiles appeared on both his parent's faces; Orville placed his hand on Marjorie's. At this point, Jeff comes over to the computer and says, "Hi Mom and Dad! We are taking good care of him. By the way, he's a great house mother!" Everyone laughs at his comedic gesture and Jeff slips away from the screen. "I am blessed to have such great guys over here," said Cam. Their call continues for the next ten minutes before Cam notices the time and tells his parents he needs to sign off. After the goodbyes, they all log off, his parents having appreciated to see and talk with him and to know he is well.

Cam's career through the rest of Veterinarian school was relatively uneventful. His progress and involvement was lauded by many of his professors and their assessment of him and his abilities were among the highest in his class. He proceeded through his training and as with most of us, he found things that he liked, he found things that he did not like. His obvious affection and appreciation in working with cats was noticeable and he needed no prodding to work with these wonderful animals. However, when considering his time in working with the larger animals, such as horses or cattle, this was not so much the case. He did perform his duties well, but he had difficulty with placing his entire arm up to nearly his shoulder when helping with the birth of a foal. His time on the farm and some of the re-living of past, less-than appreciated experiences with cattle found him not being excited toward working with them. He did it however, as was expected, and he could be relied upon to perform his duties well. There was the time however, in Dr. Smith's class where Cam was preparing to perform a rectal exam on a horse, one that was somewhat temperamental. Cam needed to perform a rectal exam for a routine examination of the horse's abdominal organs. He was properly garbed for the exam, covered from head to toe as he should be. As he approached the horse and was reaching to begin the procedure by raising her tail, the horse expelled some flatus and in doing so, sprayed Cam with some of its excrement. It didn't help that the horse had diarrhea at all! Even though properly covered, the exam was something that Cam would never forget. The ribbing from his friends did not help at all either. Tom was nice enough to capture this on his phone for posterity; something which surfaced at less than opportune times. The posting on the internet made him an overnight success, something that further enhanced his dismay. What else are friends for? Then there was the time he was learning about artificial insemination when they were working to prepare the horse for the procedure that Cam unwisely approached the horse to the left rear of the horse and something irritated the horse who rose it's left rear leg and kicked backward, clearing Cam's head by mere inches; close enough that he felt the wind from the backward thrust. Some lessons you learn the hard way, some you learn by luck. This one incident brought to light his too relaxed of a practice in approaching an animal, something that he had done like this a hundred times before; something that he would never do again. For whatever reason, it seemed as though Cam and horses didn't mix well.

Unbeknownst to Cam, Dr. Gill would touch bases with Doc to give him an idea of how his protégé was doing. "Tom, that boy of yours is quite a young man," said Dr. Gill to his old friend. "Yes he is Patrick," said Doc as he looked up at his granddaughter. "He will be I believe be one of the finest vets that Knight will have produced." The two gentlemen recanted some of their past and brought each other up to speed on their lives and families. Once the call was over, Ali asked her grandfather, "You were talking about Cam; weren't you?" "Yes," said her grandfather. "He is doing quite well. Dr. Gill is very impressed, but I don't want Cam to know we are talking. I don't want my affiliation with Dr. Gill to influence Cam in the least nor make him feel as though I am checking up on him. Ok?" "Sure grandpa; it'll be our secret." Cam and his friends completed their final year in vet school, all earning very respectable grades and accolades from their professors. Their time at Knight had prepared them for the future and graduation was looming. As this neared, each man prepared themselves for their final classes and ultimate graduation.

The proud parents of Cameron Patrick Robert were arriving at their son's house. It was graduation day; the four years of Vet school passed more quickly than anyone would have imagined. "My son the doctor! Doctor Cameron Robert. Son, I cannot begin to tell you how proud we are of you!" said Marjorie as she gave him a big hug. "Ditto, son," said Orville. "You've done it right son and we really are proud of you!" "Thanks Mom and Dad. I could not have done this without you," said Cam as he returned the hugs and smiles. Emily gave him a big hug as well and a peck on the cheek. "Congratulations, big brother!" said Emily. Doc Hughes and Ali walked up just as this had occurred, smiles were showing all around. "Cam my boy, you did it! I knew you would," said his friend and mentor,

Doc Hughes. Ali looked at him quietly and patiently, waiting for Cam to notice and speak to her. "Ali, you and Doc being here with my family makes this day complete. Thank you so much for coming to my graduation," said Cam as he walked up to what felt like the biggest hug of his life. She looked up at him and then gave him a kiss, a display of public affection that none of the others had seen before. He welcomed her affection, something that he had been shy to share with his family. "Congratulations, Cam," she said as she stepped back to take a long look at him. She looked beautiful in her pink patterned dress; the sun shining off of her blonde hair. They both wanted to stop time. "Cam, get that robe on. We need pictures and more pictures!" said his father as he dug for their camera. "Everybody, gather round; Tom, Jeff. This is a proud day for us all!" said Orville as he fumbled with the camera.

Their walk over to the arena was fairly short as the large crowd of people coming for the commencement activities had filled the closer parking spots. It was an unusually hot day on this early May afternoon. Cameras flashed around and the graduates veered off one direction to prepare for the proceedings and the parents and friends in another direction as they set out to gain the best spot possible to take the pictures of a lifetime. It was fortunate for all that the arena was air-conditioned and that the maintenance crew had made sure it had been turned on in time for it to be comfortable inside. The regalia of the university were on display as the family found a reasonable place to view the proceedings. The administration and faculty marshaled in on time and seated themselves upon the stage. Then the long procession of the graduates ensued. There were a total of eighty-three veterinary students graduating this year and there commencement was shared with the other one-hundred and two physicians, one-hundred and forty-two dentists, and the additional two hundred and seventy-five allied health and nursing students at this ceremony. The proceedings commenced and went off without a hitch, until Tom crossed the stage and after receiving his diploma, walked a couple of steps from the dean, turned to face the student body and tore open his gown revealing military fatigues. He then pulled a sign from inside his gown, raising it above his head with it saying, "I'm A Vet!" in big block letters. The student body and guests came to life and roared with laughter and began clapping loudly at his achievement. Tom then looked back to the dean, winked and then closed his gown and proceeded back to his seat. Cam, sitting there awaiting his turn to rise, sat there and smiled, shaking his head in disbelief and clapping for his friend and ally in the journey of veterinarian training. Cam was much more reserved when it became his time to receive his diploma, after receiving his diploma, he just stopped near the middle of the stage and turned to straighten his arms outward and made a fist with his other hand, then pulled back sharply, bending at the elbow as he pulled back quickly, saying, "Yes!" A photo opportunity for his parents and about the closest Cam could coming to matching Tom's display.

Cameron's achievement through his Veterinary courses and his overall grade point average (3.92) had been enticing to a number of prospective employers contingent upon passing his boards. However, Cam had decided upon specializing in canine and feline practice, similar to what Doc Hughes had done. One day he might join him and eventually take over his practice. This would allow him working with someone he respected but also allow him the ability to build a future from an established practice; besides, his parents were not getting any younger and he could be of help to them in the future as well; always the good son, he was. Along with the experience he gained while working at the clinic and through school, he opted for an internship with a somewhat new company in the animal business; CatGenus. CatGenus was conveniently located in

Louisville which made it a little more feasible for Cam to come home occasionally which was a definite plus. Cats remained the favorite breed in his life and from what the executives in this company shared, they had a passion for the feline breed as well. In his discussions with the company executives, Cameron would be working in their product development and research lab for the next three to four years as he worked on completing his residency training. As time progressed, he would also start working in the field with some other universities in collaborative research projects. This experience would allow him the best of all worlds as far as he was concerned. He would be working in product research and development which would involve chemistry-related responsibilities. As this work is being done, he would also be working with cats in evaluating their response to treatments and the research being performed for a variety of diseases and disorders. It seemed to him the perfect blend of focus. He might even be able to work it out where if direct field activity is involved, that Doc Hughes' clinic could be one of the clinics as a source of practical application and feedback. The small stipend being offered in this internship would enable him to continue his training while being able to support himself well enough during the next few years of preparing for his board certification in canine and feline practice. Things seemed very bright indeed.

On his first day at CatGenus, Cameron completed all of the required paperwork in Human Resources. He needed to view a variety of safety videos to comply with all the state and federal standards since company is governed by their regulations. The general orientation to the corporation and a review of benefits, something that did not affect him, ended early into the second day at the company. After the completion of all of the requirements, his manager came to Human Resources to pick him up. Mark Radke was the manager of the department Cam would be working in. He was not a veterinarian but had a degree in chemistry. "Cameron, welcome to our department," said Mark, as they walked down the hall. "I have been here at CatGenus for the past four years." "Dr. Lewis in my interview said that our department is working on treatment for feline cognitive dysfunction. How long has CatGenus been working on this?" asked Cameron. "It's a relatively new area for us. We started on this disorder about nine months ago," Mark said. "Our CEO believes that although this is a common occurrence with a cat's aging and that if we come up with something we will be the first to do this; and on top of this, people will willing to pay for the treatment to aid their cat." "Makes sense," said Cameron as they entered the door to his new department. "Sally, I'd like to introduce you to Dr. Cameron Robert. He's our new Veterinary intern. He'll be working with us on the FCD initiative," said Mark. "Cameron, this is Sally, our department secretary." "Pleased to meet you, Sally," said Cameron. "Likewise," said Sally, not looking up from her computer screen. "I'll be working with you shortly on getting you access to the computer system and to do some additional basic training. Mark, how will eleven o'clock be for us to do this?" she asked him, again not looking up from her computer screen. "Fine, Sally," Mark replied. "Done and sent," said Sally, as she rose and walked over to the file cabinet. Cameron and Mark passed through the lab door after he swiped his badge on the card reader. "Don't mind Sally, Cameron. She's very focused on her job and very good at it. If I died, she could run the department." Cameron then entered a lab, larger than any one he had been in before. He guessed that the lab was about forty feet by forty feet, four rows of equipment and lab counters with about twenty people working in the area. There were three separate counters in each row, with a caged holding area at the end of each bench to keep the cats close to the work area. There was a multitude of equipment, shelves and chemicals lining the outer two walls of the lab. In the room off to the far right, Cameron could see cages where the experimental cats were kept, marked Kennel. At first glance, it appeared that there were at least twenty cages in this room. "Wow," said Cameron as they continued into the room. "Hello everyone; could I have your attention for a moment?" said Mark loudly so as to be heard over the hum of the equipment. "Everyone, I'd like to introduce our newest associate, Dr. Cameron Robert. Cameron comes to us from Knight University where he recently graduated Veterinarian school and will be working with us on the FCD project. Please take a moment in the days to come to introduce yourself to him and welcome him to our little community."

Mark walked Cameron over to his workstation which was on the far right of the room, on the end of the row toward the front of the room. From here, all he needed to do was to look directly behind and he could view the cats in the kennel. "Cameron, this area is open and I hope you find that it suits your needs. Each member of the lab team has an assigned work area. Make yourself at home and let me know if you need anything. We'll go over some of your responsibilities shortly," said Mark as he started toward his office. As Cam was leaning over to put his laptop bag down, one of the other employees came up to him, extending his hand. "Cameron, I'm Greg, Greg Thomas. Welcome to the team." Cameron extended his hand to shake as well and said, "Thanks, Greg. Call me Cam." "Right," said Greg. "How long have you been at CatGenus," Cam asked him. "I've only been with the company for close to a year," said Greg. "I'm doing an internship here as well. I'm specializing in feline practice. Looks like we both are working on the FCD. Our CEO is pretty pumped about this project and has kicked a lot of funds our way." "Is that so? I'm working on canine and feline board certification," said Cam as he looked around the lab. "Are all of these people working on this project as well?" "No." responded Greg. "There are a number of projects going on in the lab. Ours is just one of the probably six or seven projects being worked on. Have you met Scott yet? He's our lead on the project." "No, not yet, but I imagine we'll hook up shortly. It's Scott Clason you're referring to, I assume." "Yep, that's him. He's out for a couple of days" said Greg. "Great guy." "I thought so. They referred to him in my interview. Sounds like he's been researching this for a few years." "Hey, Cam, I see Sally is trying to get your attention. Watch her a bit. She lets Mark know everything that is going on in here; keeps pretty close tabs on us all. Mark's in meetings most of the time and she watches to make sure we're all working and not just standing around talking." "Thanks for the advice, Greg. I'll do that."

Cam did not meet Scott after being at CatGenus until Thursday of his first week. Scott had been out at a conference and had just returned. He was a tall gentleman; about 6'3", average build, and if he had to guess, was about forty years old. His hair was thinning, a little bit of a mid-rift budge. He carried the old style briefcase. As he walked in, he stopped at the counter just in front of Cam's and set his briefcase down. He turned toward Cam, coming over toward him saying, "Well, you must be Cameron. Morning son, I'm Scott Clason. Sorry I was not here Monday when you started, but couldn't be helped. Welcome to the team." "Thanks," said Cam as he shook Scott's hand. A pretty strong handshake thought Cam. "Cameron…" said Scott. "Call me Cam, if you would Scott." "OK," said Scott. "Cam, we are on an adventure here, as I like to put it. Too many people fret and stress over their pets as they age, and for many people, these pets are part of their family, sometimes their only family." "That's true," said Cam. "So, what we are trying to do here is to extend the functional life of these animals and in doing so, we are extending the lives of many people as well. Wouldn't you agree?" asked Scott. "Well, yes, I would suppose you could say that." answered Cam. "Good," said Scott. "We've just covered the intent of our mission statement, something that I know you heard earlier. Let's get to work. Mark asked me to work with you. We will be spending the next couple of days bringing you up to speed with our research and the progress we've made to date. I understand from the information I have received that you have a good background in Chemistry." "You could say that," said Cam. "I also found Biology just as interesting." "Good," said Scott. "We will be working with many compounds to develop a substance to treat the cause of FCD, as you know. Some of our research has centered near to the medicines used in humans to treat Alzheimer's disease, but to date, we've not made any significant headway. I'm a chemist by trade, so your part in this is to help me to better understand cats and their biology. We've worked with a few Vets to date and frankly, most of them have not worked out. Greg is the only one that has stayed for any length of time." "Sorry to hear that," said Cam. "I plan on being around for a while to complete my internship. But just as I mentioned in my interview, I will give you my all to whatever project you give me, so I'm ready to start when you are."

Cam was working late. He had just finished a call from Ali, who called him every week or so to check on him. He had been home sporadically, having plunged into his work. Today had been a full day, but was trying to work out one problem. Since he was the only one in the lab, he decided to let one of the cats out of their cage. Although researchers are expected to maintain a professional distance toward the animals they work with, this particular cat reminded him of his cat from years ago, Dearfoot. The cat had all-four tan paws, colored similar to that of a deer, hence where the name came from. Along with this, the cat's mannerisms reminded him of a simpler time of life. "Come here, boy," said the young Vet as he opened the cage. For some reason, Dearfoot, or CT 292, his lab identification, was leery of the other researchers, but not Cam. Dearfoot warmed up to him fairly quickly, something the others had noticed as well. A couple of others had felt the cat's wrath even though they wore protective clothing while working with the animals and were leery of him. With the connection between the two, Cam felt comfortable letting Dearfoot trot around the lab when they were alone, but for the most part, the animal stayed fairly close to him most of the time. Dearfoot was not one of the test animals for his project. He was considered one of the control animals for another project, without any detectable problem to help the researchers gauge their treatments and the impairment of the disorders each subject was experiencing. Cam reached into his bag, pulling out a zip lock bag with some cat food inside, a practice that he had started early on. He took the small food bowl he kept in the back of his cabinet drawer and poured the food into it, with Dearfoot impatiently waiting. Placing the bowl inside the cage to the right of the counter, he was followed closely by the hungry cat. Scarfing it up quickly as usual, Cam cleaned the bowl, returning it to the drawer and the nightly ritual was completed. Dearfoot would hop up on the counter and rub against him and purr. Of those cats in his project, there were cats eleven to fifteen years of age, some older, six of them in total, Dearfoot was one of the youngest cat he associated with, being about seven years old. Each of the subjects had shown signs of FCD and the appropriate testing has been performed to rule out other conditions. Treatment to date was in using a medication approved for use in dogs (deprenyl), but the effects upon the disorder in cats have been limited. Their team would provide a weekly update to Mark who would monitor their progress as he did with the remaining projects. All in all, each member was assigned a specific area to concentrate on. Cam's assignment was to concentrate on the chemical compounds being suggested by the group either through research or practical application since he had a degree in Chemistry. Everyone did well in meeting the respective assignments. Cam looked forward to being a part of research for cats and appreciated the wonderful facilities that CatGenus had to offer. He found everyone quite dedicated to their work.

5

ENLIGHTENMENT

Cam had just returned from a long weekend at home where he was able to reconnect with his family and friends. He particularly enjoyed being with Ali. She was still working with Doc and had not been seeing anyone. There was a stronger connection brewing between the two of them and their time together was refreshing for Cam. On returning to work, he now had ten months of pain-staking research behind him with essentially minimal success. Although following all of the standards in place to assure the cats were treated humanely, about two-thirds of the cats in the study had passed away. Replacement subjects were possible through some of the area shelters who had been contacted to alert them of the need for cats displaying actions or behaviors consistent with FCD. Cam was able to work with Mark and the other researchers to bring Dearfoot into his research group of cats. He did not exhibit any of the FCD symptoms, but he convinced them he needed a couple of "control" cats in his project. Besides, some of the other researchers on the team which was working with Dearfoot were fine with this since they had experienced his wrath over time. Cam's team had developed a network of researchers from some of the leading universities, partly as a means for someone else to help them sift through the literature, but to also take advantage of non-competing research being conducted. Cam had also contacted Dr. Gill as another source for assistance. The students in training at Knight would conduct research for the team as part of their training which was a welcomed endeavor by the faculty of the veterinarian school. One thing that Cam had also considered was trying to maintain a connection with Andrew, his old friend. Andrew had graduated from Smith's State and had decided to be satisfied with going into private practice. He'd had enough school and wanted to start his career. Cam intended to contact him to see if he would be willing to assist in the information gathering and research that he might have gained from his practice, but with all of his other responsibilities, this link was one that he neglected to contact; it has slipped his mind. With the vast amount of research being performed in a number of similar areas, this network was becoming invaluable to Cameron. The week was winding down and with the upcoming board meeting; he and his team was working to compile information for this meeting since this would showcase their progress.

Cameron was waiting outside the boardroom, waiting to present his team's data to senior leadership. Scott was already in the boardroom, giving a preliminary report, doing as he put it, "Softening them up" for Cam. Mark was in there as well. Cam, as the Veterinarian on the project was felt to be the best person to present their progress to the board. He hoped that Scott had shared his research with Mark prior to the meeting. Cam looked down at his watch. Scott had been in there for the last twenty minutes. As he continued to sit there waiting, he was beginning to get nervous. "What in the world is going on in there?" he asked himself. There were some loud sounds coming from the boardroom, not happy sounds. Mrs. Johnson, the executive secretary for the "C" suite, glanced over at the door for a second, looked at Cam and smiled, and then returned to her work. A few minutes later, the door to the boardroom opened and Scott motioned for Cam to come in. Taking a hard swallow, Cam stood up, straightened his tie, gathered his materials, and walked into the boardroom. This was the first time he had presented anything to a group of this caliber before and his pulse was racing a bit. As he entered, he took note of the perfectly tailored suits and of the coiffured hair of the board members; and their stone-like faces. Many did not look up as he entered. He could feel his heart pounding as he was guided by Scott to a seat midway down the conference table. "Mr. Buck, how appropriate of a name for the CEO," thought Cam as he looked at the man that sat at the head of the table, flipping through the portfolio in front of him. Mr. Patrick Buck could be a close relative to either Harrison Ford or Kevin Costner in appearance. Cameron speculated that he was about 50 years old, with a little touch of gray flecks in his hair. He was tanned, but by the looks of his somewhat roughened hands, he was no stranger to physical activities; no tanning beds for him. "Well Dr. Robert, Scott here has said that you and your team have been working quite hard over the past year. I would imagine that he gave you the standard line that he was going to soften us up before you came in. Well, forget that. You are playing in the big leagues now, and I am as interested in results as I am passionate about helping out furry friends. What do you have to share with us?" said Mr. Buck who finally looked up from the portfolio, crossing his hands in front of him. "Well sir," said Cam as he swallowed hard again, "we have amassed quite a volume of research being conducted on FCD. As I imagine you probably know, the results with deprenyl have not been as promising as was initially hoped. There have been improvements with some subjects, but sometimes the side effects have been worse than the primary problem. I would say that the most promising research, other than our own, has occurred in Sweden. They have been using a combination of deprenyl in combination with some herbal compounds which has shown promise. Do I believe this is the answer to this disorder, I would say no." The room was quiet and all eyes were upon him. "Dr., other than data gathering, what do you have to show for the past year of work?" asked the CEO impatiently. "I have synthesized a compound using portions from deprenyl, donepezil, memantine, and cannabis which has reduced the irritability and aggression of most of the test subjects." "Cannabis?" interrupted one of the board members. "Isn't that illegal?" "No," responded Cameron. "Use of medicinal marijuana is acceptable under certain conditions and these conditions have been followed to the T; and this has been monitored and verified by multiple individuals," looking at the board member that posed the concern. "Continuing, with sample 208 there has also been a reduction in hypervocalization and an improvement in coordination in these subjects as well. This is a more substantial response than that shared from the research in Sweden," said Cameron. "You have the data from our observations, if I am not mistaken." "Yes Dr. Robert, we have your data, but to be quite blunt, with the money that we have poured into this project, we had hoped for greater success than this. Mark, Dr. Robert, we need a fairly concrete timetable of how much more time is needed for an effective treatment for this disorder. We don't have endless funds," said Buck as he sat back in his chair. Cameron felt that cold glare of Mr. Buck's eyes upon him; there was silence for what seemed forever. "Mr. Buck, stated Mark, "we believe that we can have something concrete within the next six months." Cameron looked at the man that just spoke. It was almost as though this man was someone he did not know. "Was he crazy?" he thought. "Has he lost his mind? How in the world could we ever accomplish this monumental task in only six months?" As he turned to begin to speak, Scott placed his hand on Cameron's arm as a sign that he should restrain himself. Buck noticed this action, but chose not to respond. Cameron looked at Scott quizzically, expecting some sort of explanation from him. "Six months it is," said the CEO as he closed the portfolio. Reaching over to the intercom, he pressed the button, asking for Mrs. Johnson to come into the boardroom. "See you in a few months, gentlemen. Get busy!" he said as they were rising from the seats. The board members began to whisper amongst themselves as the three researchers were leaving the room.

"Mrs. Johnson!" yelled Mr. Buck into the intercom. "Where are you?"

"So, I guess this is the corporate world," says Cameron disgustedly. "Mark, I know you are my boss, but are you freakin' nuts?" The elevator closed with the three men inside. "Cam," he said while looking up at the floor indicator. "You need to realize that I have to work both sides of the room. I have to support leadership and our team as well. No, I'm not nuts, but we have to work faster. If I had not given him a timeframe, the whole project would have been in jeopardy. Work with me here." Still disgusted, Cam didn't say anything. The typical silence of an elevator ride prevailed for the remainder of the ride to the third floor. The doors opened and they exited to the right, walking down the corridor toward their lab. "Mark," said Cam, "although I was raised on a farm, I didn't grow up in the turnip patch. I know corporate expects results, but six months... I don't know."

Each man walked through the door, Mark turned for his office, Scott and Cam toward the lab door. "Cam, said Mark as he stopped at the door, "Forget about the time frame for now. Let me worry about the C suite. Just do what you do best, keep plugging away at it. I'm confident you'll get there." Cam just kept walking, not acknowledging Mark's comments. He slammed his material down on the counter, looked at Scott and said, "I hope the hell he knows what he's doing. We're making progress, but I don't know, I just don't know." After everyone left that evening, he decided to call Ali. He felt as though he had been sold out a bit and needed to hear a pleasant and friendly voice. They talked for about an hour and when the conversation turned to his work, he side-stepped the topic. Ali knew something was amiss, but did not want to push the issue. Cam and Ali had said their goodbyes and shortly after this, Cam eventually packed up his materials and walked down to his car. He stopped on the way to his home to grab a quick dinner at a mom and pop diner just a couple of miles from his apartment. He sat there and reflected upon the meeting, Buck's business-like attitude and the response from his boss in the meeting. He was troubled by all of the events that unfolded earlier in the day and really began to question his future with this entity. He did believe that his project was worthwhile, but this was a sharp blow to his idealism, a contrast from what he had expected from a company espousing to have the desire to improve the lives of cats. He picked at his food, not having much of an appetite. His phone ringing brought him back to reality and as he fought to retrieve it from his pocket. The call was from Doc. "Hello Doc," said Cam. "Hi there Cam. I hear you got a taste of corporate America today." "I guess so," said Cam as he turned to look out the window of the diner. "I feel kind of little like a fool right now. I swallowed their mission statement and was sure that the cats were the top priority at CatGenus. I guess I was too Pollyannaish." "Well Cam, don't be too hard on yourself. We all get a dose of reality when dealing with the corporate world. Whether we want to believe it or not, the vast majority of the world revolves around money. There are only a few Mother Teresa's in the world and I can't think of any corporation that even comes close to her. We all come to this reality at different times in our lives, so I'm sorry to say, welcome to our world son," said Doc. Cam changed the subject to find out how things were going at the clinic, how Susi was, and if Ali was OK. They talked for a few more minutes and then Cam headed home.

6

A NEW WORLD

About three and a half months had passed since the board meeting and Cam remained frustrated at the situation. He was one that did not walk away from a challenge, but he was having second thoughts. This was his third twelve-hour day and his buddy Dearfoot was by his side. Dearfoot was lying on the left corner of his work station. The equipment hummed in the background as he measured out the mix of chemicals he was working with; this was sample number 213. His past successes with the combination of Alzheimer drugs was encouraging, but still was not the answer; one symptom would be affected by a combination of agents, but others remained. He changed the amounts of the primary drugs, deprenyl, donepezil, cannabis, and memantine, this time with memantine having the largest quantity in the mixture. To this combination he added a tiny concentration of hyoscine. Hyoscine was Scopolamine, better known as "truth serum" in the movies. It has pre-anesthetic qualities which might offer some advantage. Dearfoot stood up next to him and stretched as cats do after a nap and began to rub up against him. "Hi boy," said the researcher as he was pouring the mixture into

a container. He then placed the container on the counter
and because it was very late and he was tired, Cam felt it
best to conduct trials with this sample in the morning. He
retrieved the bag of cat food from his bag and the bowl, and
then placed the filled bowl into the cage as usual to feed
Dearfoot. As he leaned over the counter to grab a pencil
from his neighbor's work area, unbeknownst to him, his lab
coat brushed up against the container, spilling some of the
contents down upon Dearfoot's food. The cat is his usual
efficient manner, kept right on eating, not being inhibited in
the least at the condiment that had been inadvertently
added. Jotting down a couple a notes to himself, he still had
not noticed the accident. In a couple of moments, Dearfoot
leapt up upon the counter, sitting unusually on the edge of
the corner, erect as though at attention, blocking his view of
the container. Cameron, almost as a reflex, reached down
and grabbed the bowl, cleaned it out and returned it to its
hiding place. "Dearfoot," he said to the cat, "you need
move over here," pointing off to the left. "You are right in
my way." Obediently, the cat responded immediately. Cam
was oblivious to what had just happened while he
continued to work. The cat maintained its erect sitting pose
while he worked. Gazing over to the right, he was in deep
thought about this new mixture and the coming day's plan

for testing it, when he realized that he had knocked over the container. Seeing that it had spilled over the edge of the counter, he looked down to see a faint shadow of powder from where the food bowl had earlier been. Quickly realizing that some of the mixture had spilled into the bowl, he looked at Dearfoot, who stood there at what appeared to be attention, blinking his eyes at Cam. "Hey boy, are you all right?" he asked the cat. "Come here, let's see." The cat immediately stood up and walked obediently over to him, like usual. Giving the cat a quick exam, he appeared fine. The only thing of note was that the cat's pupils seemed larger than normal. Not being alarmed or concerned, he said to Dearfoot without much thought, "OK boy, why don't you go lay down." The cat immediately laid down right where he was. Being the astute researcher that he had become, he thought this was a bit odd, so then he told Dearfoot, "Stand up." The cat promptly followed his command. "Hummm," thought Cam. "Maybe this is a coincidence." He looked at the cat, turned to his right and walked down a couple of benches away and gave the command, "Dearfoot, jump down on the floor." As he stood there, the cat jumped to the floor. "Now jump up into my chair," he said. The cat jumped into the chair. Perplexed, but with the wheels spinning in his mind, he next instructed him to, "Go into the cage." The cat responded appropriately and entered the cage. "How could this be?" thought the young researcher to himself. Could it be the compound he had just made? Thinking for a few moments, he next told the cat to, "Come out of the cage and scratch at the floor." The cat obeyed and scratched. Sitting down in the chair next to him, he was in shock. "This is not possible. What have I developed? It seems obvious that something is going on. Cat's don't follow commands!" Sitting there stunned, he stared at Dearfoot, his mind racing. The cat looked back directly at him. After a few more moments, the rigidity of the cat began to wane and he rose upon on all fours and then jumped up onto the counter, assuming his usual posture, lying down upon the countertop. Noticing the change in demeanor, he instructed the cat to jump down to the floor. Dearfoot remained lying down on the counter, blinking his eyes at the young doctor. "Am I dreaming this?" Cam said to himself. "I know I've been working some long hours and I'm bushed, but this did happen." He reflected upon this strange occurrence and speculated that Dearfoot had followed his commands for about five minutes from the time he had noticed the change in the animal. Again, he examined Dearfoot and found nothing out of the ordinary physiologically, but he did notice that his pupils were no longer enlarged. The cat looked and acted now as he always had. He considered what he had just witnessed and then turned to his computer. Something struck him that with this odd occurrence, that maybe he should document this on his personal computer until he had a chance to validate it. Once his computer powered up, he entered his observations into it for future reference. His head was spinning and the implications of what he had just witnessed were astounding to the young researcher. He then stopped and wiped up the remainder of the spilled compound from the floor. As tired as he was, he questioned whether this had really happened and planned on trying the mixture out on Dearfoot tomorrow. Cam placed Dearfoot back in his cage and then gathered his things to head home.

He didn't sleep well that night even though he was beat. He was perplexed about what he had witnessed and partially convinced himself that what he witnessed was from sleep deprivation. He took a diphenhydramine and went to bed, finally getting some sleep. The next day, Cam came into the lab and was clearly eager to get to work. He passed Scott, who had said good morning to him, but he didn't notice. "Hey Buddy, what's up?" said Scott as he approached Cam. "Uh, what do you mean," Cam said somewhat nervously. "You seem a little rattled this morning. I said hello to you, but you missed it. Everything all right?" asked his friend. "Yah, things are good. I guess that I haven't had too enough caffeine this morning. I didn't sleep very well last night. Sorry Scott. How are you?" Cam replied. "I'm fine man. Maybe you should stop a little early today, go home and take some something and get some rest," said his friend. Scott returned to his work area and then said to Cam, "Cam, I know you've been working quite a lot lately. Maybe you should take a day off." "Maybe," said Cam as he started to prepare going over his notes. He powered up his personal laptop and started reviewing the previous night's entry. He needed to re-verify what had transpired or make certain his sleep deprivation was not playing tricks on him. If it was true, he didn't want this to leak out quite yet. Even if true, this occurrence was not within the parameters of the project and he planned to do more testing to validate his observations.

Cam stayed late the next night and after telling the last person goodbye, he waited for a while to make sure everyone had left for sure. While he waited, he played with Dearfoot a little with some string and the two enjoyed this activity. About fifteen minutes after the last person left, Cam was eager to try to repeat the last night's events.

Through knowing how much he had originally had in the container prior to the spill, he approximated how much Dearfoot had been given, since some of it fell onto the floor around the bowl. He measured this amount and added it to Dearfoot's food and placed the bowl in the cage as usual. Dearfoot responded as always and made work of cleaning the bowl. Cam waited for a few minutes after Dearfoot had finished and then started his test. "Dearfoot, come over and stand by this foot," pointing to his left foot. The cat stood up and immediately stood by his left foot. "Now Dearfoot, go over to the door," pointing to the lab entry door. The cat obeyed. He then walked into the kennel, took one of the other cats and placed it in Dearfoot's cage and then said to Dearfoot, "Dearfoot, go and get in the empty cage." The cat arose, walked into the kennel, and jumped up into the other cat's cage and turned and looked at Cameron. He was again dumbfounded. "This isn't sleep deprivation; it works. He understands me and follows my commands." Cam stood there for a few more moments, looking at Dearfoot, not really sure what to do. This break in activity was shortly followed by Dearfoot becoming again less rigid and he eventually jumped down from the cage and came up to Cam, rubbing against his leg like usual. Cam sat down and considered what had just occurred. He then recorded this information into his personal laptop for later reference. He pet Dearfoot for a while longer and thought about the discovery and where it might be of value. One thing he now knew; this was for real.

It was time for their weekly meeting and Cam gathered the information up through sample 212. The conference room was just large enough for about eight people comfortably. Each seat at the table had a computer screen to review the information being shared. As Mark opened the meeting, Cam sat down toward the other end of the table as to be less noticeable. "Well gentlemen, the clock is ticking. We have about two and a half months until the board expects results. Where are we?" said Mark as he scanned to group. There was silence for a few moments and then Scott spoke up. "Cam, you have been working late for some time. Where are you with things?" Cam was surprised by Scott's abruptness in calling him out. "Well, I've really not had much progress since we last talked. It appears that I am at an impasse, but still trudging along. It doesn't seem to matter what combinations I use or the concentrations of agents, we still are not much further along than we were with sample 208. With each sample, we make headway with one symptom; nothing with the other symptoms or another side effect pops up. I have not received any information from anyone else in the group saying they had made any progress either," said Cam half-heartedly. "Any leads from any of the research being done around the globe," asked Mark. Jim, usually the silent one in these meetings spoke up saying, "It appears that the researchers in Japan have come up with a similar formula to ours except that they have relied more upon some herbal substances with the same, maybe slightly better results." "Is this the first you're shared this with the group Jim?" asked Mark. "Yes sir, it is," he responded. "Jim, damn, it! Why are you sitting on information which might help us? What herbal substances? Pal, if you want to maintain your status here, get with the program!" yelled Mark. "We have a clock ticking fellas! Don't forget it!" As Mark headed toward the door, obviously the meeting was over. Everyone else started to gather their material and leave. Cam's cell phone rang and he looked at it to see who was calling him. It was Ali. "Hello," answered Cam. "Ali, is everything alright?" "No, not really," said Ali. "Gramps has had a slight stroke and is in the hospital. I thought you'd want to know." "Oh my gosh!" said Cam. "I'm coming home. Be there in a few hours." Looking over at Scott, he said, "Scott, I'm heading home. A friend is not well and I need to see him. I'm knocking off early today." "OK," said

Scott. "You've put in a tremendous number of hours. Get out of here. See you Monday. Hope things go well; be careful." Cam packed up his things quickly and was on the road.

7

CONNECTING

Cam entered St Joseph's Hospital, asking the volunteer where room 238 was located. After finding this out, he headed to the room. He had been in conversation with Ali for a significant portion of the trip back; it took him about three and a half hours to get back; not bad considering the traffic. The two talked about Doc, how he was such an integral part of the lives, especially Ali, him being her grandfather. Cam looked at Doc as being a second father to him and was very concerned about his condition. Passing a waiting room without looking in, he was about to enter the room when he heard Ali calling to him. He turned as she threw her arms around him. Returning the hug he asked, "How is he?" "He doing pretty well," said Ali as she wiped a tear from her eye. "The doctors say he's lucky. They were able to start the clot busters early into this and believe he will recover well," she said. "Thank goodness he was still at the clinic when this happened." "Good," said Cam as he stepped back to look at her. "Ali, I've really missed you. I should come home more often, but there has been a lot of pressure on us to get this project done. Can I see him?" he asked, looking toward the room. "The nurse said we can go in, but that we should try and keep our visits short for now so he can rest." On entering the room, Doc had his eyes closed and the two whispered to each other that maybe they had better come back later. "Do that and you'll piss me off," said Doc as he opened his eyes and smiled at the two of them. Raising his hands for the two to grab onto, Doc smiled and looked as he had in the past; something that Cam was glad to see. "He seems to have minimal deficits apparently," thought Cam as he approached. Doc had a firm handshake, something very good, thought Cam. There did not appear to be any speech loss; he just looked like someone that had come in for routine testing. They talked about a variety of things, mostly about what Doc had experienced in this scare and what they doctors had shared about his prognosis. Looked like he would be able to return to his practice, but it was suggested that he try and reduce his hours some. He was sixty-two and at this age many of the veterinarians were strongly considering retirement. That word left a bad taste in Doc's mouth.

With Doc's latest development, Cam had arranged to take a couple of days off to spend some time back home. His parents were more than glad to see him. His room was as he had left it; he paused after entering the room to look around and reflect upon the past. There was the trophy and ribbon he had won at the county fair for the science project on greenhouse emissions; his vacation pictures and pictures of his friends from days gone by were on his bulletin board; the Red Sox pennant and the Peyton Manning signed helmet were in the sports corner. And there in the other corner was the tall stack of Popular Science magazines almost as tall as Cam. All was the same, but not the same. It's tough to return to your past, a past that you often miss. However, time marches on as they say, whomever they are, and growing up is an inevitability. His mother was coming up the stairs toward his room, so Cam continued into his room. He placed his bag on the bed as his mother came in. "Cam, I'm sorry to hear about Doc. How is he doing?" she asked, walking up close behind him and placing he right hand on his shoulder and the left hand on his lower left forearm. "He seems to be doing well," said Cam as he turned to face his mother. He bent over and gave her a hug. He missed being able to do this. They were both close and he missed her the most. "Dad is at the feed store and should be back shortly. Boy will he be glad to see you!" she said returning the hug. Cam unpacked his things and once done, the two of them went downstairs to catch up on what he had been doing and what had been going on at home.

Orville came home a short time later and Cam let him know how Doc was doing and they spent time together catching up as well. Although it was for an unfortunate occurrence, Cam appreciated being home. Later, he went outside and threw the frizbee and he and Ellie played for a while; he sent some quality time with Max too. Marjorie started fixing dinner and they all sat down to eat.

Ali kept him informed on how Doc has been doing. Cam did not want to impose nor wear him out and would take Ali's lead as to when to go and see him. He stopped by the clinic the next day to see if there was anything he might be able to do to help with seeing the patients on his schedule. Altogether, Ali and Cam saw thirteen animals that day. Once out of the hospital, Doc on the other hand, did take the doctor's advice and planned to cut back; from fifty hours a week to forty-eight; no surprise. From Doc's perspective, he would be following doctor's orders. Susi was angry with him and would work her charm to lessen this number of hours. In coming home, Cam had some plans for his time off. First, he wanted to spend some time with his parents. Since taking on the internship, he had hardly taken any time away and he missed his family. Emily was in college and he hoped to get over to see her as well. Second, he wanted to spend some time with Ali.

There was a growing affection between the two of them, and although she was four years older, their attraction to one another had grown stronger. Lastly, he wanted to help Doc however he could and he wanted to approach Doc with an idea. With Doc's hospitalization and his release, Cam decided to wait to talk with Doc about his idea but made certain he saw his patients over the next few days.

Upon his return to work, Cam dove into doing more experimenting with sample 213. On that Monday, he planned to wait until all of his co-workers had left for their hour lunch to continue experimenting. After he had declined their invitation to join them for lunch and after verifying that everyone had left, he brought Dearfoot out and petted him for a few moments. He then continued his quick assessment of the animal by asking him to perform various tasks or requests. "Dearfoot, walk over to the door," he instructed the cat. The cat sat there and looked up at him. Next, he asked the cat to jump up on the chair. Again the cat looked up at him. He sat down in his chair and patted the top of the counter and called to the cat to jump up on it. With this instruction, the cat did what was asked. He then told the cat to jump down to the floor; the cat did not obey. Being the efficient researcher he had become, Cam took time to continue noting these events to this point before proceeding. After this initial assessment, Cam then prepared a dose of the drug to administer to Dearfoot.

He continued to modify the dose of sample that Dearfoot had received and gave it to him again in his food. The same results as from the previous testing occurred and its effects lasted for six minutes. He again noted these observations into his laptop. Each remaining day of the week, he repeated this experiment a lunch time or stayed late with the cats in the study that were diagnosed with FCD. Although not as pronounced as with Dearfoot, there were positive changes in each of the subsequent animals, most followed his commands. He recorded all of the results from each encounter with the individual subjects. The next week he did the same but doubled the dose. With Dearfoot, the obedience lasted for twenty minutes at this dose. With the other subjects, there were varying degrees of increased improvement in symptoms and with compliance to commands. The effects were definitely not as long lasting in the FCD subjects however. That was something that was puzzling to Cam; what caused the difference in these cats? It was amazing to him that the cats could understand the verbal commands given to them by him. "Cats do definitely cognitively understand what we tell or ask them to do.

They are just obstinate or too independent and don't want to follow commands," thought Cameron. This response did not meet the project objectives and he was concerned that he would be required put his efforts on the shelf for now or in the worst case scenario, for this work to side rail the work on FCD as a result of this was fascinating breakthrough. Cam realized that the ability to extend the research time and investigation was not possible at the lab and that he needed to look for other avenues. His hope was to elicit Doc's assistance in expanding the testing, under his guidance to develop a useful purpose for this substance. He had not brought this up to Doc yet, to give him time to work through his recent challenge. It was Friday and he started heading home; his computer and some of the sample 213 in his possession, he was ready to continue his work. Hopefully Doc would be willing. Either way, with his coming time away, he hoped to continue refining his discovery.

Cam had called Doc on his way home that Friday and after the normal conversation of how he was doing and things were going overall, he arranged with Doc to meet him at the clinic right after closing time. To Doc, Cam seemed remarkably excited about whatever it was he wanted to share which peaked Doc's interest. The only thing as close to this excitement level was when Cam and he were initially talking about Cam coming to work at the clinic, but this was different. A couple of hours later, Cam arrived and Doc greeted him and they went into his office. The two continued to catch up a bit, but Doc could tell that Cam had something more important on his mind, so he asked Cam what was on his mind. Cam quickly opened his laptop asking Doc for just a minute to get ready. Cam started to share his information and Doc sat there and listened to the young Veterinarian as he explained the high points of what he had experienced and discovered. Cameron was quite passionate in his description of the events that had transpired; he knew he was on to something. After about ten minutes of listening, the experienced Veterinarian raised his hand to stop the excited young man. "Cameron, is this really true? If so, what you are sharing with me is amazing. Of all the animals we typically encounter as Veterinarians, cats are the most independent and the most self-sufficient animals. People have tried to train cats forever and some say for instance, that they can train a cat to use the toilet; I've never seen it and believe it is bunk," said the aging Veterinarian sitting behind his desk. "You ask me if I would consider being a part of this research and the refinement of this creation? My answer would most definitely be yes!" he said. "This is revolutionary!" Cam smiled as he viewed the excited response from his friend. He had not ever seen Doc so animated as he watched him get up; walking around the room while he considered what had been shared with him. He walked toward the clinic door, stopping to look through it. "You know, if we are going to do this, we need to follow established protocol and get permission from any pet owners if we involve their pets." he said continuing to look out the door. "Well," said Cam, "that is true but I have another idea. To do that we would need to explain to their owners what the intent of the research is and I don't think that would be the best idea. What I propose is that we pick up some stray cats from the animal shelter; we would only need about four or five, to use them in our continued work. We would leave information about each cat with them at the shelter so that if an owner came in looking for a particular cat, we could still be able to re-unite them. Unfortunately most of these cats will be euthanized eventually and in doing this we might be able to extend their lives and possibly even find homes for them through the clinic. There is nothing in this mixture that would harm any of them. Make sense?" said Cam eagerly. After a short time for contemplation, Doc answered, "Yes Cam, that makes perfect sense and by working through the clinic, we would be able to document and meet all care and ethical requirements as well. And by the way, I don't know if you have considered this, but we'll also need to bring Ali into this as well. No way can we do this without her knowing; you OK with that?" "Absolutely!" said Cam confidently. "I wouldn't want it any other way." "When do you want to start?" said Doc as he turned, heading back to his office. "The sooner the better; my time off clock is ticking," said Cam as he opened the phone book to find the animal shelter number. "I wholeheartedly agree," said Doc. "I want to see this drug in action."

8

PROGRESS

Ali sat there absorbing the information being shared by the two men in her life. She didn't understand the chemical, scientific mumbo-jumbo, but she realized this was a definite breakthrough. "I would be happy to help with this and I also understand the need to keep this work under wraps," she said as they sat in the office. "If you don't mind, I have one suggestion." "What's that," said Cam as he gathered the material that had been shared with her. "If possible, I would suggest that we get another computer which would be solely use for this research. Having one separate eliminates risk and separates this work from any other in the clinic. If we need to work elsewhere in the future, it would make things a little easier as well," she said. "I think that is a reasonable and prudent idea," said Doc. "Besides, it is tax deductible as well! We'll log it through the clinic." "Done," said Cam. "Ali, would you take care of doing that? I have all of the software we would need and can download it on the new system," said Cam. "Consider it done," she said looking up at him.

Ali had contacted the local animal shelter which was more than willing to assist the request from the clinic to pick up two healthy stray cats and to look for cats exhibiting FCD symptoms. Since Doc had not seen this creation in action, it was prudent to offer him a demonstration. Once the cats were at the clinic, Cam and Doc checked them over to see if there was any medical concern with any of them. After this, Doc and Cam began to pour over the data and consider possible adjustments to the sample; something they would do over the coming days and weeks. Cam now considered the most current sample number 218. Since he had not worked with this drug yet, Cam allowed Doc to administer the drug to the first cat with the latest dose that he had given to Dearfoot and waited the short interval for it to become effective. Once they noticed a more rigid response from the cat, Cam looked at Doc and said, "Doc, it would be my pleasure for you to be the one to offer the commands to this cat." "Gladly," said Doc. He looked down at the cat and then said, "Walk in a circle," using his arm to make a circular motion to aid the cat in understanding his request. The cat rose from its seated position and began walking in a circle. "Stop!" said Doc. The cat stopped. "Jump up on the exam table." Doc pointed to the table and without hesitation, the cat jumped up on the table. "This is absolutely amazing!" said Doc as he continued to give other commands to the cat. The two men talked more about the drug and about the length of action as they prepared for performing additional tests.

In the following tests conducted with this batch, all of the cats that the sample was used on obeyed commands for over two hours; an astounding amount of time. They did not have the ability with their limited resources to make a time-released type of substance, but that was considered as a future option once this was developed to the point of bringing it to the company level. "Cam," said Doc as they were recording their findings, "have you given thought as to how and when you plan on sharing this discovery with your company?" Cam stopped what he was doing, looking at his mentor and said, "Doc, our team is on a definite time frame and we only have another two months before we need to report to the board our progress. My hope is that in continuing this work that we do find an effective agent to use in the treatment of FCD. If we do, then we will need to look at our options for this substance we are presently working on. I am afraid that if I share this development now, that it will detract their attention to the project and reduce the likelihood of success. However, if we cannot find a cure, then I will have no choice but to share this research with the company. Too many people's jobs and my reputation and the reputation of the group are at stake. We have to present some viable, worthwhile outcome for all of the research and the dollars spent during this past essentially more than two years," said the young scientist. Cam looked up at the calendar and realized that he and Ali had a date tonight, so it was time to wrap things up so he wouldn't be late. Doc said he would stay and do a little more work before going home.

"Cam," said Ali, "I really have enjoyed this evening. It's a beautiful night." The two had stopped at Highland Park to get out and sit on the hood of his car to look at the stars. "Dinner was great. I've not eaten at Tony Romana's restaurant before. Good choice, Cam." "I've had a great time too, Ali. I have really missed you," said Cam, looking into her eyes. "It's a little chilly tonight, don't you think?" she said as she pulled a little closer to him. "Oh… yah," said Cam as he put his arm around her. She looked up at him for a moment, turned and putting her hand on the back of his head, gently pulled him toward her, kissing him gently. He was taken a little by surprise, but welcomed the affection. They stopped, looked into each other's eyes and kissed again, this time more passionately. They got down off the hood of his car and went for a walk through the park. It was a perfect night, clear with stars twinkling in the distance. The remainder of the evening went by all too fast for them both, but each seemed to have one of the best nights of their lives.

On getting to the clinic the next morning, Cam found Doc hard at work. It was unusual for them to see patients on a Sunday, but Mrs. LeBlanc's dog was in distress. Ali had just arrived a little earlier and she seemed to have a little bouncy step to her this morning. "Morning, Cam!" she said, glad to see him come in. "Ready for another wonderful day," as she touched his arm as she passed. "Yep," he said. "I only have a couple more days before I need to head back to work." "Cam," said Doc as he exited an exam room, "I want to share something with you once I'm done here." "OK," said Cam as he entered the exam room that had been converted into a mini-research lab. Once done with the patient he had, Doc came into the room and closed the door. "Cam my boy, I have something to show you. Mrs. LeBlanc will be here in about a half-an-hour, so we have a little time. I worked late last night and think I have come up with an improvement in the combination of agents. I've been thinking about this for a while and thought that there had to be something we could use to lengthen the duration of action of these agents. In doing some research, I went to the health food store and bought some ginkgo. I added about two mg of this to the 218 sample and watch. He opened the door and said "Gracie, come in here." In a short moment, the calico cat named Gracie walked through the door, looking up at Doc. "Gracie, jump up on the table," he instructed. "Now Gracie, pick up that piece of paper and while keeping it in your mouth, jump over to the other counter." The cat bent down, picked up the piece of paper, and leapt over to the other counter as asked. "Cam, now you tell her to do something," Doc said. "Gracie, jump back over to the table." The cat stood there looking at him. He repeated the command, this time pointing over to the table as well. Again, the cat sat there. "Gracie, jump over to the table and put down the paper," said Doc, and the cat did as requested. "That was one thing that I was wondering about; was the subject willing to take commands from anyone or was it specific to the person giving the medication. This is kind of like an imprinting that happens with animals at birth. Another thing that I half-way wondered about also and we still need to verify is, is it the person giving the medication or does this attachment relate to the first person seen by the animal; the imprinting perspective. "I had asked Ali a little before you came in to see if Gracie would follow her commands and she didn't. I wanted to re-verify this with you when you came in this morning," said Doc as he then told Gracie to it, which she did. "Could you work with Mrs. LeBlanc, Cam?" asked Doc upon seeing her bring her dog inside. "I need to keep her Gracie with me today to see how much longer the medication will last. "That's fine," said Cam. One other important point you'll like; I gave this medication to Gracie did last night before going home. It is still effective after being given over ten hours ago." "Wow!" said Cam. "A simple herbal agent this made that much of a difference? There must be something about this that has altered the breakdown of the agents through the cat's system." "By the way," said Doc. "We can't call this sample 218, excuse me, sample 219 now, forever. Have you come up with a name for this?" "I have been giving it some thought and I believe that I have. I am naming it, Oboedīre; the word from where obedient is derived." "Sounds good!" said Doc as he patted Cam on the back. Ali came in just then. "Cam, don't you think this a great?" she asked. "Yah, the increased length of action is wonderful," he said a little stunned. Cam then left to work with Mrs. LeBlanc's dog while Doc and Ali continued there evaluation of Gracie.

The effects of the medication wore off about two hours after their conversation. With the dose given, that meant there was about a twelve hour duration of action. With Mrs. LeBlanc's dog having been treated, Cam and Doc decided to lower the ginkgo dose to one mg and Cam gave the dose to another cat without the cat knowing who had fed it. Once the food was eaten, and as had been the case in the past, the medication should take effect in about five minutes. During this time, no one approached or was seen by the cat, so as Cam entered the kennel, the cat looked up at him. He approached and gave the command, "Fluffy, go stand over by the back wall." The cat obeyed. Bringing a chair into the room, he opened the cage door and sat down in the chair. "Fluffy, come and jump into my lap." The cat jumped into his lap. Ali came in next as was planned and gave the cat a couple of commands which she did not follow. Every command that Cam stated, the cat followed. There still needed to be a little more evaluation of who would be in control of the cat once the medication is taken, but this appears to be the first person seen after it takes effect. The remainder of the day passed without incident. The medication given to Fluffy lasted for seven hours. The three researchers knocked off around dinner time, heading to Doc's house for burgers on the grill.

9

REALITY

The weekend ended all too quickly and Cam returned to work on Monday. Doc was able to get a couple of cats from the shelter that had been dropped off with what initially appears to be FCD. Further evaluation and testing revealed they did have the disorder. Both Vets agreed that it would be good for Doc to continue to try and modify the medication to see if he could find a mixture which would address the symptoms of FCD. Shortly after coming into the office, Mark and Scott approached him, asking if he enjoyed his week away and expressing that little to no progress occurred recently. Mark looked over at Scott, who looked back at him as well. Cam noticed this which made him curious that something was going on. "Hey guys, what's up?" he asked. Mark again looked at Scott and paused. "Cam," he said, "the time frame for presenting our progress to the board has been pushed up. We have to deliver an update next Monday." "What! Are you kidding me?" said Cam, "We should have about three weeks to go. We're not ready if you didn't make any progress," he said frustrated. "I know," said Scott, "but when the big boys and girls tell us to jump, we ask how high on the way up," he said almost apologetic. "Did you make any strides at all that I am not aware of?" he asked. "No, nothing of any significance," said Scott. "We're in a pickle," said Mark. "We still have this week, so keep trying. Whatever you need; let me know, but focus on the task at hand and try and not worry about next week. Something will break." Cam's head was spinning; he couldn't believe that there deadline was moved up.

Later that day at lunch, Cam called Doc to give him an update to this situation at work. He expressed his frustration with the advancement of the timetable, but there was nothing he could do about it. He called Doc to vent, but really to get some advice from his friend. "What do you think I should do?" asked Cam. "Somewhat of a tough question, my boy," said the older Vet as he leaned back in his office chair. "I guess unless you guys or we have a breakthrough in the next few days, you have little option; you'll have to share your results." "Yah, that's what I think, but I don't know… this has some pretty far reaching consequences possibly, both medically and ethically. This medication could be used to help with a number of challenges with cats. It could help with the cat that has litter box issues in the home; it could be used to help with some of the FCD symptoms, but not completely address this; it would be of immense help in helping Vets treat cats in the office; but as with anything, there could the dark side…" said Cam while turning to look at the kennel area. "I know that you may not want to hear this son, but CatGenus has been paying your way during this internship and is helping you gain the experience needed to sit for the exam. You do have an ethical obligation to them, you know," said Doc, trying to gently as possible remind him of reality. "I know," said Cam after taking a deep breath. He hung up the phone sitting there dejected hoping that something would break in the coming days. He wasn't optimistic.

Monday morning came without any progress worth mentioning. Cam and a couple of others on their team posted some long hours in the lab over the previous week, but nothing meaningful came from their efforts. The meeting with the board was a one o'clock. Cam hadn't slept all night even though he had taken a diphenhydramine pill. Everyone appeared to be on edge this morning; they knew the board meeting was today and that it did not look good; their futures at CatGenus were on the line. He knew what he should do, but he also knew what he wanted to do. He had no aspirations of getting rich, which this discovery without a doubt would probably do for him or anyone else if they desired. Cam knew what the right thing to do was but he wished he had more time.

Mark had scheduled a meeting for 0900 that morning in their conference room. All team members were to attend as this was an important meeting. Bring your research, résumés optional was the pessimistic word that was unofficially passing around. It was believed that everyone understood the ramifications of this meeting. Hopefully what had been accomplished would secure their jobs, but most were realistic enough that they had updated their résumés; some had begun looking. At 0900, all had arrived at the conference room, it was eerily quiet. Mark started off the meeting by expressing his appreciation to the team for their hard work. Even though they had not completely accomplished their goal, they had made strides forward and he expressed his hope that the board would be gracious enough to allow a further extension. Most in the room expressed that another six months to a year would allow for success. Enough said there was a final review of the research and of the material to be shared with the board as was standard practice in these meetings. Cameron sat quietly in the room and during the meeting took time to reflect on the people in the room. There was Jonas, he had a wife and two young children; Kevin, a widower who although unmarried, helped support his son and his family due to his son's job loss; and there was Rita, married with a child on the way. These were the people to be affected by the outcome of today's meeting. His conscience, either that or Doc's conversation, led him to a decision of what he needed to do. "Well everyone, is that it, did we cover everything?" asked Mark prior to closing the meeting. Cam stiffened up in his chair, cleared his throat and said, "Mark, I have one thing to share with the group. Doing this might take longer than our usual meeting time. Are you OK with this?" Mark nodded, showing a quizzical look on his face as he sat down. Cam stood up and as he was walking to the door, he said, "I have something to show you all." With that, he opened the door and called for Dearfoot to come into the room. The cat came in and stood in the room. Mike snickered at the site saying, "OK Cameron, so the cat came in; big deal." Cam looked at him with an unapproving look and said, "It is a big deal, just watch." Next he looked at Dearfoot and said, "Dearfoot, go untie Mike's shoe, pointing at him." The cat looked at Mike, walked over to his shoe, bit the shoelace and pulled it, untying the shoe. "What?" said Mike. "Dearfoot, jump up on the table and sit on Mark's papers." The cat responded with a robot-like response. He was sitting on the papers as requested.

"Dearfoot, lie down in front of Mark now and place one of your paws on top of his hand." The cat obeyed his request. Mark sitting there stunned said, "Cam, what is this? How is this possible?" Cam spent the next hour going over his research and results, leaving out the part about where Doc assisted in the research, and how the combination of the mentioned agents offered a way to have cats not only understand what they were asked, but to also display an unwavering compulsion to obey commands. He reiterated that this reaction of obeying the commands of an individual were apparently tied to the first person the cat saw after the drugs took effect. Everyone in the room was astonished, never seeing anything quite like this before. The room came to life with a number of side conversations and whisperings. He went on to state that there were some additional benefit to the FCD-affected cats, but not a complete reversal of the disorder and not as long in duration of action than cats without the disorder. The mood in the room changed entirely. Mark pulled Cam off to the side while the other researchers jabbered among one another. "How long have you had this? Why have you been holding back?" asked Mark sharply. Cam looked at his manager and said, "I've have been working on this for about the last month to month and a half. I had not shared this with you since it was not really a cure for FCD. I didn't want this to detract from any of the group's efforts." Mark had an obvious look of anger on his face as he continued. "Cam, this should have been shared before now. With this discovery, who knows; we might collectively have been able to arrive at an answer to our project mission. We'll never know now. Get you material together and be in my office in fifteen minutes. We need to develop our presentation and portfolio around this new information within the next two hours." "Meeting adjourned," Mark said loudly to the group. "Sally, I need you now!" he snapped over the intercom.

10

JUDGMENT DAY

Mark, Scott, and Cam sat nervously in the waiting room. They had been here before, but this was different. They sat there with their material, waiting for their turn. The minutes seemed like hours. This meeting would define the fate of the entire team and whether they all would remain gainfully employed or re-assigned to another team. Eventually the door opened and they were asked to come into the boardroom. They each gathered their materials and they all walked in. The same stone faces and well-dressed and manicured members were there just as in the past. Mr. Buck was standing off to the side, looking out the window of the seventh floor boardroom, which was toward the parking lot. He turned his head upon their entry and gazed at the newcomers to the room. Cam glanced at him while walking to an open chair. Scott seemed oblivious to what was going on. "Afternoon gentlemen," said the leader of the company. "I trust you have been working hard and have something to show us." "Yes," said Cam. He noticed how they were like gargoyles sitting on the roof of a building, with the same cold stare, none uttering a sound. "Let's get down to business," said Mr. Buck. He turned and took a seat at the head of the table, waiting to hear their presentation.

Mark started off the meeting with updating the board on the group's progress and the results from their final test sample, the one prior to Cam's presentation to their group. It showed promise, but was not the answer as of yet. In his presentation, he displayed a timeline of this team's efforts and the progress they had made along with a future timeline, where he was confident that if allowed to continue, this group would indeed unlock and answer to the cure for FCD. A few questions were asked by a couple of the board members along the way, from those members ironically that were Veterinarians; the remainder were silent. A few took notes. Cam watched the room for positive signs; he did not see any. But from the memory of his previous experience, this was a stoic group; he shouldn't read too much into it he thought. At the end of Mark's presentation, Mr. Buck received a call and indicated that he needed to take it, so he instructed there would be a fifteen minute break while he took the call. Most everyone got up and refilled their coffee; a few decided to use this break and head to the men's room. Mark and his two reports stepped out into the waiting area for a mini-conference. "Well, how do you think things are going?"

asked Scott to Mark. "I don't know," said Mark. "I really don't want to speculate. Buck is the major player in the room. Everyone seems to follow his lead. Cam, we will sit on your information and use it only if we have to." "Great," said Cam. They waited outside until it appeared that Buck was returning.

The meeting started shortly after Buck's return and everyone had taken their seats. "So," said Mr. Buck. "Let me get this straight. You have had a slight amount of progress, but still have not found an effective cure for FCD, right?" "Well sir, you're right we do not have a cure, but we are making progress, albeit it be slow, we are getting closer," said Mark. "So, we've been at this for a couple of year and we still don't have a cure," Buck replied. "Yes," said Mark, "we project that another six months to year tops; we'll have this cure." "We've pumped two million dollars into this project so far," said Mr. Peters, the CFO of CatGenus, "with essentially nothing marketable to show. And you're asking for probably another million on top of that? PB, I think we need to cut our losses and refocus our strategy." 'With all due respects and in not wanting to minimize the money spent, Mr. Peters, as you know, many of the new agents coming to market have cost in excess of four million to produce, so by our projections we will be under the industry average with our proposal," retorted Mark. "I know that sir, but your focus is on this one project. With the other projects that are on-going, this board has a fiduciary responsibility to weigh all operations and to be quite frank, we have a number of projects which are in about the same position as your project; bleeding profusely without a bandage," said Peters. "OK gentlemen, we see each of your points, and as valid as each may be, I believe that Mr. Peters is right, we need to start looking at all our projects with a critical eye. I want us to be a cutting edge company, but it may just be that we tried to swallow too big of a bite of the whale at this time. If projects become non-funded, it doesn't mean that they will be scrapped; we will put them on the shelf for a while until a time where some of our more promising projects begin to pay off. Our return on investment is our greatest concern at this point. Your work has been impressive, but I am questioning the ROI on this project in light of others at this time," said Mr. Buck. It felt as though a hot knife was just thrust into Cam's chest. Seeing the heads beginning to nod around the room, Cam knew it was time. "So sir," said Cam, "what is the probability that our project will be shelved?" "There is a strong probability that it will," Buck stated coldly. "We really are not interested in shelving any initiatives, but with the number of projects that have stagnated, our expenses are exceeding our revenue and that has to be turned around and turned around fairly quickly. I'm afraid yours stands to make one of the least profits for us. The room went silent for a moment. "Mr. Buck, could you give us the liberty of about a ten minute break, there are a couple of things we need to get sir," said Cam quietly. "Is this germane to the outcome of this meeting?" asked Buck to the young Veterinarian. "Yes, it is. I believe you will find this interesting enough to re-consider," said Cam. "We will re-convene in exactly ten minutes, not a second more. This better be worth the extra time. We have a full agenda," said Buck as he prepared to speak to Peters. Cam headed out to the lab to get what he needed.

The meeting reconvened after the break. "This had better be worth our time," said the grouchy Mr. Peters." "Before we start, is anyone in the room allergic to cats?" asked Cam. No one indicated that they were. "Mark, would you please open the door?" asked Cam. "Dearfoot, please come in here and jump into the empty chair." In trotted a cat that subsequently jumped up into the empty chair. The room was unimpressed. "OK, so a cat comes into the room, big deal," said Peters. "Is there relevance to this?" he challenged. "There most certainly is," stated Cam confidently. "Dearfoot, please go over to the phone and press a button on the phone. Then go over and sit on Mr. Peters' note pad," pointing to Mr. Peters. The cat responded and pressed a button, then turned, walked over and sat on the pad in front of Peters. "I need an explanation now," demanded Buck. "Mrs. Johnson, put the rest of the items on the agenda on hold for now." The gargoyles in the board room changed their faces for once.

Cam spent the next hour providing background on his research, much like he had done in the earlier day's meeting. Whispers occurred throughout the room at various times, but no one stopped his report. Dearfoot sat in the chair at what appeared to be attention for the entire presentation. If anyone ever had the full attention of an audience, Cam had them beat today. "So what we have here is an obedience drug; how really marketable is that?" asked Peters smugly. "That might be what is largely appears on the surface sir, but we have more than that here," said Cam. He presented a number of options where this new drug could be marketable. He further re-emphasized that this drug in its present form, does offer some relief of the symptoms of FCD and with more refinement, eventually would lead to a cure for this disorder. All this time Mr. Buck had sat quietly listening to the presentation, its demonstrations, and the sharp-tongued comments from a few of the board members. "Cameron, I definitely believe you have tripped onto something here. I understand the points of marketability you suggest and agree with you. However, I believe you have been a little short-sighted into the full potential of this discovery. Mr. Thomas, I would like you to gather this material and give it to Mrs. Johnson. I believe this is something that needs to be shared with our friends on the tenth floor. This should be shared with Murphy so we need to get a meeting arranged with the two of us as soon as possible. Please ask Mrs. Johnson to make this happen immediately. Mark, you and your team and especially Cameron need to be available for consultation with these people," said Mr. Buck as he rose. "Good work Dr. Robert, although I would have preferred a more straightforward approach, and gentlemen," glancing over at Mark and Scott, "you will retain your funding for the FCD project based upon the findings from Cameron's impressive report. This funding will follow your recommendations; for one more year at the maximum. Unless anyone objects, this meeting is over. After gathering their individual materials and entering the elevator, Cameron asked Mark, "What is on the tenth floor? I didn't realize we had a tenth floor." "Government research offices," said Mark as he looked up at the floor indicator. "What are government offices doing in this building?" asked Cam.

11

FRUSTRATION

"Cam you really saved our bacon," said Mark as they walked back into the lab. "Mark, I don't feel good about what just happened up there," Cam said angrily. "I thought CatGenus was a company interested in furthering animal care. I can't imagine that the government really has the best interest of animals at heart." "Cam, settle down a bit," said Mark. "Knowing Buck's track record, if he thought something wasn't above board, they would not be here." Their conversation continued for the next half-hour. Cam eventually settled down a bit, but really wasn't convinced that everything would be all right. Mark had announced to the team that they would be funded for another year which was a great relief to all. Mark also gave Cam the primary credit for their being able to continue. Back slaps and smiles were shared as were phone calls and texts to loved ones. Everyone was happy; all but Cam.

John Murphy sat at his desk as he poured over the documentation forwarded to him from Buck. John was the senior advisor to the U.S. Navy, scientific division. He had served as a Seal in Dessert Storm, being on one of the lead teams in to reconnoiter the landing area prior to the initial invasion. He was a decorated war veteran and his accomplishments in the military could be the basis of a book easily. The scientific jargon was BS as far as he was concerned; whatever happened to an executive summary. Murphy's secretary told him that Patrick Buck was here to see him. "Morning, Patrick. I trust things are well with you and your family," said Murphy as he extended his hand to him. "We're fine, John. Hope the same is with you," replied Buck. Murphy nodded. As he leaned back in his chair, Murphy said, "Patrick, I don't have time to sift through all of this crap. Feline dysfunctional whatever. What does this shit have to do with us?" Patrick Buck in his earlier life was in the military, specifically, he was a Navy Seal also. Seals are called on to do many things, most of which are never spoken outside of small, protected circles. "John, you should know that I would not waste your time. When I was posed with the possibility of renting this floor out to you guys, I never envisioned that I might be sharing something that we are working on with you. The revenue generated from the leasing of this floor was considered by many on our board as a stroke of genius by me, especially since the money from this goes directly into funding our research. However as developments do occur and opportunities present themselves and as a company CEO, I must do whatever I reasonably can to improve our financial stance. That is why I sent you all of this shit as you say." "Go on," said Murphy. "John, you know that we did some pretty hairy shit while active. We all placed our lives on the line more times that we can count, always knowing that the next assignment could be our last. Well with this most recent discovery from our labs, I believe that it can be used to help save the lives of future servicemen and women, to help us better protect our country, and to enable us to possibly get intell like never before," said the CEO confidently and passionately. "Just what the hell are you proposing?" asked Murphy suspiciously. "John, one of our teams has developed a drug that can allow for cats to be controlled and by controlled, I mean they follow commands. Once given, this drug enables someone to give a command to a cat and it will obey. The possibilities for the use of this drug could be significant. We, for instance, could put a mike on a cat and send it into a room and hear everything that is going on without placing anyone in jeopardy. How many times have we had to sit on our asses while waiting for substantial enough information to act? I would also imagine that some of our CIA friends would love to be able to get their hands on this as well. I personally don't condone putting an animal in harm's way, but unless a person hates cats, they could present an inconspicuous presence in a room. Obviously additional testing needs to occur, but I consider this a strong development." Murphy sat there for a while, allowing what Patrick had just said to soak in, it was so incredible. This information, the significance of it and its worth to certain governmental agencies shot through him like an armor-piercing bullet would. He got up and walked over to the mirrored outside window, mirrored to keep prying eyes from snooping, and looked out it for a few moments. "We need to do more testing, to verify the response as you say, but there definitely may be other useful purposes for this drug across a spectrum of our governmental agencies," said Murphy as he continued to look out the window, "Time will tell."

Cam was telling Ali how the meeting went and his frustration with the outcome. He was glad that his friends were secure for the coming year but it was bitter sweet to the involvement of the government. He shared how everyone expressed their appreciation to him; some had wanted to take him out for dinner, some sent thank you cards. He appreciated it, he told her, but he really had trouble believing that the government had the best interest of animals in their sights. Ali tried to console him and present possibilities. Maybe their interest was through the Department of Agriculture. With some additional work, other species might be able to be better controlled, make those working with these animals safer. Without a doubt, it would be of immense help to Veterinarians. With the almost unlimited resources available to the federal government, the opportunities are endless, she said. He agreed, but still had the fear that other agencies might use it for other negative purposes; the military, CIA, Homeland Security, just to name a few. With his lunch over, he told Ali goodbye and that he would be in touch soon. Cam continued to dwell over the possibilities and his distain of the possible inappropriate or dangerous use of any animal for the benefit of their masters was enough to bring Cam's blood to a boil.

Shannon Purdue and Meghan Krieg were research scientists with the U.S. Department of Defense. Both had been with DOD for some time; Shannon for eight years and had a PhD in chemistry. Meghan had been with the agency for six years, having a PhD in Biology. Both very gifted scientists, they were provided the files with Cam's research and findings. Both were instructed to collaborate with Cam and his team. They were to evaluate the validity of the research and findings and report back to the advisory committee within one month. After the committee had reviewed the information, if there was enough interest to pursue investigation of this drug and once verified, the next step would be considered. Their first meeting was set for later today, at three o'clock on the tenth floor of the CatGenus building. Both women had spent the past couple of days going over the material and found it interesting but it seemed far-fetched. Cats are some of the most independent creatures and to be able to direct their actions seemed implausible. However, the research and findings were there as were video clips showing the cats responding to commands. Time would tell and these two very competent scientists would complete their research in an efficient manner.

Cam and Greg were with their escorts while waiting for the elevator. "If nothing nefarious or sensitive was going on here, why the security escort?" though Cam. The two gentlemen were also dressed as though they were scientists with their long white lab coats on. "This is also unusual for security. Why hide who they are?" thought Cam. Cam looked over at Greg who returned the gaze. Neither said anything as the elevator doors opened. Once on, one of the guards pulled a card from his coat and held it over an inconspicuous spot above the floor button; the door closed and the elevator started upward. "Interesting," though Cam. "The ten button on the panel must be a dummy." The elevator stopped; the ten on the floor indicator lit up and the four exited. Both men looked around the room. It was a very plain waiting area and in front of them was a closed glass-paneled door leading to the hallway of the other side. Diagonally to the right was an office and inside there sat a single individual in the small room. One of the escorts waved at the person in this room who reached over and pressed something; a button or switch of some sort and a mechanical buzz sounded and a click was heard. The escort reached for the door and opened it. Everyone proceeded into the hallway where it was necessary to stop and sign in. They were also required to pass through a metal detector after emptying their pockets. A second solid door then again required an access card for them to pass. After Cam and Greg had passed through the metal detector, one of the escorts said, "Come this way, sirs." They walked down the hallways to the third door on the right where once again, an escort pulled a card from his pocket again and swiped it and opened the door. As Cam and Greg walked in, they noticed two women sitting at the end of a conference table to their left. Again, a relatively plain room; no pictures or adornments, just a conference table with six chairs in the room. "Please come in a take a seat, gentlemen. My name is Dr. Meghan Krieg and this is Dr. Shannon Purdue. Thank you, Drs. Robert and Dunn for coming today." The escorts exited to room. Both men seated themselves and once seated, Cam immediately said, "Ladies, could you tell me which agency you represent?" We work for the federal government and a number of different agencies, Dr. Robert," said Shannon coolly. "Which one today?" asked Cam. "We are representing the Department of Homeland Security today, Dr. Robert," said Meghan, slightly annoyed. Both scientists were instructed to indicate that they were from Homeland Security as a means to keep the veterinarians unaware of who was conducting the review of this medication. Valuable information is always on a need-to-know basis and these individuals did not need-to-know. "What does Homeland Security need with our discovery," demanded Cam. "Dr. Robert, we are charged with the responsibility of verifying and evaluating the results of your work. What is done with this review is over your pay grade and mine. Shall we get to work now?" said Shannon indifferently.

The following day, the two scientists working for the Department of Defense were back in Washington at their primary office. The office also housed an extensive laboratory and research area. This division occupied the entire 4th floor of the building located on E Street NW. The building housed many other governmental offices, but this was the only laboratory on site. It was a plain, indistinguishable building to avoid detection of its occupants. This work was slightly unusual for the two and to accomplish their task, special arrangements needed to be made to conduct their evaluation of the drug. Obtaining a cat from a local shelter was not a significant issue, but a veterinarian assistant was needed to comply with legal requirements for animal testing. Security clearance for this individual was rushed to assure safety and confidentiality issues were addressed. Once all of the logistics were handled, Shannon and Meghan began their evaluation, building upon the information that they extracted from Cam and Greg. "Shannon, have you measured out the dose to administer yet?" asked Meghan. "Yes, I did this late yesterday after you left so we could begin first thing this morning. The veterinary assistant had just arrived with their test subject and was waiting in a conference room. He was instructed to not feed the cat after six o'clock the previous night and to not to feed him this morning to help assure the cat was hungry for testing purposes.

Both scientists entered the room with the pair waiting for them. "Has the cat not eaten since six o'clock last night as requested?" asked Meghan. "Yes, that's correct. He should be good and hungry," said the veterinarian assistant. "Good," said Shannon. "Let's get the evaluation started. A research assistant had set up the video equipment earlier that morning to capture the sequence of the morning's events. "Are we good, Jim?" said Meghan to the gentleman operating the video equipment. "Yes we are. Starting the recording now," he said. "This is research analysis 071513, titled Feline Command. I am Dr. Shannon Purdue and this is Dr. Meghan Krieg, representing the Department of Defense and we are conducting this evaluation to determine the effectiveness of a newly discovered medication which is purported to allow humans to control the actions of cats receiving this medication." Upon the request of the researchers, the cat was released from the cage and a variety of commands were given to determine the cat's response prior to the administration of the medication. Once it was established that the cat did not follow any of the prearranged commands, the cat was returned to its cage. "We are now adding a thirty milligram dose of this medication to the food for this cat," said Meghan as she poured the powered medication onto the cat's food and then mixed it thoroughly together. She then placed the food near to opening to the cat's cage, releasing the cat immediately after this. The cat cautiously came out of the cage again and after surveying the area, the cat approached the food; initially smelling it, and then began eating. "If this medication works as claimed, within approximately five minutes after ingestion, the medication will take effect. During this time, the other individuals will exit the room, leaving me as the sole person in the room for the five minute period. They will be observing the following steps on the other side of the two-way mirror in the adjoining room," said Meghan as the others then exited the room as instructed. Once the cat had finished the food, Meghan pushed a button on the timer to count down the five minute interval, capturing this activity on the video. Meghan silenced the timer alarm at the end of this time period and then stood back. She looked at the cat and repeated the commands previously given to the cat earlier to evaluate his response. In each case, the cat complied promptly with all given commands. The next step was to have Shannon come into the room and repeat the exact same commands to determine the cat's response. On doing this, the cat did not follow any of her commands. The veterinarian assistant then came in, repeating this set of commands without response from the cat. Meghan then repeated the commands at which the cat followed each command as before. Looking at the camera, Meghan then commented, "We will continue to assess the cat's responses to the willingness to follow commands and will do this at five minute intervals with different commands each time to determine the longevity of the medication's effects. Recording of this time period will continue until it has been determined that the medication is no longer effective and a time noted of effectiveness."

Without their knowledge that this would occur, a senior officer from the intelligence section from the Pentagon had entered the adjoining room to personally witness the testing. The report of this new medication had made its way to the Undersecretary of Defense and he was uniquely interested in the results and had instructed the program director to view and report back in person to him the results from this evaluation. He was awe-struck by what he witnessed and happily he shared his observations with the Undersecretary in the early afternoon that day. The amazing results and the opportunities that this remarkable new medication could provide was the brightest hope toward combating the forces plying against our great country. Plans were made for a more robust assessment of this medication and how it could become another source of use within the military's arsenal.

With their work substantiated, Drs. Purdue and Krieg's report was sitting on Murphy's desk. He had representatives from the Departments of Defense and Homeland Security sitting in his office with him. "Gentlemen, we have some rather interesting research that has been done in the private sector. This information was shared with us by the leadership of CatGenus, owners of the building in which we sit. Ironically, we have leased space from them for many years, and quite frankly, I never considered any other their work crossing my desk, but it has, and this is significant," he said in starting their meeting. "What was developed accidentally by the scientists within this company could be of immense help to our government and the resultant use could save an innumerable number of lives along with providing us with droves of valuable information. CatGenus has developed a drug which when given to a cat, an ordinary house cat, allows for them to not only be able to understand commands, but obligates them to comply," said Murphy as he got up to pour himself a drink. "Help yourself, gentlemen," he said. Upon returning to his desk, Murphy tapped on his keyboard and a projector came to life and a video screen descending from the ceiling. "Gentlemen, watch this initial test we have performed." The lights dimmed slightly just prior to the video starting. On the video titled, Feline Command, started and after watching the video for eleven minutes, the lights came back up as projector turned off and the screen returned to its hiding place. After taking a sip, he continued. "I can see where both of your agencies would probably be interested in evaluating this work. Mr. Fields, I could see where in using this drug and cats, you would easily be able to infiltrate cells or drug cartels to obtain real-time information which could allow a faster response to situations and possibly avoid the repeat of Lebanon and 9-11. General Turner where I see this could be of use for the military is with reconnaissance and intelligence gathering, but I think that I am just scratching the surface." "John," said Turner, "are you shitting me? Relying upon a cat for a soldier's life; are you kidding?" "Ralph, think about it. A cat that can be controlled can infiltrate a home or camp more stealthily than a ninja, and with a camera or a mike, it could be your eyes and ears in an enemy camp. You know, cats are instinctively effective hunters and are quiet as anything. These creatures have the natural ability to move about undetected and they don't have to be taught how to do it.

These abilities will more than qualify their value in a project such as this and will be quite useful. The intell on this drug is that it can last as long as twelve hours at this time. Think about it Ralph! Having real-time information fed back to your command post about IED's and planned attacks, about the locations of bomb-making houses; the services are near limitless. Christ, it would be like you sitting right in the room! Ralph, I imagine your department could begin the process of testing the validity of this agent as soon as you desire." "If this is true," said Mr. Fields, "then the accuracy of information and the ability to intercede prior to attacks; it unimaginable." "This report; it validates the drug's effectiveness?" asked General Turner. "Yes, it's all there," said Murphy as he takes a sip of the scotch he poured. "John," said Turner, you have a convincing argument. How soon could you get me this drug?" "Soon," said Murphy.

12

GAMES

Murphy had requested a meeting with Patrick Buck to discuss his associate and the substance he had developed a little more. Buck arrived up to his Murphy's office at the arranged time and was led into the office, carrying a file with him. "Patrick, how are you?" asked Murphy as he rose to meet him and to shake his hand. "I'm fine John. Hope everything's well with you," he responded. "It is. It is," responded Murphy. "Take a seat Patrick. I thought it prudent that we talk a little bit about this Robert fellow so I have a better knowledge of him and to get your insight on how we might better deal with him." "John, Dr. Robert has been with us for a couple of years now and he is quite a bright and talented Veterinarian and scientist. This drug that he concocted is amazing from some of the preliminary tests you have shared with me and some uses have definitely crossed my mind. We ought to be able to rid the world more easily of some of the filth out there." "I totally agree. The use of this is extremely promising. It's got everyone on point." "Patrick, what do you know about the man, Cameron Robert. What's he like, what makes him tick?" "I have limited knowledge of him John, but from what I glean from those he works for and the comments of those around him, he is someone very dedicated. He works around 60 hours a week and is very thorough in his work. Comments about him have surfaced that he is very committed to his animals, almost driven to provide for them. He also seems something like a Boy Scout. I would be surprised if he has ever done anything wrong in his life," said Buck, with his leg crossed over the other, sitting upright in the chair. "So you are saying he is a passionate person who always does what's right?" responded Murphy. Buck thought for a second, and said, "I guess that I would say that pretty much sums him up pretty well." "Where's he from?" probed Murphy further. Buck grasps the file from the table next to him and opens it up. "I know he's a farm boy, but from there… yes, here it is. He is from Indiana, Russiaville specifically. He has one sister. He graduated second in his high school class and at the top of his veterinary school also. Pretty smart cookie." "So he's a farm boy from the conservative state of Indiana; Boy Scout; Smart kid too." said Murphy as he walked over to the window. "He's also got a strong work ethic." A pause ensued as Murphy considered this young man. "You know Patrick, under normal circumstances I wouldn't give two shits about what someone thinks about what we need to do to keep this country safe. But with this young man, I think that if we can keep him appeased, he might be valuable to us in the future." They continued this line of thought for a while and discussed the pros and cons of appeasement versus submission. In the end result, both finally agreed that in this case, due to his abilities, it would make sense to give this young man the appearance that his discovery was being used for positive purposes. The two men finished their conversation on the matter and then talked about plans for the two of them to get together for a round of golf this coming weekend. Murphy was a scratch golfer who beat Buck every time they played.

Murphy borrowed Buck's personnel file on Cameron to review the information more thoroughly to try and get a better picture of this young man. He was impressed with what he read and was hopeful that one day he might be able to convince this bright young scientist of the benefits of using his talents for the government. He asked for Homeland Security to establish a monitoring of his activities for the meanwhile to gain a better understanding of the young man. One of Murphy's valued talents was his ability to see opportunities and work toward using them in beneficial ways. Such as the case with this new drug that was passed his way; possibly the young inventor would be the same. Time would tell and Murphy waited while his resources worked toward getting a clearer picture of Cameron Robert.

A few weeks had passed and after having learned more about Cameron from the in-depth research performed, Murphy was more convinced than ever that trying to keep Cameron appeased, or at best, to give the appearance to him that he was in the loop and that the proposed use was the right thing to do. It served no positive purpose for this brilliant young veterinarian to sit somewhere conjecturing what was being done with his development; after all, he knew they had it. The less his wheels were spinning, the best for everyone, thought Murphy. Murphy had decided to take an even bolder move; he decided that it would be more productive to go to Cameron than to call him up or have him escorted up to the tenth floor, so he made the call to come to Cameron's lab. In preparing for this meeting, Murphy had arranged with Buck for him to use a conference room down the hall from Cameron's lab and made sure the A-V equipment was available. He started down to meet with him in the late morning.

"Dr. Robert, would you please come up to the reception area? You have a visitor," said Sally over the lab's intercom. Cam was working with Greg at that moment and they stopped and looked at each other. Cam had never had a visitor at the lab before and was surprised by this announcement. "That's odd," said Cameron as he stood up, holding in place for a second. "Greg, I'll be back," said Cam who eventually started moving toward the door. Cam opened the door leading into the reception area and on walking in to that area, he saw Sally sitting at her desk as usual, but there was a man standing there in a suit, turning to face him upon hearing the door open. He was about six foot three inches tall; square shouldered and looked solidly built. A tint of gray was noticeable in contrast to his dark black hair. Upon turning, Cameron surmised that he was in his late forties. "Dr. Robert?" said the man, extending his hand to shake. "Yes," said Cam, still unsure who this person was, but reaching to shake his hand anyway. "Dr., my name is John Murphy; I work up on the tenth floor. As Cam grasped his hand at this point, upon hearing his name, Cam realized this was the person that Buck had referred to earlier and upon grasping his hand, tried to squeeze it hard, but he accomplished nothing. This man's grip was more solid than Cam's and it didn't budge. About this time, Mark came into the reception area as the two were introducing each other also. "Dr. Robert, I came down because I wanted to thank you for your valued research and ultimate development of this new drug. We have studied it so far and have found it to be very effective and if you have some time, I would like to show you some of the testing we have performed. If you do have the time, I have arranged to use a conference room down the hall from here to show you this to you and to give you an idea of where we are with it. I would like to alleviate any concerns that you might have about this and want to be as transparent with you as possible. Would this be a good time for you?" "Mr. Murphy, right now is probably…" Cam was interrupted by Mark who said, "Cam, I think that we can work things out so you can take a look at what Mr. Murphy has for you. Go right ahead." Cam snapped an unapproving look at Mark. "All right Mark," said Cam reluctantly. He did not know Murphy personally, but since he was the one that Buck had provided his information to, he was essentially the enemy. "Cam, let's head down to the conference room. If you have any reservations or questions about what we are doing with your remarkable discovery, I think this should help to address these concerns."

Both men walked out the door and turned right, going down three doors on the left and they entered the conference room, being the sole persons in the room.

"Have a seat Cameron while I get this video started for you," said Murphy as he started to work with the computer. Cam took a seat without eliciting a response. Murphy fiddled with the computer for a couple of minutes and then the projector displayed a pattern on the screen. Before he started the video, Murphy turned and looked at Cam and said, "Cameron, there is one thing that I would like to ask of you before I start this video. I ask you, as sort of a gentlemen's agreement, that what I am about to show you here, that you keep this between ourselves and not divulge this to anyone else. You obviously know about the drug and its actions, but what we discuss here should not be for dissemination. A large part of my job is to save lives, and with this drug, I believe this is possible. Do I have your word about not sharing this with anyone else?" "Mr. Murphy, at this point it is hard for me to say how I may respond based upon your video since I have no idea of the content. I can keep a secret as well as the next guy, but if animals are being put at risk in any venture you're planning on using them in, then I have a problem with that." "Dr. Robert, the main plan for the use of this drug is to use these cats to gather intelligence; information which can aid us in reducing the terrorist threat to our country, to smash the illegal drug trade, basically to gather information on these scoundrels and bring them to justice. That is our main plan," said Murphy sincerely to the young veterinarian. "I see," said Cam. "You assure me they will be safe; just as safe as someone walking the street?" "Will I sit here and tell you that one will never be hurt; then I must tell you that is not the case. Just if you walked home tonight and were mugged; we don't have total control of every facet of life. But we will do everything within our power to keep them as safe as possible" said Murphy. "I understand you can't control everything. The cats will be safe?" asked Cam. "Yes," said Murphy. "I will keep this to myself, based upon the comments you have made here," said Cameron. "Thank you Dr. Robert." The video started right up after this and both men sat their listening to and watching the tests performed by Drs. Purdue and Krieg. At the end of it, Murphy turned to Cam and said, "We have done this initial test and as a result of it, we are confident your discovery will help save lives and/or give us so much valuable information. If the testing continues to prove to be as positive as this initial test, we will not place the cats we need in undue jeopardy."

"Mr. Murphy, you are a stranger to me. I met you about twenty minutes ago and up to that time, you were just a name to me. I appreciate the fact that you have taken the time to personally share this with me. But forgive me if I remain leery to what use is planned for my drug. I will keep my word and not disclose what we have talked about or to what I have seen. But hear me say clearly to you, if you have said is ever proven to not be true, then all bets are off. I will do what I have must to put a stop to the use of this drug for inappropriate purposes." Murphy sat there for a brief moment, looking at Cameron and then said, "Dr. Robert, I believe we have an understanding. I will keep you apprised of any change or new development that is germane to the use of this drug, Dr. Robert. Thank you for your time," said Murphy as he stood to shake Cameron's hand. After this, Cameron left the conference room, leaving Murphy there and he returned to his lab. "What a pompous shit," though Murphy to himself. Doesn't he realize the evil we are trying to combat in this world? Time will tell how or if we will need to deal with him in the future."

Cam returned to his lab, thoughts swirling around in his head. "This was somewhat a bold move on his part. I didn't expect for this to happen, but it did provide me some insight into where they might be headed with this, but I don't know…" He came back to reality upon Mark coming up to him as he was entering the lab and said, "Well Cam, how did things go?" "Mark, can we step into your office?"

asked Cam as he pointed that direction. "Sure," said Mark.
"I hope it went well." After each took a seat in the office,
Cam looked at Mark and said, "as well as could probably
be expected. I agreed to not discuss our conversation, but
let's just say that if he follows through on his end with what
he said, and it is used conservatively, there should not be a
problem from my end. But, I'm cynical toward whether
everything he said was true or not. I don't know the guy
and although he seems sincere; well let's just say time will
tell." "This sounds fairly good Cam. I hope that it does
work out as you hope too," said Mark. "If anything
pertinent is shared with me, I will keep you apprised."
Mark stood up and started to head to his door and then Cam
rose as well. "Have a good and productive day, Cam," said
Mark as he opened his door. "Thanks, Mark," said Cam as
he started back to his work area.

"Things go well?" asked Greg. "I guess," said Cam.
"I am surprised that they wanted to pull me into their loop.
But the closer they keep me, the better they can get an idea
of where I am with things as well." "Very true, Cam," said
Greg. "What did they talk about or show you?" "Both
things occurred, but at this point, I agreed to keep our
conversations under wraps and I'll abide to this as long as
they keep their part of the bargain," said Cam. Greg nodded

his head as a note of understanding and gave Cam a pat on the shoulder before saying, "Well then, I guess we had better get back to work." Cam looked over at the kennel and looked at the cats housed in there for a while and thought about what had just occurred. "Part of me wants to believe him. But I have a gut feeling that I can't trust him; they're leading me on. I developed this drug and they must feel like they have to keep me happy for some reason." Cam then got up and walked into the kennel and opened Dearfoot's cage and started to pet him; thoughts continued to swirl around in his head.

13

TRUE SPOTS

"The testing we've done so far sir, has been impressive. I can't say as much for working with Dr. Robert. He's been kind of a jerk!" said Jones to Felthoff. "Well Jones, this may be the first time that the DOD working with Homeland Security has paid off. Imagine how disinterested Dr. Robert would be if he knew our plans." "Oh, yeah," said Jones. "By the way, I have a recommendation to make. If we use the Maine Coon cat, I believe this cat will better serve our needs." "Really," said Felthoff, "what the hell is a Maine Coon cat?" "Well, the Maine Coon cat is a cat that is larger than your typical house cat and their claws are stronger and longer as well. The damage one of these cats can do will be more effective. Also, due to the slightly larger size, they will be more difficult to fight off; males weigh between fifteen to twenty-five pounds." "And it looks like a regular house cat?" asked Felthoff. "Other than the size difference, yes. To some people, they would consider them similar in size to that of a Tom Cat," responded Jones. "You might have something there, Jones. Have we done any testing with them?" "Not yet, but we have a couple coming in later this week," Jones said. "Good. Keep me posted," said Felthoff as he headed up the stairs to a meeting with project leads.

Everyone in the meeting had ample time to review the reports. "So Felthoff, report," said General Turner. "Well sir," said the Lieutenant, "it appears that in the tests performed, the cats receiving the drug codenamed, Houdini, were instructed to attack a variety of animals of various breeds and sizes, and in all cases, they completed the assignment successfully. All subjects died from exsanguination; they bled to death. They were extremely effective and lethal. Another thing that we noticed in all of the attacks that occurred; was that when two or more cats were employed, each one could be programmed to attack a specific area of the body, and once an area was neutralized, then the other would attack the secondary area; or the attacks could occur simultaneously. For instance, cat one was instructed to attack the eyes and neutralize this area. It did this with relative ease.

The testing began by using these Maine Coon cats to attack a variety of different sized dogs, starting with smaller dogs, eventually leading to attacks of larger breeds such as Rottweiler. A typical scene depicted from the recordings of this assessment was that the medication was fed to the cat as before and an operative provided instructions to the cat. The stray animals obtained from the animal shelter were released on opposite sides of the room through a sliding door. Once each subject had noticed the other, the dog typically would bark and snarl at the cat who would sit there as instructed by the operative to give no response to the dog's aggressive behavior. This was allowed to go on for three to five minutes, the dog pacing and being more provocative with time. Then the cat would be instructed to walk around the perimeter of the room while maintaining visual awareness of the dog's location. As determined in previous testing, it was determined that the instructions for the cat's attack needed to be specific to how the cat would attack or the cat would routinely use it's claws, scratching at its prey as the primary response. For the attack to be truly effective, it was determined that the cat's most success potential would be in disabling the victim's eyes and then for the cat to focus in on attacking the throat area to either sever or puncture the victim's carotid arteries leading to exsanguination. Based upon the success from these attacks, more menacing animals were tested. Here is a video clip of two Maine Coon cats attacking a mountain lion. The mountain lion was chosen because of its size and the fact it is more than capable of defending itself." They watched in shock as the two Maine Coon cats ripped the mountain lion to essentially shreds. The attack from start to finish lasted for twelve minutes. "My God!" said Turner who was just as shocked as anyone in the room. "Imagine how this would go down it they were attacking a man," he said still stunned by what he had just watched. The deathly silence of the room was interrupted by Felthoff who went on to say, "it is important to reiterate that detailed instructions were necessary and when given, they followed them to a T. The other thing of important notice is that typically when cats fight, there is a lot of hissing and meowing or verbalization. When instructed, these cats are silent." "Ralph, imagine the possibilities if these cats were part of a Seal team," said Murphy who recently had entered the room. The General by this time had regained his composure. The results were astonishingly impressive. The buzz around the room was overtaking the meeting. General Turner sat and watched the participants for a while and then pulled everyone back together. "The implications of this are almost mind-boggling," he said. "It is not very common for the military to work with outside agencies, and the present association with Homeland Security has been a good experience to date and I am confident it will continue. Besides, this collaboration was mandated from high above. There are implications for use in both agencies in combating the terror threat to our nation and the world. What I am about to propose is something that has not been well accepted within the military ranks, but must occur for the overall benefit of our nation. Murphy, would you contact the CIA and bring them in; the sooner, the better." A simple nod from Murphy indicated his acknowledgment but was something that Murphy had already planned to do.

John Murphy was a visionary of sorts, someone that was able to see the larger picture and someone whose reputation garnered the attention of many. When the encrypted transmission was received at CIA headquarters, it was immediately made aware to the Director of Field Operations. Bill Fisher was a man of immense influence and power and his authority was questioned by but a few of the highest ranking members of our government. With the information having made it to his desk about an hour ago, and seeing that this was forwarded to him by Murphy, Fisher reviewed it in his usual efficient manner. When his door was closed, no one dared to interrupt him. It was a sign that interruption had better be something equal to the dropping of a nuclear device or of the assassination of a senior world leader if one wanted to maintain his position within the agency. "Get Ryan in here," he commanded over his phone to Helen, his secretary. Within minutes, Matt Ryan appeared at his door and knocked. "I said get in here!" Fisher bellowed. Ryan entered saying, "Yes, Bill, what's up." Fisher had a great respect for Ryan. He was someone that could see things, could always be relied upon, and would listen and speak when appropriate. These were traits that Fisher expected of those close to him. "Ryan, I just received some astonishing information from John Murphy. Close the door and sit down, this might take a bit." Ryan closed the door and before seating, poured himself a glass of water; offered one to Fisher who waved off the offer. "Matt, what would you say if I told you we had the ability to control a cat and that this cat could be used to obtain information, to even kill if requested. What would you say to that?" "I'd say you were full of shit," said Ryan as he took a sip from the glass. "Well it appears that we have just such an agent and the DOD and DHS have each tested a medication that can allow this to happen. From what I'm seeing it's not smoke. We need to look at this and the complete data. Doing more research and testing into this to absolutely verify their abilities to gather information needs to be done straight away. If it is true, then it most definitely needs to be in the field. Matt, you are point on this. Make it happen and keep me apprised," said the temperamental Director as he handed Ryan the file for him to review. "Will do, Bill," said Ryan as he grasped the file and headed for the door.

Within a few days, it had been arrange for additional testing to be performed based upon the findings from Purdue and Krieg, as Ryan wanted to see a further evaluation this medication's effectiveness and worth. The scenario planned was for one cat to be fitted with a remote microphone and speaker which would be attached to its collar for data collection and give instructions. This cat, after receiving the medication, would be taken to a local city park to observe and document its use in a real situation, simulating a surveillance assignment. The two agents assigned to this were, Tyler Jones and Rachel Simon, who would conduct the experiment and be the primary handlers in this situation. Tyler would be the agent controlling the cat and Rachel would record any observations noted while this occurred. Each agent used a wireless communication device to assist each other's effectiveness as a team. Their instructions were to transport the cat to James Monroe Park which was near George Washington University a little before noon, to catch the lunch crowd which was common there to find subjects to overhear their conversations and put this idea to the test.

Tyler and Rachel arrived about eleven-thirty with their accomplice Edgar, a domestic cat. Upon reaching their site, Tyler gave Edgar the order to stay while the two were exiting the car. The cat obeyed while Tyler turned on the microphone and speaker and then was instructed to follow them. After locating a hill where he thought he could sit unnoticed, Tyler and Rachel decided she would sit on a park bench that was about twenty yards from a picnic table. She would be able to observe both Tyler and Edgar easily and make take down notes about the process. Rachel took a seat on the bench and Tyler and Edgar walked over to the hill. Once a couple sat down on the picnic table to eat their lunch, Tyler instructed Edgar, "Edgar, go and sit under the picnic table close to Rachel and stay there until I tell you otherwise." Edgar stood up and began trotting over to the picnic table. Once there he positioned himself under it as instructed. Tyler attempted to listen to the couple's conversation, but was having some difficulty in hearing everything that was being said. "Edgar, move closer to the people," Edgar edged closer and the conversation became more distinct. This activity was being recorded using the equipment in their car, but Tyler was able to hear their conversation about work and the exercise was proceeding well. After about twenty-five minutes into the exercise, one of the couple noticed Edgar. She bent over, looking at him and tried to coax him to come to her. He remained motionless. Upon seeing this and her continued attempts, Tyler said, "Edgar, go over and smell the lady's hand." Edgar stood up and proceeded over to her and sniffing her hand. The lady reached out to pet him and he backed away. "Edgar, jump up on the bench and allow her to pet you." Edgar complied and the lady smiled and started petting her new found friend. Rachel jotted down all of this and any other observations she thought pertinent. This continued for the next ten minutes until one of the ladies noticed that it was time for them to return to work. They both stood up and after petting Edgar said their goodbyes and headed off. Edgar sat there and watched the ladies leave.

Tyler considered this as meeting the criteria established for the exercise and called for Edgar to come back. Edgar immediately jumped off of the bench and started trotting over to him. On his arrival, Tyler petted the obedient cat and said, "Let's go back over to Rachel." The pair walked over and joined the other member of the team. As they were walking back to their car, Rachel spotted a shallow reflection pool nearby and said to Tyler, "You know Tyler, cats don't like water. Let's do another test and see if Edgar will walk into the water or not. "OK," said Tyler. "Let's see how deep it is first." They walked over and after determining that the reflection pool was only about four inches deep, Tyler looked around and on finding that no one was around close enough to hear him, he told Edgar to walk into the water. The cat again stood up from his seated position and casually walked into the pool. "Walk around in the water," said Tyler. The cat obeyed and continued to walk until Tyler instructed him to stop. "Sit in the water Edgar," was Tyler's next command. The cat sat down in the water, looking at the pair. Unnoticed by the two agents, an elderly man was sitting about fifty yards from them on the other side of the park and he came over to them. "That's quite some cat you have there," said the man. "I have never seen a cat do anything like that before. How did you train him?" Both Tyler and Rachel were taken aback by their breach of protocol and attention by this new conversation. The ever quick-thinking Tyler looked at the man and said, "Well, we have been working with him since he was a kitten and he has gotten to the point where he is like he is almost drugged. He indeed is one of a kind!" They all laughed and stood there looking at the unusual site. "Well, we had better go honey," said Rachel. "You should take him to Vegas," commented the elderly gentleman as they started to walk away. "Not a bad idea," said Tyler. The two then headed back to their car and returned with Edgar to their office.

The report which was compiled by the team was reviewed by Ryan who passed it on to Fisher. Fisher sat in his office, noting the success of the cat being able to capture the conversation from the couple chosen, but was troubled by the closeness that was needed for the team to hear what was transpiring. "That's something we need to work on," he said to himself. What he did like in the report was its thoroughness and the important fact that the cat was very easily accepted by the couple being spied upon. He had felt confident that this would occur. He was pleased with the team's off script idea of having the cat walk into the wading pool to additionally determine the effectiveness of the cat's ability to follow any order. Upon finishing reading the report and the de-briefing of the team that conducted the field assessment, Fisher knew that the next step lie in improving the reliability of the microphone. The wind blowing across it was one of the detected challenges as was the cat's fur brushing across the top of the microphone. "Helen, get Ryan here again." Within about ten minutes, Ryan arrived and the two reviewed the report together. "Sounds impressive," said Ryan to his chief. "Yes it does," said Fisher confidently. "But you, just as I, see where we need to proceed. Ryan, I want you to work with R&D to have them work on improving the microphone for this operation. Get back with me when this has been addressed," said Fisher.

Ryan, on his way back to his office, he started to review the information more closely. Upon returning from this informative meeting, he asked his secretary, Kathy, to contact Miles Donahue in research and development. "We need to improve this microphone. I would imagine that this report is accurate, once we can work out the bugs, this development will be one of the most significant advances in quite some time," he said to himself as he walked through his office door. He continued to scan over the report that Murphy had provided and a few minutes later, his secretary informed him that Mr. Donahue was on the line. Ryan picked up the phone saying, "Miles, this is Ryan. I've come across something new which if true would be something we could use to fight those bastards that are endangering our way of life. I need your expertise to improve something. Could we get together sometime this week to talk about this?" "Sure thing, Matt. When would you like to do this; I'll clear my calendar whenever it works out best for you." "Miles," said Ryan, I'd like to do this as soon as possible, so I'll put you over to Kathy so she can schedule a time. Let's meet here at my office. This material is sensitive and there isn't a better place than here to keep it that way." 'Fine, Matt. I'll see you soon." With that, Ryan passed the call over to Kathy for her to schedule the meeting. Once Kathy had arranged for the meeting, she shared the arrangements with Ryan.

The following Wednesday, Miles Donahue walked into Matt Ryan's office and sat down across from his old friend. "Matt, how is the family? You're doing well I hope?" said Miles. "I'm fine and so is the family," said his old friend. "Miles, this job is going to be the death of me. We send people to God-forsaken places and they get blown to pieces by pieces of shit that we can't even see let alone find. It's gotta stop somehow and if the report in front of me is accurate, we may have a new tool to make this happen. It's better than a drone." "Really?" said Miles. "Tell me more." Ryan then took the next hour to review the information gather and testing completed by the DOD and HHS. Miles sat there quiet as a church mouse, listening to the unbelievable story that Ryan was unfolding. "So, the DOD & HHS has tested this and it has proved positive, right?" asked Miles. "Yes, their reports indicate that this agent's use is completely effective and relatively long-lasting. But our use of it may be different in some ways than that done by them. We've tested it briefly and the results were positive as well. I'd like us to test it more since it will be my ass hanging out in the wind if their report and the initial testing is a bunch of shit," said Ryan as he leaned forward, his elbows on the desk and hands clasped so his chin could be supported. The traditional mistrust between these governmental agencies continues to haunt them although they were willing to work together on this. "We can test this if we have a sample of the drug. How would you like us to proceed?" asked Miles. Ryan opened his desk drawer and pulled out a plastic bag with some powder in it and he tossed it on the desk top. "Miles, here is a sample of this drug. What I want you to do is to validate their findings with the following differences. One, I want us to continue to evaluate how effective this drug is and the cat's ability for information gathering. I think that this if true could without a doubt enable us to obtain volumes of valuable information some of which we can never get through conventional sources. The assholes out there we're watching become our best informants. Two, we know it works on the typical house cat, but on this Maine Coon cat, and on some other types of cats, we need to do further testing. It makes sense to me that if it works, we probably would want to use cats that are common to the area we would use them in to help avoid detection. And thirdly, we need to develop a small collar that could provide us an audio feed to the cat; a video feed for us to watch, has a GPS, and that also has an explosive charge in the collar. On the initial test we performed, the microphone used during this proved to be inadequate. Wind and cat hair were the main problems detected. We need you to overcome these issues." "Well that's a pretty tall order," said Miles. "We can do it, but how quickly do you need it?" "Everything but the explosive charge, as soon as possible. I want to continue our assessment of this drug, not that I don't believe our counterparts, but my ass is on the line and I've grown kind of fond of it," said Ryan chuckling. "I'll get right on it, Matt," said Donahue as he started out the door. Even though there are reports substantiating its effectiveness, it's like they were all from Missouri, the show me state.

A little over a week later, Miles contacted Ryan to let him know that he had a prototype of the collar he had requested. "This wasn't a major deal," said Miles to his friend. "The biggest problem that we had was in finding a battery source that would last for a while. Not having much success with that, we installed a miniature solar power source which can keep the battery charged, much like what is found on watches. The camera pulls quite a bit of power which was a problem, but we took care of that." "Great!" said Ryan. "When can you get one to me?" asked Ryan. "I can walk one over right now if you like." "That would be great, but I'm getting ready to walk into a meeting right now, so how about I call you when I'm finished?" asked Ryan. "Sounds good. I'll be waiting." "I knew that I could count on Miles," thought Ryan. "Man, if this really pans out, the possibilities...how much more effective we'll be." Ryan continued into the conference room with a slight smile on his face. After his call to Miles, Ryan had the new collar in his hand and was looking to move forward.

Ryan contacted Fisher as requested and brought him up to speed on the new collar development. Fisher was pleased and instructed Ryan to complete some additional testing of the cats and the device to determine the viability of them both. After a number of test situations, a summary report we prepared and provided to the Field Operations Director's desk. Fisher came in early that Wednesday morning, and on finding this report on his desk, he quickly reviewed it and had his secretary contact Ryan. "Matt," that was the first time that Fisher had called him by his first name, "this is Bill," again highly unusual. "I want you to work on getting this into the field as soon as possible. Contact someone that you personally have worked with in the past and get it started now. From what we have done so far, this is about the most exciting thing I've seen in thirty years! If everything goes as well as expected, it sounds like we will be hiring some new people in short order to help take care of our new agents. Good job Matt."

Federal agencies have a strong history of dislike and distrust of each other. This is partly due to a multitude of factors, the main ones being; budgetary allocation, competitiveness, esprit de corps, and power. Situations do at times force these "children" to play well together, but it is usually with teeth grinding and fake smiles. None the less, William Nystrom, deputy director for the South American CIA branch was assigned by Ryan to attend a meeting with the other federal agencies. The desire from upper leadership was to work toward fostering an atmosphere of collaboration early on in this venture due to the expected magnitude of this new opportunity for them all. Nystrom was not briefed as to why, just told to report. Having flown back from Tel Aviv overnight, he was a little spent, but this was nothing new in his job. He reported to the CatGenus building and after passing through security, was waiting in a conference room for God knows whatever reason from his point of view. He couldn't imagine why coming to a place such as Louisville was such a crucial need. Ryan had shared this move with Fisher and his belief that there was in fact a tremendous potential that this new medication could bring to their operations and the outcomes of these endeavors. Ryan sat with Nystrom during this meeting and afterwards, planned to pull him off to the side for a discussion about the future events.

After the usual necessary but guarded pleasantries, Nystrom received a complete briefing on what has recently been named Operation Subtle. Ryan had personally spoken to the Middle East chief himself prior to the arrangement of this meeting to let him know they would meet immediately after this collaboratory meeting. He sat incredulously listening to the initial information being shared. "What is occurring here is totally outside of the usual interdepartmental boundaries, and I must say I am impressed." As they replayed the video, he sat there in amazement. "Seriously? Cats being used for surveillance and information gathering?" he said to himself. "You know, if we would have had this agent years ago; some of us probably would be out of work today," said Nystrom to the group. A few eyebrows raised and Murphy sat there with a slight grin on his face. "Yes and some of our past friends would probably still be with us as well," said Murphy. Nystrom and Murphy were right, but it was a moot point. "We started with this project initially thinking that we could use these cats for recon and information gathering, you know. Placing a mike for instructions and a miniature video camera on a collar would provide us real-time intell and be priceless to our mission. However, and I don't recall who it was that brought it up, with the instinctive hunting and stalking abilities that cats have, using them for eradications was investigated and review is underway. The Maine Coon cat was decided upon due to its larger size but even though bigger, still gives the appearance of a common cat. Slides of the Maine Coon cat in comparison to the typical domestic house cat were displayed on the screen. These cats have demonstrated the ability to inflict deadly attacks through biting or clawing through major arteries in the victim's neck, leading to a quick bleed out," shared Murphy to the group. "Thank you John for your insight and wisdom. Without a doubt, from what I have seen we definitely want in on this," said Nystrom. Ryan was pleased at Bill's interaction with the group. "We have honestly been considering something along these lines for some time but have not been successful. The specifics on this operation are included in the file that I am giving you today for you to share it up your chain," said Nystrom. "Thank you for this consideration Bill. This intense collaboration between agencies is something that needs to go into the record books. This is an unprecedented occurrence, one long overdue," said Murphy as the two shook hands. There was a mumbling of conversation that was occurring around the room. At the close of the meeting, Ryan and Nystrom each got a couple of cups of coffee and left together, to discuss his further involvement with the field testing of this drug. "Bill, you need to know that we have already been looking at this drug and have performed some initial testing with it," said Ryan as the two walked away from the coffee urn. "Upstairs believes that we need to get this into the field as soon as possible to really evaluate the benefits in a real situation." "I see," said Nystrom after taking a sip of coffee. "Just point me the way you want me to go and we'll get this taken care of post-haste. Who would have ever thought of a furry ninja?" They both laughed as they walked down the hall.

Cam sat wondering what was going on up on the tenth floor. It was almost like he had a sixth sense. The meeting between the governmental agencies had just ended, unknown to Cam. He had been in a number of meetings with government officials up there in the recent past but had not heard anything for the last few weeks. "Apparently they scrubbed everything out of me that they needed," he thought. His distrust of where this involvement might go still resonated in his brain. His sixth sense still bothered him over the meeting he had with Murphy a few weeks ago and since then there has been no additional communication. "I need some fresh air," he thought. "Greg, its lunch time, I'm going for a walk outside; need some fresh air." "Hey," said Greg, "mind if I come with you? Sounds like a great idea." "Sure. Let's go," replied Cam. As they waited at the elevator, Cam noticed that the elevator stopped at the tenth floor. Shortly it stopped on their floor and only one man was on it; that the two did not pay any attention to. Cam and Greg both got on and the doors slowly closed. The ride to the first floor was the typical silent ride and all exited after the doors opened again. Cam and Greg out the main doors of the building and headed off to the right while the other gentleman to the left. Cam turned upon hearing something occur, behind them off to their left; apparently the man bumped into someone on his way to his car. As Cam continue to look in that direction, the man walked a few more steps toward the parking lot and when he pulled what appeared to be his keys from his right coat pocket, something shiny fell into the grass next to the sidewalk. He stopped and got Greg's attention, heading over there to try and find the item the gentleman dropped. "Hey wait!" he called to the man, but a semi passing their building blew its horn about that time, interfering with the man's ability to hear his call out. The two stopped about where they believed the man had dropped the item and started looking for it. Cam looked up and the man had gotten into his car. He waved his arm to try and get the gentleman's attention while glancing back and forth from the man to the ground. The man pulled away, oblivious to Cam's attempts to get his attention. "Well if we find whatever it was, I'm not sure how we can get it back to him," said Cam frustrated. Greg said, "Here it is. It's a flash drive. Maybe we can take it back to the lab and there will be something on it that will provide some contact information." The two decided that since the man had left, that there was no tremendous hurry in checking out the flash drive, so they continued with their walk. The fresh air felt good to Cam as since all of this transpired, Cam had found it increasingly difficult to come into CatGenus each day. He thought about the private meeting that he had with Murphy and the queasy feeling that still remained within him about their use of his drug and his fear that it will be used for other perverse purposes. Cam came back to reality with Greg's comment about the weather. Cam shared his concerns with Greg as they continued their walk and the two discussed their options. Greg did his best to re-assure Cam and expressed his hope that there would be a positive outcome. But down deep, Greg too had his concerns about where this would lead.

Upon returning to the lab, everyone had gone to lunch, so they plugged the flash drive into a computer and once open, a number of files appeared. Most they were unable to open; most files were encrypted and required a password. Of the ones they were able to open, they were mostly general notes and did not provide any contact or identifying information. "It doesn't look like we're going to be able to identify the owner," said Greg. "I guess not," said Cam as they continued to scan the files. There was however a video file that was loaded on today. They looked at each other and although both doubted that there would be contact information on it, they decided to open it if possible. On opening the video file, an empty room was initially displayed. A man's voice came on saying, "Houdini trial number five." On the left side of the room, two large cats appeared. "Sit down," the voice commanded. Both cats responded by sitting down. Each cat had what appeared a larger than usual collar on. Then on the right side of the room, a cat significantly larger than the previous two cats that had appeared. Once the larger cat observed the two smaller cats, it crouched down and made a snarling sound. The cats of the left side of the room sat there motionless to the presentation and actions to what appeared to them to be a mountain lion. The mountain lion slowly started to creep toward the two cats that still remained motionless. The voice on the recording then said unemotionally, "Lou, attack eyes. Bud, attack throat. Maintain silence." Both smaller cats rose from their seated position, each now slinking in opposite directions each approaching the sides of the mountain lion. Neither smaller cat made a sound. The mountain lion, upon seeing their movement began growling, eventually hissing as each of the cats came closer to their prey. "Bud, distract target," said the voice on the recording. The cat on the left approached the larger cat and lunged toward it, swiping at it with one of its paws. This activity happened a couple of more times with the mountain lion focused more on the aggressive of the two preys. "Lou, attack eyes now!" called the voice on the recording. The suddenness of the sound startled the mountain lion for a second and in a blink of an eye, Lou had jumped up on the back of the mountain lion, clawing his way toward its head. The mountain lion responded by rearing upwards to try and throw the cat from its back but this attempt was in vain. His claws securely sunk into the coat of the mountain lion provided Lou with secure footing. As the mountain lion landed on its front feet, Lou lunged forward to its head and began to rip his clawing into the area of the mountain lion's eyes. The mountain lion screamed in pain as the attack continued. It instinctively tried to swipe at the small cat with his paws but could not effectively reach the attacker. It then rolled onto its back, further trying to dislodge the assailant from his head. All the while, the attacking cat continued to rake the eyes of its prey. With the mountain lion fighting for its life with the first attacker, the voice came on again saying, "Bud, attack the throat now!" Instantly, the second cat lunged toward the mountain lion, sinking his long, sharp teeth into the sides of the mountain lion's neck. Cam and Greg sat there in horror. Blood started to flow and then spurt from the mountain lion's neck. Bud jumped away from the mountain lion as he anticipated an attack from the mountain lion and began to stalk his prey for a second attack. Lou's attack continued and the mountain lion's efforts to dislodge him were finally successful, but not before significant damage had been done to its eyes. The mountain lion yowled and screamed in pain and apparently was unable to now see its attackers. The mountain lion tried to wipe its eyes with its paws ineffectively. Bud crept inaudibly to the side of the mountain lion and then thrust himself toward the mountain lion for a second attack on its throat. Sinking his teeth deep into the side of the mountain lion's neck then led to a greater amount of blood spurting from the mountain lion's neck. Bud then pushed himself against the neck of the mountain lion to inflict more damage and to escape the wrath of the mountain lion. The mountain lion raised his right paw just before the cat pushed off and as the cat flung away from its victim, he caught the cat in the side with his sharp claws. In the ensuing minutes that passed, the blood loss began to take its toll on the mountain lion that it eventually slinked away and posed itself against the wall. Shortly after this, the big cat remained motionless; its life had gradually slipped away; the room was a bloody mess. "Bud, Lou, come to the door," said the voice. The cats walked to the door, one limping and bloody, eventually moving through the door which had opened for them to exit. The door closed and only the decreased mountain lion remained.

Cam's worst fears materialized in moments as they viewed this very graphic movie showing the two cats attacking a mountain lion. The shock quickly turned to rage. "Oh my God!" shouted Cam. Both men stood there watching this gory event unfold. Upon viewing it, their shock turned to anger quickly. "How could anyone do this?" Greg shouted. Cam stood there looking at the blank screen. Enraged, he stormed over to Mark's office, finding he was not there. Next he headed out to Sally's area. "Where is Mark?" he loudly asked. "He's at a meeting and then was going to lunch," she said sardonically. "Where?" Cam demanded. "I'm sorry, but the meeting is off site. They are expected to be back later this afternoon," she replied, looking over her glasses at him. "Fine! Tell Greg I'll be back." As Cam threw open the door, he was angrier than he had ever been in his life. Greg came running out saying, "Cam, where are you going?" "To that bastard Buck's office," said Cam as he waited impatiently in front of the elevator. "That son-of-bitch Buck has some explaining to do!" as he paced while waiting for the elevator. "Cam are you nuts?" asked his friend as they stood there waiting for the elevator to arrive. Cam did not respond. "Cam, think through this before going up there. Again, no response from him as the elevator doors opened. Cam hurried in and turned to look at Mark. His eyes said it all; there was no stopping him.

The elevator doors opened and Cam stormed down the hall to Buck's office door. Upon throwing open the office door, Mrs. Johnson was sitting at her desk and was surprised by the unexpected brash entry. "Is Buck here?" demanded Cam. "Well sir, he is in a meeting at present and can't be disturbed," she said kind of flustered. "The hell he can't!" yelled Cam as he started for his door. "You can't go in there!" said Mrs. Johnson as she attempted to stop him. Cam brushed past her and threw upon the office door. She quickly returned to her desk and called for security immediately. Buck coolly looked up from the drawing he and another gentleman were looking at. "Buck, we need to talk and we need to talk now!" ordered Cam. "Dr. Robert isn't it? I'm in a meeting at the moment. I don't appreciate this interruption. Mrs. Johnson will set an appointment for you at a later time. Now get out!" said Buck angrily. "I really don't give a shit Buck! You're responsible for those governmental bastards getting access to my discovery and they have twisted it into something incomprehensible and it's your fault!" Cam yelled. Buck, looking over to the gentleman with him said, "Would you please excuse us? I see that this is something that I must deal with. My utmost apologies to you. Mrs. Johnson, would you please reschedule this meeting for me?" The gentleman nodded his head, gathered his things quickly and looked at Cam as he exited. Security had just arrived and Mr. Buck waived them off. "Everything is fine here. I can handle this," he said. Security hesitated, looking at Cam and then Buck but started to leave. "We'll be just outside, sir," one security guard said, closing the door behind them. "I imagine that you've found something out that isn't to your liking. I figured we might have a meeting like this someday, Dr. Robert. You have no idea of how your discovery will save the lives of countless people in the future. I've personally been involved in some more than hairy situations where something like this… well, I just can say that some of my friends would be with us today if we had this in the past," said Buck relaxed as he seated himself behind his desk. "Buck," said Cam, "you know this was not the intent for this discovery! I can't stand by and watch innocent animals be turned into murderous agents for any reason. You're a son-of-a-bitch and so is that bastard Murphy! When we met, he gave me his assurance that no animals would be put in jeopardy. That was a crock of shit! How in hell could anyone consider doing this to an animal? You're vision, what you say this company is about; it's all bullshit!" said Cam, as red in the face as anyone could be. "Let me tell you something, you little prick! While you were sleeping in your comfortable bed all these years, men and women have been out there putting their lives on the line so you could live the easy life you do today. Being a Navy Seal, I've seen it; I've lived it, so has Murphy. This drug without a doubt is more valuable to us in intelligence gathering and the defense of our country than you would ever know. Imagine, sending in one you these cats to just sit and listen in on conversations of those wanting to do harm to our country. My God! If we had something like this before 9-11, maybe it wouldn't have happened! This really isn't about killing people; it's about using whatever resources are available to save lives. If some bad guys die along the way, so be it! You pompous, pious, puffed toad! You don't know the first thing about what is really going on in the world out there from your protected little lab, your precious farm home! Robert, just go back to your little safe world and let the big boys and girls keep getting their hands dirty for you, you preppy little shit. Now get out!!" Buck said. "Get out or I will gladly throw your out!" as he rose from behind his desk in a challenging manner. "Mrs. Johnson, come in here!" he said over his intercom while straightening his tie. "You've not heard the last from me Buck," gnashed Cam as he rose to leave. Cam brushed past Mrs. Johnson and the security guards as he stormed out the door, heading to the elevator. Buck took a moment to re-compose himself after this unexpected intrusion and bout with Cameron. Once his blood pressure came down, he picked up the phone and called Murphy. "John, we probably had better meet sometime soon. Dr. Robert must have come across some information he should not have and we just had it out in my office."

Cam returned to the lab and gathered his things. Greg was there and on seeing him return, approached him. "What did you do up there, Cam?" he asked not trying to attract more attention than Cam had already done with him abrupt entrance. "I told the son-of-a-bitch that I wouldn't stand for this use and that he had not heard the last from me," lashed back Cam. Cam started walking toward the door with Greg following closely behind. Entering the hall, Cam said, "The bastard told me he was a former Navy Seal and that my discovery would save lives. Some blood might be spilled along the way, but what the hell; it's for our glorious country!" yelled Cam. "Wow! No wonder the government is in our building. He's been involved with them for years," said Greg as the got on the elevator. "Where are you going?" he asked. I don't know but I have to get the hell out of here for now!" said Cam angrily. The elevator stopped at the ground level and the doors opened.

As they both exited, they saw a couple more security guards that usual upon walking into the lobby. "This whole thing really bites," said Cam as he walked through the building doors outward. Cam continued to storm toward his car. "Cam, just be careful. I don't know that we really have any idea of what or who we are dealing with here. I completely agree with you that this is wrong, but flying off half-cocked isn't smart. Think about it, my friend," said Greg as Cam jumped into his car. He started his car and then looked forward for a couple of seconds. "I know you are right Greg. But we have to do something; I can't stand by and know that my discovery is being used for illicit purposes. And animals are being misused and killed. It's just unacceptable!" said Cam as he put the car in reverse. "Be careful, Cam," said Greg as Cam backed up. Cam squealed his tires as he turned the wheel to head out of the parking lot. He was quiet for the remainder of his drive back to his apartment. Buck stood there in his office, looking down at Cam's departure. "I really ought to get rid of that little prick," thought Buck. "But with him here, we can keep a better eye on him."

Later that afternoon in the day of the impromptu meeting between Cameron and Buck, Buck made his way up to the tenth floor to meet with Murphy. "John, apparently Dr. Robert has come across some information which leads him to believe that we are using this drug for unacceptable purposes. He stormed into my office this morning and confronted me about it. The last I heard we were testing it for intelligence gathering but that was as far as things had progressed. Have we gone further into another use?" "Patrick, we both know that there has been discussion about using it for more covert methods than just eavesdropping purposes. Well, we have done some additional testing. There is a push to consider its use as more of a new stealth weapon. Our preliminary testing has shown these animals to be very lethal in their attacks, so the direction is for us to consider looking further into their use in eliminations of bad guys across the globe.

"Eliminations?" said Buck. "I know we deal with some serious bad guys, but this to me even seems extreme and remote as a possibility. I remember when we first talked about this that I couldn't condone putting an animal in harm's way. There's no way you could use them in assassinations without doing this." "Patrick, you've been out of the service for that long?" asked Murphy incredulously. "You've gotten soft my friend." "Not soft, but let's just say that my life has a little different focus now than earlier in life," said Buck a little miffed. "I still support our country and our troops; don't you ever forget that John!" "Whoa, there Patrick. We're getting off on the wrong foot. This development could save so many lives; what's a few cats here or there?" "If they can save a soldier's life, that's one thing, but I get a feel that you're leaning toward the thought that cats as disposable," said Buck, shifting in his chair. "No Patrick, cats are not disposable, but they can make a difference," said Murphy confidently. "Well OK, John. I think we are closer to being on the same page now," said Buck as he relaxed a bit.

The two continued their conversation and came to a more mutually accepted understanding of the direction and the ethics of using cats for future purposes. As far as the topic of Cameron was concerned, both felt that there should be a closer review of what was transpiring with him while he worked at CatGenus. Buck would have a routine report generated of his computer use activities and would monitor all in-coming and out-going phone calls involving him. Buck stated that he believed that although Cameron was highly committed to animals, that he did not see him leaving CatGenus, at least until his internship commitment was completed. He had too much to lose by doing this. This would allow there to be a more complete assessment of his professional actions in the meantime and whether he was working on something subversively. It was agreed that both would keep each other abreast of any concerns that might surface. With the direction meeting both men's satisfactions, their meeting ended.

Ryan, following his orders from Bill Fisher had arranged for the CIA to perform further tests on this drug. Ryan had taken the collar that Donahue's group had designed and had provided it to the research team for their appraisal. As Ryan had requested, the team was putting together the resources to check on the different types of cats around the world. This was a fairly daunting task and one that would be performed in a progressive pattern. As each group of cats was evaluated, the same group members would perform these evaluations. It was relatively easy to obtain the typical house cat and a Maine Coon cat for this trial. These tests were performed at Quantico, where their main research facilities were housed. Just as demonstrated by the previous video, each of these two cat groups responded appropriately and the results were re-verified with additional test subjects. With the ensuing next tests, it was necessary to contact research and development for them to provide prototypes of larger sizes of collars for the next breeds. Breeds that were considered for this assessment were the Chinese desert cat, and the African golden cat. Each of these was chosen for their particular traits. The desert cat was selected due to its color which would allow it to blend into more of a desert background and also due to the soles of its feet which protect it from hot sands. The golden cat had been chosen due to its typical twice the size of a domestic cat; the thinking being that one of these might suffice in place of two or more cats attacking or that it might be able to inflict damage more quickly and ultimately subdue the target quicker.

Testing performed with the desert cat was quite positive. Since dogs are commonly used for security animals, is seemed prudent to test them against these animals even though an earlier test had been performed. In the first of three tests, once an appropriate dose of Houdini had been determined, the cat was tested first against a Doberman pincher. In this experiment, with the proper instructions given to the cat, it only required six minutes for a successful attack to occur with the cat receiving no injuries. Similar tests were performed against the Rottweiler and the Bullmastiff. The attacks were successful although both dogs were capable of providing a much better defense and were more challenging for the cat. They dogs eventually succumbed to the onslaught, but in each case the desert cat suffered significant injuries which required medical care. Overall, it was determined that the use of the Chinese desert cat would be better suited for human attack and for information gathering in certain world environments.

The African golden cat however was a different situation. Partly due to its size and to its quickness, this cat performed much better than the Chinese desert cat. When placed up against all three dog breeds, the cat made quick work of them all. The Doberman was incapacitated within three minutes of the attack without any injuries being sustained. The Rottweiler was incapacitated within seven minutes of the attack and the cat suffered no injuries and with the Bullmastiff, it required six minutes for the incapacitation to occur; again with no injuries. Incapacitation was defined as when the dog no longer was actively trying to be an aggressor and became defensive in nature. Each of the dogs tested all eventually died from exsanguination within minutes after their incapacitation.

From the results of these tests, it was determined by upper leadership that a combination of cats could be used together as was deemed appropriate, but that the routine domestic cat would be excellent for information gathering on subjects and that the Maine Coon and Chinese desert cats would be used for this and for information gathering and human neutralization. For larger prey or stronger opponents, the African golden cat would suffice as the primary animal for these situations. The larger size of this animal would lead to undue attention in most other applications. Additional tests were conducted to determine their flexibility in working together and that once an initial dose of Houdini has been administered and they had worked together, then there was not conflict between any of the breeds. The desire of leadership was to use the domestic and Maine Coon cats as the primary tool since they were more universally known throughout the world; so as to not attract any undue attention. The need to keep this activity secret was paramount.

14

FIELDWORK

"This is fantastic," said Jack as he was listening to the conversation occurring on the veranda of an apartment around the corner. "We can sit here and be totally undetected and have access to information like never before," thought Jack as he continued to monitor the conversation. He was monitoring a conversation of a known drug kingpin who was in town for supposedly a vacation, but this intell was giving him the time, place and route of delivery of a large shipment of drugs. The cat was lying on top of the wall to the compound, just a stone's throw away from the encounter. The team which he was attached to was receiving this information as well and was using it to develop their plans for intercepting the shipment and to successfully capture the suspects. "Strange how things change," he thought as the meeting continued. "Before this, we were doing everything in our power to get dirt on these guys to get them off the street and now they are our biggest ally." It was projected that as a result of this development that sometime in the near future a lot of these high rollers and/or their compatriots would be either dead or off the streets as a result. They would be looking for reasons why their shipments were being intercepted and would believe that someone from within was selling information or as a deal to avoid jail time. As the shipment interceptions increased in frequency, it would only be a matter of time before cartel members would disappear or show up dead in horrendous ways. Either way, the streets would become cleaner and safer eventually.

Being in Miami, now on another mission, these two agents were part of a newly gathered team. Jack and Rick had been briefed on this new and incredible instrument to combat the flow of drugs into the country. Nystrom had arranged for this operation with two agents he had not worked with before, but that had an impeccable dossier. They were instructed to complete their assignment and send their final report to him. Considering that cats were the new tool being employed, each member of the team was evaluated to see if they had any allergic response to cats before becoming involved with this venture. Based upon the suspected explosion of use of this new tool, plans for allergy screening of all field personnel was starting to take place and is something that would become part of the agency's initial medical physical. Jack had been with the

CIA for the past eighteen years and he had never seen so much excitement or hub-bub over a new development before. "No expense had been spared over the past four months to bring this into operation and in other undertakings, a boat load of information and success had occurred during their evaluations.

In this particular mission, they were assigned to track and monitor a suspected terrorist cell operating in Miami. It was believed that this cell was planning an attack in the future at the next Super Bowl to be held in New York. A few of the operatives within the cell have been identified and as of yet, no definitive information has been obtained; at least enough to justify any action be taken. One of the suspected members of this cell works as a landscaper through the day hours and receives phone calls somewhat often. With the use of the cats, it is hoped that additional information could be obtained regarding their actions, meeting times and places, etc. Their team had arrived in Miami about a week ago and had the time to set up their house and reconnoiter the area before proceeding.

The first day found the team following the company that the cell member worked for and once at their work site, the cat was instructed to stay in the shadows for now. The subject was kept under surveillance from a distance. If he received or made a phone call, they would have the cat move in closer to attempt to listen in on the conversation. The crew worked for about two hours before taking a break. At this point, the subject walked away from the other workers and pulled his cell phone from his pocket. "Sparky, walk over close to the man talking on the phone," instructed Jack to the cat via the speaker on the collar. The cat trotted over near the subject and his conversation was able to be lightly heard. "Move closer Sparky," said Jack. The cat edged closer, unnoticed. The talking became more distinguishable. "Yes," said the subject. "I will meet you tonight at your apartment." There was a pause while he listened to the person on the other end of the line. "No, these fools have no idea. One of them asked me to come over to eat their vile food. If I only had a gun!" he said. He looked over and the others were returning to work. "I have to go now. Meet you later tonight." He then saw the cat and kicked some dirt at him, telling him to go away. "Jerk," said Rick as he watched through his binoculars. The cat did not flinch. "Sparky, move away from him and go back over by the trees," Jack instructed. The cat obeyed. Nothing else of significance happened for the remainder of the day.

The surveillance went on for the next two weeks and each encounter provided a small amount more insight into the cell, its members, their resources, and their plans. Some of what was overheard did not make complete sense to the intelligence team. Why would this cell be making arrangements to purchase three motor coaches? Were they planning on packing them with explosives to ram their way into the stadium for a detonation? For sleeping? There still remained unanswered questions and what appeared to be little time. The group seemed to becoming more active and their time frames for completion of tasks were shorter; this coincided with the date of the game getting closer. The cats were able to listen in on a number of the known meetings that the team was aware of. Some of the meetings were located in private dwellings and the cats did not have an opportunity to enter successfully or safely. The majority of these meetings were held outside; probably from the belief it was safer. Parks, walking trails, an occasional restaurant when weather permitted were perfect sites for the cats to come within close proximity to their subjects.

Finally, a stroke of luck occurred. On one of the walks in the park, the answer to the questions about the motor coaches came out; they would be using the vehicles as mobile bases and sleeping quarters for the cell since finding hotel rooms was a virtual impossibility. As they gained intell, Samir it appeared was the cell leader so the team focused on him. Samir and one of his members were walking in the park and their main topic was how they were going to inflict the greatest casualties at the event. Cell members had infiltrated the maintenance and concession areas a number of months ago. The maintenance workers would in the early morning on the day of the game would use devices made to bore small holes safely into the natural gas lines within the infrastructure of the stadium at various key points. The job of the concession workers was to, at a predetermined time, loosen connections to the grills in their areas to add confusion and possibly a little more of an igniting source to help create more injuries and damage. The final step in their plan was to have four small private planes that would take off from separate airports within a reasonable distance from the stadium. These planes would be loaded with as many propane tanks used for home grills as possible. Boxes of nails were inside the planes as well. They would fly low, each coming in from different directions. The ultimate goal was to then fly to the stadium, sharply rise to an altitude of one thousand feet and then plunge directly toward predetermined locations in the stadium, crashing into it and causing huge explosions and fires to kill and maim as many people as possible. The shrapnel from the explosion would also increase the death ratio. The cell was planning to leave for New York within the next week, using the coaches as their source of transportation. All the while this conversation was taking place, undetected by the two conspirators; two cats had been following, one with the primary responsibility of video recording their walk, the other maintaining a close proximity to two plotters for recording conversation. "Holy shit!" said Jack as he absorbed what was just revealed. "Get these recordings to Nystrom at Langley as quickly as possible," said Jack.

"The volume and accuracy of the intell gathered as a result of these cats and this new drug; well I can't say how much this will help turn the tide against these cockroaches we are battling," said Fisher as he watched and listened to the recordings. "We need to bring in representatives from all local, state, and federal law enforcement agencies into this discretely. We need the additional manpower to insure success of this mission. This is one time where we need the FBI to run with this since this is on American soil. They're usually a pain in the ass to work with, but considering the magnitude, we have no choice. We will not reveal how we got this information to anyone. Get them on the horn," he said as he was getting up heading for his office. "From what I understand there is an enormously long list of big wigs that are projected to attend the game. They have to be stopped at all costs!" The calls to the various agencies started immediately and the meeting was arranged for two days from now.

All agencies had been pulled into the situation, were briefed and ready to implement the plan developed. The desire was to maintain this group as small as possible to diminish possible detection by the terrorists. Airports within a one hundred mile radius were covered, watching for planes scheduled for flights on the day of the big game along with pictures of the known cell members being available for fast identification. The planes were the first priority and needed to be stopped at all costs. Area military bases would have attack helicopters in the air prior to and during the game. Teams were also assigned to the stadium; personnel from the FBI had been working with engineers to identify the most likely areas for the terrorists to puncture the gas lines. Employment records were reviewed along with information on the known cell members and anyone they were known to associate with also occurred. All workers coming into the stadium were required to pass through metal detectors, something that was not normal procedure, to try and identify any unknown persons entering with wrenches that were to work in the concession stands. If detected, they would be allowed to enter without incident; a weapons check was the reason to be given for the change in practice. Additionally, if tools were found in this assessment, then an FBI agent would be placed to work with this individual. The crowning jewel in this planning was the cats. Three dozen cats would be used to help in identifying and tracking known terrorists and to slip around the stadium and broadcast their video signal back to a control room with each cat's feed being monitored individually. One handler was assigned to each of the cats roaming the stadium to help with faster response to and/or communication of their activities. All agents in the stadium had natural gas monitors as well. With all areas covered, the team waited to spring their trap.

Fisher waited in the command center and with the aid of drones and satellites, had each all areas of concern under surveillance. The command center had area for forty personnel to monitor screens and activities. Each team and their communication traffic were monitored for leadership to follow any questionable activity or intervention. They waited for the moves of their targets. Slowly, the patterns emerged. Video feeds from the cats provided the location of some of the maintenance workers and their activities. These individuals were quickly apprehended and of the twelve involved, only two were able to puncture a gas line which these were quickly sealed. Of the concession workers, eleven were identified and neutralized by agents many while they were in the act of loosening connections. Eight other sites of gas leaks were detected, some as a result of the reports of the other workers smelling the leak in the concession stand, some from the portable monitors that agents carried. Most of the concession workers were apprehended in the act of tampering with the lines and were arrested before any threat occurred. All individuals were held in the areas where found as feasible, to avoid sharing the progress and tipping off other cell members. Of the four planes that were involved, all but one was stopped before take-off. One pilot eluded the team on the ground and with its successful take off, was in the air heading for the stadium. Helicopters were dispatched to intercept; its location was easily determined for interception with radar and satellite imagery. Communication with the plane was attempted and after numerous tries, the order was given to shoot the plane down. This was an easy target for the experienced helicopter crew and the plane exploded in a huge fireball above an empty field. Ground crews moved in to protect the area and for assessment of crash site for any additional information.

"You know," said the crotchety Field Operations Director, "I never have liked cats and they haven't liked me either. But there is no question in my mind that they have jumped up a peg or two on my board!" The game went on as planned with the Colts beating the Patriots, 34-21, must to the chagrin of the Fisher. "Damn those Colts!" he said disgustedly. The teams began to shut down their operation when one of the assistants quickly came into the command center and approached Fisher. He leaned over and whispered something into his ear; Fisher's response indicated he was taken aback, something most never ever saw from him. "Well I'll be damned!" said the aging Director. "I've been doing this job for the last twenty-two years and have been involved in dealing with some pretty hairy, high level shit before, but this takes the cake!" He stood up sharply and picked up the phone on the counter directly behind him as he cleared his throat. "Mr. President, this is Bill Fisher," he said, standing more upright than was his usual fashion. "Fisher," said the President, "I wanted to call you and congratulate you on an excellent mission and tell you that even though the world does not know what just transpired, you need to know that I do and you have my utmost admiration and appreciation for saving the countless lives of our citizens and by putting down one more assault against our way of life. Well done, Director! By the way, I was just apprised about the use of these cats. We need to sit down sometime soon and discuss this fascinating new tool." "I'd like that, Mr. President. Thank you sir," said the Field Director. Fisher hung up the phone and stood there for a moment. The rest of the world would never have any idea of what happened here today; no press conferences; no medals or commendations, but Bill Fisher had just received the biggest accolade of all.

15

BROADENING SCOPE

The members of the Marine patrol were reconnoitering the area around Garmsir District, Helmand Province in Afghanistan. These Marines were working out of Patrol base Khodi Rhom, a company from the second Battalion, second Marine Regiment that had been on station here for the last eight months. For weeks they had been working to rout Taliban forces from the area with limited success. IEDs have been a particular problem in this area and efforts toward reducing have occurred, but it was a long way from being curtailed. In response to this problem, William Nystrom was walking along with this company on this particular patrol. He was introduced as an intell officer although he was really a CIA representative and was along to evaluate the effectiveness of a new tool in recon; trained Chinese desert cats. Due to the nature of this work, all of the company's soldiers were informed that this activity was highly top secret and was ordered to maintain the strictest silence concerning what they were about to be involved with. Dishonorable discharge and jail time awaited anyone who wavered from this expectation. Each of the two desert cats was outfitted with a special collar having a GPS, miniature video camera, and a two-way communication system. The road side bombs were such a problem that resupply had to occur by foot to observation posts due to the IEDs. The plan was to use each cat differently. One would be used to scour around the nearby town by day to help locate collaborators and insurgents involved in this undertaking or to gain any other type of information on enemy activity. The other cat would travel down the side of the main roads at night, listening for the insurgents planting these devices and then coming close enough to locate and listen in on those involved to help detect the deadly pursuit. On the second night, the one cat was able to sit nearby on a road commonly a problem for IED's, remain undetected and locate and provide a glimpse of the infamous practice. The cat had been out for about two hours after dark when it heard some sound off in the distance. Nystrom sat there and on noticing the cat's movement on video, he instructed the cat to move toward the sound. The cat obeyed and in doing so, the sounds became more distinct. Nystrom could hear voices, so he instructed the cat to proceed. When the cat was close enough for a view of the activity to be seen, Nystrom instructed the cat to stop. The specially designed night camera allowed them all to watch the work of these three men who participated in the burying of the device in this situation. The group was amazed as to how nonchalantly the group handled the explosive device. Once their evil act was complete, the men moved off. The cat was then instructed to follow the men back to build information on where the bombs are being built and to capture their associates. Having the coordinates of the bomb, on the following day the disposal team was able to move in and safely remove the device. About a week later, from the intell gathered by a cat, it allowed the troops to raid a bomb-making house and arrest the occupants without any loss of life. Nystrom had more than enough proof that not only did the drug work effectively; it already had saved lives and provided a wealth of information. His lengthy report on the positive aspects for the use of this medication was received back at the Pentagon and the CIA, to be reviewed by senior leaders.

The CIA is one of the principal US agencies responsible for intelligence gathering and the analysis of information for national security and for specific tactical response against these persons, groups, or governments which pose a threat to the United States. After they had tested the new drug and their testing was complete, the value of this new asset was beyond comprehension. Intelligence gathering, locating persons of interest, and being an agent of death; all of these and more were envisioned by upper leadership and analysts with the use of this drug. The CIA, just like the FBI has developed their top ten-list of perpetrators that needed to be captured or eliminated, whichever was possible. The lethality of the cats had been tested numerous times on animals, but had not been evaluated on humans. The need to verify this ability was there, but even the CIA has moral boundaries. So, over a significant period of time, the decision was finally made to test the capability of these animals in carrying out a neutralization, as it was termed, of a person which was well-considered a threat in most corners of the world. This person had been on a kill list for many years, but he was never seen, so a sniper's bullet was not possible; he was one the CIA's top ten list members. He was a recluse in a French villa, content with his self-imposed exile but was still more than able to control his minions. He was an international arms dealer, someone who would sell anything to anyone if they had the resources and money to purchase his wares. The man in question was Jean-Pierre Chevalier.

He had been in this very profitable business for twenty-two years and the list of customers was as a who's who of the world's most notorious characters. The operation, code name "Chaser" started with a cat visiting the compound for three weeks to establish a pattern of habits and routines that Chevalier and his closest associates followed; and his security forces. This monitoring of fact gathering provided so much intell that a couple of shipments were able to be intercepted; but not too many though. They didn't want to spook the target. One afternoon, it was determined that a cat would sneak into the villa with the regular delivery of fresh fish. Chevalier demanded his fish be bought as fresh as possible. Slash, the name of the cat assigned to the team, had been able to sneak into the house on an earlier occasion, was able to identify Chevalier and had sent the night in Chevalier's bedroom to gain a better understanding of the lay out of this area.

On the day of the planned attack, once he gained entry into the house, the cat was instructed to hide in an inconspicuous place until evening. At approximately 1500, Shepard, the agent in charge, administered the Houdini dose to Slash and waited with him until the medication took effect. He was now ready for the mission. "We need to get him going," said Pate, the other agent on this mission. "The fish delivery should be coming in about an hour." "Right," said Shepard after he had validated that Slash was following his commands. "Slash, head to Chevalier's villa." The cat stood up and hopped off their veranda, heading to toward the villa. "Isn't science and technology wonderful?" said Shepard later as he was watching the video feed from the cat's camera while heading toward the villa. "What?" said Pate as he was turning around from replenishing his supply of coffee?" "It's just amazing, the science, and the technology. Here we are, sitting in the room where we are seeing and hearing most everything that is going on in the villa with a cat as our bug in the room. Tag that with the most amazing feature that we can give instructions to the cat and it obeys! Who'd ever figure? The last part is what blows me away," said Pate after taking a drink. "Cats are so damn independent. This drug, the implications are tremendous. By the way, who named this cat Slash?" he asked while watching the video monitor, sitting with his feet propped up on a chair. "Don't know. Probably some Guns N' Roses fan. Appropriate though, don't you think," responded Shepard. The night wore on and about one-thirty, Jean-Pierre commented he was going to bed. On hearing this, Shepard responded by sending a command to Slash. "Slash; make your way up the stairs to the second door on the right. Hide under the table and once he opens the door, run in right behind him." Within moments, the cat crafty began up the staircase, ultimately hiding under the table just outside the room. "Amazing," said the two almost simultaneously. "The recorder is running, right?" said Shepard. "You bet," said Pate. "If we did not record this, it would be our asses!" About five minutes later, someone could be heard coming up the stairs. As the two watched, a figured approached the room and as he came closer, it was Chevalier. He turned and opened the bedroom door and as he passed through the opening, Slash darted out from under the table and continued into the room. Chevalier stopped for a moment and looked back as though he had heard something. Finding nothing, he closed the door and headed to the bathroom. "Whew!" said Pate as he anxiously watched. "He made it." The cat chose to hide under the bed to avoid detection, waiting for his prey. "We'll let Chevalier get to bed and go to sleep. Once he seems to be good and asleep, we'll sic Slash on him. This will be pretty gruesome, but considering all of the pain, suffering, and deaths that this son-of-a-bitch is responsible for, maybe this will be a pay-back for those poor souls," said Shepard viewing the monitor with a stern look on his face. "Yah, he's one guy that won't be missed," said Pate. A report came from another operative that the lights have been out at the villa for the last hour and a half. From the sounds in

Chevalier's room, he was well asleep. "Man, this guy snores like a freight train!" said Pate. "He should do something about that." "How about us giving him a hand?" said Shepard quietly. "Slash, it's time to go. Come out from under the bed and jump up on the night stand." The two men sat there with their eyes glued to the monitor as they watched the cat come out from under the bed and jump up on the night stand by Chevalier's bed. Slash held there for a few moments before proceeding. "Move over onto the bed," said Shepard. He then slowly passed over to the bed, using his instinctive stalking and hunting skills to avoid detection. He crept toward his target slowly, a slight pause with each step. He eventually was told to stop by Shepard since Chevalier was sleeping on his side. "Not a good attack angle," he said. The cat crouched down and patiently waited for Chevalier to roll to his back as instructed by Shepard. Twenty minutes passed until Chevalier rolled onto his back. The cat tensed, ready to jump off the bed if needed, but was unnecessary. Once the snoring started again after a few moments, the cat rose up and moved closer to his victim. "Aggro! I repeat, aggro!" said Shepard. Aggro was the code word for Slash to attack. It was chosen as the code word because it was feared that if too common of a command word was used, there could be inadvertent bad consequences as a result, so something very obscure was chosen. Aggro means, wild almost to the point of losing control, but effective. "Never heard that word before this mission," said Pate, "but how appropriate." "Aggro!" said Shepard again to make sure the command was remembered. In an instant, the cat sprang into action. He sank his long, sharp teeth into the right side of Chevalier's neck while sinking the front claws of both paws deep into the left side of his neck. With a combined upward and outward thrust, the cat propelled itself away from the victim who instinctively was reaching toward his throat. Blood began to spurt wildly from both areas of his neck and with the force of the attack, he was coughing and choking and gasping for air. He rolled from the bed, clutching his throat with both hands, bleeding profusely and tried to call out, but was coughing and only a loud gurgling sound eventually emanated from him. As he tried to stand up, upon Shepard seeing this, he instructed Slash to jump on Chevalier, which effectively knocked him down to the floor. In shock, Chevalier eventually struggled to his feet and began to stumble his way to the door, trying to get the attention of his guards who were downstairs. The grasped the doorknob but his blood-wet hands slipped on the knob. He tried again to open the door again but was unsuccessful, but eventually he was able to get the door opened. The guards remained oblivious to what was occurring upstairs. With the ensuing interruption of blood flow to his brain, Chevalier was starting to become lightheaded and with the resultant blood loss combined, he braced himself against the wall for support and slid down the hallway slowly, stumbling as he went, a bloody streak on the wall followed him. After about ten feet, the haziness caused by the attack and the resulting blood loss took hold and he slid down to the floor, his blood saturating the plush carpet beneath him. He was slowly losing consciousness and began to hit the floor with one of his hands that he removed from his throat. The thick, plush carpet deadened the sound of this pounding on the floor. The lights dimmed in his eyes as he lost his struggle. He laid there in a pool of blood; a stark contrast to the cream-colored carpeting. His guards could be heard downstairs laughing.

Slash, as part of the instructions from Shepard, positioned himself so that Chevalier's struggle for life was caught on video. The two CIA agents sat watching the action without missing a moment. After seeing Chevalier making his ineffective attempt at getting his guard's attention and from the stopping of blood flow from his neck, once they saw no movement from him, they instructed Slash to approach Chevalier and to bite him on the foot to view any response. No response, no jerk or motion of any kind was seen. He was dead. Both agents, although stunned for a moment about the effectiveness and the gruesome nature of what they had witnessed, turned to each other and high-fived each other. "Wow!" was all that was said. While Pate transmitted the code word, Hamilton, to their branch chief to indicate a successful mission, Shepard returned his attention to Slash. "Slash," he said, "search for an open window or door and get out of there. Once out, walk through the wading pool on the grounds to wash away any blood that might be on you and return to our location." The cat, after checking to see if anyone was around, started to look for an exit. As he slinked around the villa looking for an opening, he paused at times to make certain he was not spotted. After a short time, he found a slightly opened door heading toward the pool and he slid through, on his way home.

Shepard and Pate both were sitting on the veranda of their apartment when both were slightly surprised by Slash jumping over the railing onto the floor. "Hi there boy," said Shepard, as he reached down to pet the cat who was still somewhat wet from his rinsing. "Good job, fella. How about a treat?" said Pate as he lifted his glass to the cat and then tossed him a piece of his dinner." "You know," said Shepard, "we are sitting here with probably the best weapon we've ever had." With that, Slash jumped up into Shepard's lap, and started to purr as he indicated he enjoyed the petting. The response to their communication came through as a "Ding!" was heard by the two. "Good job. Fisher."

16

COLLABORATION

Doc sat there listening intently to what Cam had to share. He knew something was up from the tone of Cam's voice when he called telling him he was on his way home. Combine this with the fact it was Tuesday. Cam rarely missed work and had only taken a vacation once in his time at CatGenus, so he knew something was troubling the young man. He purposely gave Ali the rest of the day off since he felt there might need to be some privacy with the coming conversation. Doc was pretty astute. He checked on the animals being housed at the clinic since he didn't have any upcoming appointments. Doc also called Susi and told her that they would probably be having a guest for dinner, but to keep it to herself for the time being. He did not know what was up and still wanted to protect Cam's privacy. "If Cam wanted anyone else to know he was coming, he would handle that himself," thought Doc as he checked the bandage on the golden's paw. About two hours later, Cam pulled into Doc's parking lot. Doc saw the reflection on his office wall and looked out into the lot. He got up and greeted Cam at the door. The young man looked as though he had not slept for days and was honestly, a little smelly.

"Son, you look a little worse for wear," Doc said as he shook Cam's hand. He knew he didn't need to ask what was wrong, he'd find out shortly. Cam came into the office and sat down. Doc pulled a soft drink from the refrigerator and pushed it over toward Cam. After taking a drink from the soft drink Doc had provided, Cam then took a deep breath and then shared with Doc the whole story of what had transpired at CatGenus and the discovery of the flash drive and its contents. Doc listened attentively to the story and in due to his years of life experience, he was not completely startled. "Cam, why in the world would a corporation like CatGenus be leasing out part of their building to the government? That seems weird to me," he said as he took a sip from his coffee. "It all comes down to money, Doc. Buck said that he did it to bring in money to support research, but this swung way out into something more than I ever imagined," said the young Vet rubbing his eyes. "The government has their hands into almost anything, and has done research on animals for years. The government has used animals in many situations, the military particularly, but never in this manner that I know of," said the elder Vet, with a concerned look upon his face. "I have proof, but I don't want to put you at any risk by showing it to you" said Cam, pulling a flash drive out of his pocket. "I know you said you've seen it in use, but a video?" said Doc incredulously. "I got it by accident, but couldn't find the owner after he dropped it and we looked at the files trying to find contact information. Don't know what agency this guy worked for, but it really doesn't matter, it's pretty graphic," said Cam. The elder Vet sat there and said, "I want to see this video. You need someone else to corroborate this situation if necessary. I'll accept the risk," said Doc. Cam reluctantly handed the flash drive to Doc who plugged it into his computer. After the drive was recognized and opened, Doc started the video. He sat there in revulsion as he watched the explicit video and stopped it before the end, almost pale from the experience. "Somehow we need to stop these bastards!" said Doc as he sat there stunned. "I am not completely surprised that this drug has been adulterated for this type of use. Probably the things that most governments get into, the extreme steps that some take in the name of justice or country; we probably don't know the half of it," he said in disgust. Doc and Cam continued to talk for a short time. Cam walked back into the kennel area, stopping to look at the animals housed there. "I could go along with the idea of using cats to record or capture information. But I can't understand why anyone could ever think about it, let alone condone using animals in this way. It just sickens me," he said quietly as he looked down at the animals. "Just remember Cam, you're not responsible for this. You're creation has its place in the world and can and should be used for positive reasons. Don't beat yourself up over this," said Doc as he walked up behind his protégé, placing his hand on Cam's shoulder.

That evening, the two went to Doc's house and upon his recommendation, Cam showered while Susi washed his clothes. After about fifteen minutes, Cam came out of the bathroom in Doc's robe while he waited for his clothes to dry. Susi was concerned and knew something was wrong, but waited for them to share what was up until Cam came out. Knowing that they could trust her with keeping this information confidential, they all sat at the kitchen table while both men shared most of the story to Susi's disbelief. "How in the world could anyone be so sick as to use an animal in this manner," she said staring out of their window. "Some people are just sick!" "Obviously they have your formula and can replicate the drug at will, so there is no way to effectively respond in that arena," said Doc. "How about going to the press?" said Susi. "That's an option," said Doc, "but how do you know who to trust? I see postings on the internet all of the time from independent sources that never are found in the mainstream media. Where would you start? Who could you safely talk to and be assured they would run with it?" Cam sat there soaking in the comments from both and looked up, "If these people or agencies are brazen enough to use the drug for this purpose, what makes you think that they would not hesitate to use them on you or someone you love?" he asked. Doc and Susi stared at him. "Doc, people bring cats to you every day. Susi, an unfamiliar cat walks up to you while you are gardening. The prospects are more than frightening." There was a dead silence in the room as the couple looked at Cam. "Let it be known, I am not saying that we should do nothing; far be it from that. What I am saying is that we need to think this out and come up with a solution that is as safe as possible, but effective," said Cam as he picked up the phone. "And we need to think through this carefully for everyone's safety," said Doc. "I'd better head over to Mom and Dad's," said Cam after their short dinner. I called them earlier to let them know I was coming home tonight. I called in sick at CatGenus to cover my absence."

The next day, Cam contacted those closest to him and arranged for a meeting to be held at his parent's house. Ali, his parents and sister who happened to be home from school, Doc and Susi were in attendance also. Cam had decided, although fearing that he was probably being paranoid, to hold the meeting outside by the basketball court where the picnic table was. It was isolated far enough away from the house and anyone sitting in a car nearby would be able to be seen easily since the crops were just harvested. It would be possible for any strays to be seen approaching; his shotgun was in his car nearby. There would be no listening in by Lord know who by holding it outside as well. His family was perplexed by this unusual request and for him to come home through the week, but they welcomed his coming. Cam had purported that his visit was to get together for some cake and ice cream, to talk over old times but he asked everyone to park their cars in the barn. They all thought this odd and they knew something was amiss, but they would comply. His parents, knowing that Ali was coming had at one point considered that maybe an announcement was forth coming concerning the two of them, but by the demeanor of Cam, they knew this was not the reason for asking everyone to get together. Cam was now twenty-eight and they were eager to see him settle down; they also wanted grandchildren but this was hardly the time. Cam and his parents were setting up for the table as everyone started to arrive. Both parents were becoming more concerned over Cam's quiet and reserved behavior. As everyone arrived, the usual welcomes and small talk ensued. After everyone was served, Cam stood up and looking at them all said, "Everybody, thank you for coming on such short notice," said Cam as he looked downward. The eating was slowing down as he spoke. "I have something that I need to share with you all, Doc and Susi both already have heard what I am about to share. Something has occurred at CatGenus and with a discovery that I have made which is extremely concerning to me and which I don't handle this right might be placing each of you at risk," he said as serious as anyone could be. The eating stopped and all eyes were glued upon him. His mother stood up and placed her hand on his shoulder. "Cam," as she started to speak. "Please have a seat Mom, I'm OK." His mother slowly returned to her seat, the obvious worry for her son showing on her face. Orville put his arm around her. "I asked for us all to meet out here since there is a reduced possibility that this conversation could be monitored, although still not impossible, but reduced. As some of you already know, to different degrees, that I have made a discovery that enables a human to control a cat's behavior. It is very reliable and the cat follows commands without exception. That is where the problem lies. My company has shared this with certain agencies within the federal government who has tested it and I believe have used the drug to have cats to perform various inappropriate functions. Things such spying on people could be one possibility. However, based upon a video that I happened to come across by accident, there is no doubt in my mind that they have move sinister plans for the drug's use. The video that I found more than supports this belief." Marjorie sat there, her mouth open, with her hand covering her mouth; Orville, sitting on the edge of the bench, not missing a word or the mannerism from his son. "To help assure your safety, I will not show you the video, which is the only proof that I have concerning this situation. I have to put a stop to this, but don't know how. I also believe that because they know that I am on to them, we all are potentially in danger, so we needed to talk about it." "Why would they come after us?" asked Marjorie. "To keep Cam quiet," said Orville, "To control him." "Exactly," said Cam as he continued. "And they have the formula, right?" said Ali. "Yes, unfortunately," said Cam. He looked down the roads leading to their house and saw no cars were in sight. With none seen, he continued. "I am not advocating that you do much different in your lives, but one thing, definitely do not share this information with anyone; I mean anyone. Two, any cat you see with an unusual or large collar or is not a cat familiar to you, get away and/or get with other people as fast as possible. Three, keep your doors and windows locked at all times. "Cam, do you really think they will come after us?" asked Emily. "No, probably not. I am the one they will be the most concerned about and hopefully this conversation is for naught. To try and further help protect those I care about, I now have a pay as you go cell phone so as to not be tracked by GPS and to reduce wiretapping. You all should get the same so we can talk without being tracked or recorded. I now also rent a car and pay cash whenever going out of town. I'm really not paranoid, but you need to know where things are and I think that taking some precautions would be smart. But really, the other reason that I got you together other than to inform and warn you all, is for you to think about any contacts you might have in the media or any ideas that you might have for how I can stop this from continuing." said Cam as he looked at those he cared the most about in the world. The ice cream melted and not much of the cake was eaten after the discussion. They all gathered around to discuss some thoughts and ideas which might be fruitful, might not. None of them had a direct contact with media sources.

Cam and Ali walked away from the group, talking about what he had said and she expressed her concerns for his safety. "Ali, I am sure I will be all right; at least at this point. I'm probably still a source of information for them. They know that I personally am not much of a threat at present, but that would change if I find an avenue to respond and they become aware of it," he said. "Only a few other people have viewed this video and I want it to stay that way. It's extra security for you all," he said as they continued down the path. "Cam," said Ali as she grabbed his arm, "You will take care of yourself and not do something stupid! Whether you realize this or not, I care too much about you to see you hurt. Cam, I love you!" Cam looked down into her hazel eyes and a stared for a moment. He too had similar feelings for Ali but based upon the situation at hand, felt it best not to share it. "Ali, I care for you too," he said as he gave her a peck on her cheek. "Don't worry, I'm not stupid." They returned to the group and helped clean up from the gathering. The Hughes' and Cam's parents went into the house to take the remaining items into the kitchen. Cam and Ali decided to take a walk down toward Brian's farm to spend a little more time together and catch up. They were quite a ways down the road when a car passed Cam's parent's house, neither of them noticed black the car that passed down to road, heading west.

17

BIG BROTHER

Sunday night after dinner, Cam left his parent's house to head back to his apartment. Everyone understood the gravity of the situation and all indicated that they would be careful and would get the phones he suggested. He had been pretty preoccupied with the events that had unfolded and his focus was off a little. It was late and as Cam neared the exit about twenty-five miles from his parents, he noticed he was getting low on gas, so he pulled off of the interstate to fill up. After filling, he pulled his car away from the pumps, moving it over to the side of the building. He needed to use the restroom and wanted to get something to drink so he headed into the convenience store. After addressing his needs, when he returned to his car he found that the back tire on the driver's side of his car was flat. "Great!" he said out loud. Remembering that he saw a can of flat tire fixer in the Quik-Mart, Cam went in a bought a can and started to return to his car. As he rounded the corner, a Sheriff's car had parked along the left side of his car. The deputy stepped from the car, looked down and said, "Looks like y'all got a little problem here." "Yah, sucks this late at night, but that's life," said Cam looking

down, fixated on the tire. "Need a hand?" the deputy asked.
"No thanks. I'll fill it with this can and with the air hose
over there and be on my way. Thanks though," Cam said as
he shook the can while bending over preparing to fill the
tire. Once down and unscrewing the cap on the stem, he felt
a hard object touch the back of his neck. "I wouldn't move
too quick if I were you," said the deputy. "Y'all have
something that belongs to me and I need it back," "What
are you talking about? I have never met you before in my
life," said Cam nervously and confused. "Well we really
haven't met before, but I dropped something that you and
your friend picked up a while back. Does that ring a bell
with you now?" said the deputy as he looked around
quickly to see if anyone was around. "I know y'all have it,
so why don't y'all pull it out carefully and hand it up now,
y'all hear?" said the deputy who pushed the barrel a little
harder into his neck. Cam slid down onto his knees and
slowly straightened up at bit to be able to reach into his
pocket. "Well what a good boy y'all are," said the deputy,
as Cam pulled the flash drive slowly from his pocket and
raised his hand with the flash drive in it. "Now I imagine
that y'all have copied this onto another device of some sort.
I would highly suggest y'all erase it as soon as y'all git
home. And a…if you'n don't, well let's say y'all or

someone y'all care about; hey, how 'bout that cute little thing that were with at your parent's farm with this evening? Would hate for her to have an accident," said the deputy coldly and sternly. "Thank you much. By the way, you're lucky. I'm leaving now and that you are staying alive is why. Now as I leave, if I see your head bob up to look over at me or try and go for help, well let's say your headache will be a short one. Got me?" said the deputy with a little chuckle at the end. "OK," said Cam as he stayed motionless.

Cam heard the car door close. The car started and backed up and then the car pulled away. He did as instructed and after he could hear that the car was in the distance, he sat down on the ground next to his tire. His hands were shaking and his heart was racing. He sat down on the curb next to his car for a while and on collecting himself, he finished filling the tire with the can and then filled the tire with additional air from the station's air hose and began is trek back to his apartment. "There isn't any doubt now," he said to himself. "I am being watched. They knew where I've been and went to pretty elaborate steps to retrieve the flash drive." The remainder of the way he checked his mirrors frequently and arrived at his apartment about ten-thirty. As he exited the car, he looked around to see if anything seemed out of the ordinary outside his apartment. Not seeing anything or anyone that concerned him, he went up to his apartment. On coming to his apartment door, he checked and the door was locked. He opened it slowly, flipped on the light and cautiously entered the apartment, closing the door behind him. Nothing seemed out of order. He quietly went around the apartment, checking each room and found nothing. He checked to make certain all of his windows were locked. He threw his keys on the table and sat down on his couch and turned on the TV. He sat there thinking about the night's events not hearing a thing from the TV.

After this encounter, he experienced another sleepless night. He reported to work the next day and located Greg quickly after arriving. They went into the kennel and on Cam's request acted as though they were examining a cat. "Greg, hold the cat so I can act as though I am examining it. No matter what I say, do your best to not act surprised or look around. This is serious. OK?" said Cam. Greg responded by nodding his head and was a bit taken back and perplexed by this introduction. "Remember the flash drive we found?" asked Cam. "Uh huh," said Greg. "Well the owner found me last night and had a gun to my head wanting it back and telling me to erase it from everything that it might be copied on," said Cam while checking the ears of the cat. Greg pushed back slightly, shocked from what he had just heard. "Really?" he stammered. "Really," said Cam, continuing to exam the animal. "He was dressed as a Sheriff's deputy, with car and all. Apparently their resources are extensive." Cam said looking slightly at Greg. "Oh shit. What should we do? What they are doing isn't right and something needs to be done," said Greg as he starred at Cam. "If they knew how to find me, they know where I work and they probably know you were there when we found the flash drive. If there are any of the files from that flash drive on any system or device, delete them immediately. Whoever they are, they probably are monitoring that, wherever stored. I am sure our computers are definitely being monitored here for activity. Deleting any files that we have here should help improve things," said Cam as he removed his gloves indicating they were finished. "Anything else we should do?" asked Greg, looking out of the window. "No, just keep your wits about you. You're not who they're concerned about, just me," said Cam. "Everything will be fine."

Greg and Cam returned to work. Both felt as though they were being watched and for good reason. CatGenus prided itself in the advanced technology their corporation employed and for "security" purposes, video cameras were everywhere except bathrooms. Monitoring computer activity was a very common occurrence in most every industry today and CatGenus was no exception. So, from the tenth floor, it was a simple process for Murphy and his team to gain access to the monitoring of employees. It was especially easy since Buck had little problem with their oversight and had approved access, but he retained the right to determine what and where. Buck, due to his background had a soft spot for the military, not necessarily the government as whole, but he was a patriotic citizen. He had experienced some horrors of life and could live with a giving the "good guys" as he was known to say, an advantage. Besides, it was business. He had a company to run and was more than fine with the government supporting research he had a personal interest in. Also, this new development would provide CatGenus with some badly needed additional of income since he would be expecting the government to be paying his company for the use of this drug. Mr. Peters was pleased.

As Greg sat down in from of his computer, he was nervous, wondering if he was being watched that very second; he was scared and had every right to be after what happened to Cam. After sitting there for a moment, he said to himself, "No matter. If they are, then they will see what I am doing which will help get me off their radar screen." Once logged in, he accessed the file in his computer where he had stored the video clip and deleted it. "I hate to do this, but I am not a soldier, just a researcher." He then emptied his recycle bin immediately after that. The files were gone and he took a sigh of relief. Cam did the same thing as well on his computer. He was certain that if anyone's computer and activities was being monitored, it was his. As he was erasing all of the information from the drive from his computer, he couldn't get his mind off of Ali. "She told me she loved me!" His heart raced a bit. "Wow! That was neat." He had the same feelings for her, but with this situation, he couldn't put her further at risk. "I have to be careful what I do. I don't want Ali hurt, nor anyone else I care about!" he thought. "What a crazy time to think about this now." He in fact had erased everything off of his work computer. But he still had multiple copies. He had copied on the computer at Doc's. He had a hidden data card in his apartment and he had mailed another one on to Andrew, his friend from years before. In the letter he sent with it, he asked Andrew to hang onto it for him and to keep it sealed and keep it in a safe place; he would tell him the details later. The same thing was done in sending this to one of his oldest friends, Brian who he knew he could also count on. Both men then did their best to focus on their work, but they were distracted.

Cam went home after a long day. He had been assigned to another project by Mark. Mark was concerned that even though he was the developer of a new drug, that due to the challenges involved, he needed to be separated from the project. He was now working on Uveitis, which is an inflammation of the inner pigmented structures of the eye. It is a painful disease, and although not life threatening, it is hard to treat and can lead to further eye problems, ultimately blindness. This was not as rewarding of an assignment, but since he was close to finishing his internship, he was happy to be able to continue. He'd be happier to leave CatGenus altogether, but he had too much to lose at this point. He would have to stick it out.

Cam stopped for dinner on his way home and on arriving home; he collected his mail, placing it on the table with his keys as he finished looking at what he had received. Bills and junk mail; the usual. He sat down on the couch and took off his shoes and put his feet up on the table. It felt good. He stretched out and turned on the TV, channel surfing, not looking for anything in particular, to see if something caught his attention. All of the sudden, his screen turned blue. He sat there for a second, punched the buttons on the remote, nothing happened. "Shit," he thought. "Just what I need now." He put down the remote to check the cable connections when as suddenly as the picture left, a voice emanated from the screen. "Hey dumb shit," the voice emanating from the screen said, "good job with y'all and your friend's file deleting. Smart, man, real smart." "The voice…the voice; wait a minute, it's that deputy!" thought Cam. "Looks like y'all can listen even tho' you're guys. Ya' know, they say us guys don't listen well, but not y'all. You're on it man!" he continued. "Now I was purty confident that y'all had saved it somewhere's else and thought about it for a spell. Came to me that y'all probably kept it at home. Most people would y'all know. Well… I'd suggest y'all go into your bedroom. You'll find something in there that a smart guy like you will understand. Nice working with you Doc. Hope we don't have to meet again. By the way, purty smart place to keep the toy I found. Give that purty little thing a peck for me now, y'all here?" With a slight flash on occurring again on the screen, the picture returned on the screen. Cam stood there dumbfounded. He was shocked; he stopped for a moment for things to soak in. His head clearing, he slowly started to make his way back into his bedroom. On initial glance, nothing looked out of order. As he looked to the left, there was something small on the dresser, the back of it reflecting on the mirror. He walked over. It was one bullet, standing upright on the dresser. Cam pulled the second drawer down on the left side of the dresser. The data card was gone from the slit he had cut into the back edge of the drawer. "That son-of-a-bitch!" thought Cam. "These guys know what they're doing. Good thing that I sent copies to Andrew and Brian." He returned to the living room and sat there, not paying any attention to the TV. He got up and checked the door and windows, all were locked without a signs of forced entry. The stress of it all hit him shortly afterwards and after taking a diphenhydramine, he went to bed.

18

LIGHT'S OUT

Either emboldened or encouraged by the success of Operation Chaser, the CIA decided to work in a different arena with this new asset. Illicit drug traffic was rampant everywhere and even though interruption in business has occurred, it is speculated that their efforts are just a drop in the bucket of the total activity. Drugs can be obtained about anywhere and there are just not enough assets to fight the battle. It's kind of like trying to kill ants; you think you made head way, but later find them everywhere. It had been decided that another team would utilize the new tool for the eradication of a well-known drug kingpin. The desire to continue fighting the war against illicit drugs brought a team and three cats to Columbia. The plan, Operation Brothers, was as in France, was to infiltrate the inner circle of their target, a one Alberto Gomez. Gomez had a reputation for being very elusive, successful, and ruthless. The Mendez cartel has been operating for twenty known years and is the largest cartel in Columbia. Many groups have sought the capture of Gomez; the CIA is known to have lost six agents, the DEA has lost fourteen and this list goes on. The Operation Brothers team had arrived on the ground in Columbia July seventeenth and has been there for the past seven weeks. Their goals are to 1) gather valuable intell on any illicit drug activity possible while searching for Gomez, 2) locate Gomez, 3) infiltrate his location and at a time appropriate, eliminate him using the new tool, 4) leave the country undetected.

Groucho, as one of the cats was named, didn't seem to particularly like the Columbian weather. Who blamed him with the scorching heat and high-humidity it was a definite change for him as it was for everyone else. He did his job though and was as reliable as anyone or thing could be. Over the past seven weeks, he had provided an immense amount of intell, as has the other two Maine Coon cats, Harpo and Chico. Names, locations, distribution points and times were the main benefits from their help. These cats could go almost anywhere and blended in like the vegetation of the land. Occasionally they did have to outrun a child who wanted to play or a mother looking for something to feed her children but for the most part, their presence went unnoticed. Groucho was bigger than the cats there in Columbia which made him stand out a little, but not enough that it caused an issue. Toward the end of the seventh week, Groucho had been able to find one of the lieutenants of Gomez, a guy named Sanchez. Gomez was

almost like a ghost and although he moved around freely
without fanfare; one of the secrets to his anonymity, his
loyal followers would die before relinquishing any
information about him. Partly this was due to the fact that if
this ever occurred, and it had three times previously, the
family of the offender would die a horrible death; not just
immediate family but anyone related to that person, no
matter how remotely related or insignificantly affiliated.
One such transgression led to the deaths of seventy-eight
people. The Columbian people well knew of his reputation
and exploits and would not take a chance with their
family's lives. With this new found link to Gomez, all three
cats were sent to the area where Sanchez was known to
frequent in hopes more information could be obtained.
Once the he was located, their plan was to listen in and if
there were people with additional ties to Gomez, each of
the other cats would trail that person to gather more
information to hopefully get closer to Gomez. After nine
days of listening to trash and boastful comments from these
individuals, a break occurred. Sanchez was meeting with
some individuals at a local cafe and they were discussing
the need for a large shipment to be sent to the US and some
of the challenges related to problems with government
officials. Sanchez, on delving more into the specifics of the

situation, realized the challenges were from someone in a high governmental position and as such, the influential muscle of Gomez probably was needed, if nothing else, he should be aware of the problem. Arrangements will be made for the meeting. The group of three men finished their lunch with Sanchez noting he would be in touch shortly. The cats tailed the other men to obtain more information.

The meeting that Sanchez had asked for was to be held on a vast complex location six miles from Cartagena. According to the information revealed through Groucho's efforts, this complex was owned by Gomez and a place where he was the most comfortable. Gomez was one individual that had been very secretive and few pictures of him were known to exist, and the existing photos were indistinct. He was a man from the shadows but with the aid of the three cats, his identity could more easily be determined. The meeting was scheduled for the evening of September ninth, at seven o'clock at Gomez's compound, four days away. An advance team was dispatched to reconnoiter the area and the compound and all three of the cats were sent four days prior to the meeting to prepare. This was necessary to identify security measures, patterns of persons in and out of the compound, and to gain valuable information about the layout of the villa and potential entry points for the cats. This information was relayed back to the command post located within the rented house about one mile away as the crow flies, where the team lead would be based. This house was perfect since it was gated and had a privacy wall surrounding the property. Two cats were sent in each day on three separate occasions to perform this scouting. Once this intell was received, it took a short time for this experienced team to arrive at a plan of attack. To minimize any detection or attention, a man and woman team would transport the three cats to a remote location about one-half mile from the compound around one o'clock in the afternoon. This would allow the three cats more than ample time to traverse to the compound and to also gain access well before the scheduled meeting. The cats would be released from a side road where traffic was light. Each cat would be guided remotely from the command post, by Nelson who was the lead agent. A backup command post was established about half of a mile away from the compound to minimize any risk of communication problems and Brown and Miller would be at this location. The plan was that once at the compound, each cat would gain entry into the compound at different sites and would stagger their entry to not arouse suspicion. They would be there in plenty of time to utilize the normal in and out traffic that occurred in the villa to gain entry.

With the plan initiated and the cats on their way, things looked good. No communication glitches, the GPS provided the ability to track their progress from the signals received from the satellite. The cats separated as planned as they traveled and each moved quickly through the jungle toward their objective. One of the cats, Chico, was about half way to the objective, when he encountered a bushmaster snake. As Chico was moving toward the compound, when after jumping over a fallen tree and after taking a few steps, the rustling of the leaves to the left made the cat jump to the side just seconds prior to a bushmaster's strike attempt. The cat, noting the snake, crouched down, its hair standing up on end, and surveyed the situation. The snake moved slowly to the cat's right, the cat watching every move. As the snake moved, the cat pivoted himself slightly away from the snake. This action happened so quickly, that the agents did not initially notice the clash, being distracted by a recent communication. The cat, now considering its options, prowled around the snake, as the snake tried to do the same. The cat hissed and menacingly lunged at the snake. The snake responded by rising into the air to avoid contact. About this time, Seele, the agent monitoring the cat became aware that something was wrong and reverting his attention to the video and audio feed. "Shit!" he yelled, "Chico found a snake!" Nelson rushed over to assist and when the snake came into view, he said, "Oh hell! That's a bushmaster! Tell the cat to avoid the snake and move on!" As the Seele began to transmit this order, the cat once again lunged toward the snake, using his left paw to attempt to strike at the same time that the snake attacked, and the snake struck the cat's left paw. "Did he get hit?" asked Nelson. "Tell him to get the hell out of there! Now!" They could see the cat back up from the aggressor snake and it stayed in place. With the command given to Chico, he did not respond. He continued to sit where he was for a moment and then slowly started to move away. "Was he hit? Is there any way we can determine if he was?" said Nelson. "No," we did not incorporate any kind of vital monitoring device with these cats. There wasn't any perceived need," said Seele. Chico began moving further away from the snake and back on course, but at a slower pace than usual. "Tell him to get a move on," said Nelson, "He's behind schedule." With the order given, the cat started to speed up, but this effort was short lived. He pace slowed and soon after this, he stopped. "Oh shit!" said Nelson, "the snake got him!" Both men at the command post and those at the back up post who had just come on line watched as the cat ignored any additional orders. Within six minutes after the attack, Chico would not move. No signs were detectible from the audio feed. The video picture did not alter from the bush it was displaying. He had succumbed to the venom of the bushmaster. "Damn!" said Nelson. They stood there fixed on the screen for a few moments. "Seele, we can't afford someone coming across this collar. Detonate the device." Seele looked up at Nelson and then turned to the control panel. "I hoped that I would never need to do this," he said somberly. Seele pressed in a code for this collar and in an instant, the screen changed to fuzziness. "We had to do it," said Nelson as he walked away. "Well, we'll need to proceed with Groucho and Harpo as our plans just changed," he said frustrated. Both of the other cats were making good progress toward the compound, being less than four hundred yards from their objective.

Groucho and Harpo had reached the outer perimeter of the compound as scheduled. They were instructed to sit there for a while for the team to look things over. There was an increased number of guards present today as expected, but with their ability to move about relatively undetected, this helped assure their success. Each of the remaining two cats received the command to enter the compound and then to work their way into the villa. Groucho would enter through the door leading into the kitchen since there probably would be foot traffic in and out of the kitchen for the meal preparations. Harpo would enter through the doors located close to the pool which was typically left open for the ladies to walk in and out without being hindered. Even though there was a fair amount of activity in this area, the lush vegetation adorning the area would provide more than ample cover for their movements. Within twenty minutes, each feline was in the house, making their way to the master bedroom as planned. The plan was a little different than that used in France. It was planned that the cats were to follow Gomez into the bathroom which they had previously visited, unbeknownst to anyone, and then attack him while there, after the door was shut. With the door shut, any potential noise would be muted and lessen the possibility of detection. The elaborate and huge bathroom provided many places for the cats to hide without detection. In the massive bedroom, one of the cats, Harpo, was assigned the responsibility of perching himself in the window at the side of the room that overlooked the front door to the villa. "You know," said Seele, "we don't have stealth bombers, but we do have stealth meowers," looking up at Nelson, while laughing at his feeble attempt at humor. Nelson just looked at him. "Great," he said. "I'm stuck with you all day." As each person arrived at the villa, Harpo, who was poised on the window sill would follow the commands from Seele to ensure that video of those arriving could be captured. This activity would be videoed for additional information and future need. "There is Sanchez and the other two guys from the café," said Nelson as the three exited from their car. A few minutes later another car pulled up and four men exited who were unable to be identified by the two agents. "Langley will run their pictures through the international data base and the facial recognition software with ID them," said Seele. Finally, Gomez arrived. Interestingly, he came by himself. He was in a rather plain car and had no driver or bodyguard. The two agents were surprised at this, but in comparing the hazy pictures available, this person had to be Gomez. Once Gomez had arrived and it appeared that no others were coming, the cats then were instructed to wait under the massive bed for their prey to come to bed. The desire for his death far outweighed the need for information so the cats would wait patiently. This would probably be one of the few if not their only chance to catch

Gomez and kill him. The cats obediently responded and patiently waited under the bed.

Even from the remote location of the master bedroom where the two cats were hiding, the sounds of yelling and what appeared to be disagreement was occurring downstairs as the night drug on. It was too indistinct to be heard completely, but there no doubt it was happening. Gomez had arrived about thirty minutes prior to this boisterous exchange and the cats remained in hiding as instructed; their backs were up against the back wall to avoid possible detection. Occasionally what was perceived to be a guard would come into the room, look around and would leave. The meeting, dinner, and evening events lasted until one o'clock in the morning. The laughter of men and women could be heard downstairs now. The cats and their agents waited patiently for the events to die down; the hardest part of the night. While this was occurring through the night, each agent took turns grabbing naps at two hour intervals to help them remain sharp through the night. An increased commotion and some laughter ensued just before one in the morning. The sound of cars coming to the front of the villa was detected. The closing of car doors was heard outside the villa; things were coming to a head. "Wake up," said Nelson to Seele. Being in the dimly lit room, there was not much to see on the video and it was not worth sending the cats out to look; listening was the only option. A short time passed where things became quiet and after a number of minutes passed, the sound of footsteps could be heard on the tile floor, coming closed to the bedroom door. Both men sat there glued to the monitor, waiting to see if the door opened. The footsteps stopped just outside the door and an exchange of conversation was happening right outside the door. As the door opened, one man could be heard saying, "Thank you Manual, I am fine. This was a productive meeting. Have your men keep an eye out tonight. We leave at six o'clock in the morning for the airport. Get a good night's sleep" "Very good boss," said the other man, as the first man walked into the room saying, "Good night my friend." The cats crept to the edge of the bed so that one could get a glimpse of the man with his video camera. It was Gomez.

Nelson and Seele were tense in the seats. This was the closest that anyone has ever gotten to Gomez and their hopes were high that this would be a successful mission. Gomez apparently was not ready for bed because he walked over to a writing desk and opened a laptop, sitting down while waiting for the computer to come to life. Once open, he spent about twenty minutes working on the computer before closing it down, all happening under the watchful eyes of the surveillance team. He sat back and rubbed his eyes, taking a deep breath. "Shall we let the cat go now?" said Seele. "No," said Nelson. "We should stick to our plan. We can't screw this up." Gomez rose and after stretching and yawning, he turned toward the bed and in doing so, Seele said to the cat, "Get back!" The cat quickly darted back under the bed skirt. Gomez hesitated for a moment, thinking he saw something move. He stood there for a moment and even though the tequila flowed freely during the evening, he was a cautious man; he didn't get where he was by not being very careful. He walked over to the bureau and retrieved this forty-five caliber automatic and then moved over closer to the bed, getting down on the floor to check under the bed. Nelson and Seele heard the closing of the drawer and this movement toward the bed. Gomez walked over to the bed and after getting down on both knees, bent over to look under the bed. He reached for the bottom edge of the bed skirt and quickly raised it with the forty-five pointing toward the underneath the bed at the same time. "Aggro!" yelled Seele, the command for the two cats to attack, on seeing the hand grasp the bed skirt. Instantly, the two cats leapt from their hiding spot under the bed. "Harpo, eyes!" yelled Seele. "Groucho, throat!" Each had practiced these attacked on other animals. One spent time getting practice attacking the eyes, the other practiced on attacking the throat to neutralize their victim.

"AYEEEEE!" shouted Gomez as Harpo attacked his eyes with his razor-sharp claws, ripping deeply into his eyes with both paws. The sudden and unusual attack caught him by surprise; he dropped the weapon to protect his eyes instinctively. He reached up and grabbed the cat and reflexively threw the cat from his face, causing a further ripping away at his eyes. Simultaneously, Groucho jumped upon Gomez's throat and began to sink his teeth into the right side and his sharp talons into the left side as trained, as Gomez lie on the floor on his back, fighting off Harpo. The nearly simultaneous, vicious attack had Gomez fighting for his life. As Harpo was forced away from his face, Groucho made quick work of his deed and Gomez was profusely bleeding from both his eyes and throat. Harpo reflexively sprang back to Gomez's face, working on his eyes again. Gomez again grabbed the cat and threw him off of his face, with more damage being caused by the vicious attack. Yelling for help, Gomez made his way up to the edge of the bed on his knees, clutching his throat, blood intermittently spurting from his neck wounds. The cats pounced on the bed and again, Harpo attacked

Gomez's eyes, his hand responding again to this attack. Groucho waited for this momentarily and then repeated his attack on the throat. The cats and Gomez were covered in blood. The commotion caught the attention of one of his guards who came rushing into the gory sight with pistol drawn. His leader was leaning on his knees propped up at his back by the night stand next to his bed. The cats, knowing they had been discovered, shot from the bed toward the door. "Come home!" instructed Seele to the cats on seeing this intrusion. The guard pointed his gun toward the cats and fired. He continued to crudely aim at the cats as they were bolting for the open door as he headed toward his leader. Others now in the house were alerted to a security breach with the gunfire. As the house came to life, the cats fled down the stairs heading toward their planned exit in the pool area; their bloody paw prints being left behind them as they ran. As the situation unfolded, some of the guards and compatriots raced to Gomez's room, others chose to follow the trail of footprints left by the bloody cats. As the cats raced toward the open pool doors, their pursuers caught a glimpse of them and began spraying the area with automatic weapons fire. As the bullets danced around them, the cats took advantage of their speed and prowess to move quickly around the corner away from the gunfire. By now the outer compound lights had flipped on and the compound was a flurry of activity. The cats darted across the open grassy area heading toward the wall. When they were about two-thirds of the way to the wall, their attackers had rounded the corner, a few stopping to get a more accurate shot, others continuing on after the cats. The spray of bullets commenced again, kicking dirt up around the two cats. One of the running attackers was foolish enough to run into the line of fire and was gunned down in his desire to kill the cats. This allowed for a momentary cessation of fire from one of the guards which enabled the cats to reach the wall. Scrambling up the thick vegetation on the side of the wall, both cats were nearly to the top when one of the cats, Groucho, squealed out in pain; his tail was struck by one of his assailant's bullets. They both bounded over the wall to freedom, heading for their extraction zone. The assigned agents watched as the cats jumped into the darkness. Since the attack was carried out, it was decided that it would not be a good idea for anyone to be in the general area of the compound, so the cats were guided back to the command center using the GPS.

The scene in Gomez's room was one of a mad frenzy. Men rushed to their leader's side and had gathered towels from the bathroom to try and slow the massive bleeding from his neck. He could no longer see as the one cat's assault was completely effective. He was hoisted up by four men who rushed downstairs with their leader as quickly as possible. Orders were yelled to pull a car around to the front but by the time the group had arrived at the front door, no car was there. They all rushed, with their severely injured leader in tow toward the garages. A car then raced toward them and due to the driver's desire to get there quickly; his erratic driving struck one of the first men carrying Gomez, knocking them all to the ground. The remaining able men snatched up their leader and threw him into the car. "Head to the closest hospital in Cartagena!" ordered one of the men. "Paulo, call the hospital now! Tell them we are coming" said another man. The nearest hospital was ten miles away. Their leader lay in the back of the car with his men holding pressure as best they could to stem the flow of blood. As they traveled down the road, the response from their leader lessened. The wounds across his face and eyes, something like this none of them had seen before. His face was a mass of blood along with some thick grayish substance. They spoke to him reassuringly that they were near the hospital and to hang on, all of them covered in his blood. They were making fairly good time since at this time of night, the roads were pretty much deserted. The signs of life continued to slip away from Gomez, but the men continued to try and support him as best they could. "The hospital is just up the road a bit more; how is he doing?" asked the driver. "I don't know! Keep driving," yelled one of the men. As they reached the hospital, the driver slammed on the breaks near the hospital emergency entrance, throwing the men forward in a heap. They threw open the door and drug their leader's non-responsive body from the back of the car, as the hospital attendants brought a gurney from the entrance. Heaving Gomez on the gurney, his men rushed him inside with blood dripping from Gomez's limp hand that flopped from the side of the gurney as the doctors and nurses began their work toward saving their leader and friend. This activity was being monitored at the command post through a camera that had been positioned off in the jungle and by the satellite feed. "How could this have happened?" yelled one of the men. "Cats? Is that what attacked him?" said another. Against the wishes of those in the emergency room, two of Gomez's men stayed in the trauma room with their guns automatic weapons in hand. The doctors and nurses worked feverishly to save the stricken man who they had not identified as of yet. The damage was extensive and the care he needed was somewhat beyond their capabilities. A surgeon had been summoned and was on his way and should be there in a few minutes. IV lines were rapidly placed, a breathing tube inserted. The reading on the monitor showed a heart rate of forty beats per minute without a blood pressure. Bags of IV solutions were hung with medications being pumped into each IV as fast as possible as they continued to try and save their ravaged patient. The staff began chest compressions as the ER doctor worked to the best of his ability to try and evaluate the wound in his neck. A portion of the artery had been severed on both sides of his neck which were the life-threatening injuries. The massive blood loss was causing the low blood pressure and other staff had just brought in units of blood to give to their patient. Looking at the armed men in the room and believing that this individual was someone not to disappoint, he barked an order to one of the nurses to get two sixteen gauge IV catheters. Once obtained, he tore the device apart and attempted to force the catheter into the destroyed left carotid artery. Hopefully, he thought, this unorthodox repair might be sufficient to save this man. Having been able to accomplish this on the left, the repeated the procedure on the right, but the destruction was more extensive and he yelled for a scalpel. He needed to expose the artery move to attempt his make-shift repair.

As he began doing this, the surgeon rushed in and on surveying the scene, yelled for them to transport him to the OR immediately. They hurriedly rushed Gomez to the operating room while a therapist continued to push aggressively on his chest. The guards were in close pursuit. The surgeon looked back and seeing them starting to walk through the door, he said, "You cannot come in here!" One of the guards ripped off a burst of rounds from his weapon and said, "Stop me!" as he pushed the gurney further inward. Once in the operating room, the surgeon barked orders to all as he started to attempt to save his patient's life.

The surgery attempt lasted for thirty-eight minutes and during this time, multiple numbers of staff filtered in and out of the suite to be able to continue with the chest compressions. This movement made it difficult for him to do his work, but he had no choice. Knowing that this effort was probably futile, the surgeon wisely elected to continue for as long as what might be considered possible before ending their heroic efforts. Correcting these injuries was almost impossible, especially when considering the limited supplies on hand. He looked at the closest guard and said, "I am sorry, but he is gone. There is nothing more we can do." The guard stood there, looking the old surgeon in his eyes and said, "Keep going! There is something more that you can do to save him!" yelled the young man. "No. We have done all that we can. He has been without a heart rate for the last eighteen minutes. I am sorry. We can do no more. God be with him, I am sorry," said the surgeon. Rage and disbelief filled the young man as he looked around the room. "You are all incompetent!" he yelled as he took a step back. "You quack! You old fool!" he roared. With this, he then pointed his weapon at the surgeon's head and pulled the trigger. The old surgeon fell to the floor. His partner came toward his friend and both then began to spray the room with gunfire as the hospital workers scurried away for their lives. Most were dropped where they stood, a couple were able to escape out of the door but were mowed down as they ran down the hall. "Bastards! They are all bastards! Whoever did this will pay!" yelled the young man as he emptied his remaining ammunition into the ceiling. After close to an hour after arriving at the hospital, Gomez's guards began coming out of the hospital, all six of them. On seeing this, it was obvious to the team that their mission was a success. Smiles and pats on the back started.

19

PLAN OF ACTION

Cam had worked past the shock of his abode's violation. He had returned to work and started to develop a routine work habit, while he established a plan to respond to what had transpired. The turn of events with the encroachments and risks within his personal life enraged him even more. He was certain that his activities at work were being monitored and he would present to his viewing audience a positive review of his efforts toward finding a more effective treatment or possibly a cure for Uveitis. The need to resolve this issue with Buck and Murphy remained on his mind and would until resolved. "These assholes really don't know who they are dealing with," thought Cam. The resources these people had and their abilities were astounding and scary. "This is like the spy novels and movies," he thought. The exception to this was it was real and his family and friends were at risk. He and Greg continued to work together on this project and had made some limited progress, something that had been reported upstairs. He made it a point to not let Greg know what had happened; he didn't want him more involved. Mark now checked on his work more closely than in the past;

probably something that was mandated from above, but he took it in stride. "It's probably part of the way to legitimately keep track of me," he thought while looking at the test subjects. Another group was now working on the FCD project and due to the new Uveitis project; other cats were needed for his project. He had worked it out with Mark that with the limited cage space and the Dearfoot was not a subject with FCD, that he could take Dearfoot home as a pet. A little unusual, but better than having the cat euthanized like is what occurred with the others that left their lab. Cam had been back at his work for about two weeks and he asked to take off a couple of days to have a long weekend. Being approved, the next day he would start this time off.

Cam did not feel safe working on developing a plan of action on how to address the adulteration of Oboedīre at his apartment, so he began to work at the local university. He had been racking his brain on how to effectively bring the government's covert operation to a close, but needed help without placing himself or those around him at risk. On this day, Doc was meeting him at the university to talk about it. Cam purposely chose an interior room within the library to minimize the possibility of being videoed and/or listened in on by snooping eyes and ears. The small conference rooms that the library offered were perfect for this. He had been there for a few minutes when Doc walked through the door. "Morning, Doc!" said Cam as he saw his friend come into the room. "Morning, Cam. It's great to see you." Doc responded. After a few minutes of catching up, the men began their discussion. "Doc, you need to know that someone broke into my apartment and took a data card that I had hidden that had the video file on it. Whomever it was also was able to break through my cable connection and let me know that he was successful and to essentially let me know I'm being watched." "Cam, maybe this has grown to a point where it's too dangerous to pursue it. With the odds as they are, you know that we have a lot stacked against us. We will only have one chance at this, and it better be good," said the elderly Vet from across the table. Cam sat so that he could watch through the window those that may pass by their room. "I know Doc," said Cam, "but I've been racking my brain trying to come up with a sound plan of action. We could march up to the CNN headquarters and present our information to them and see where it goes. They have a large audience" "Not smart," said Doc. "Yes, they have a large audience, but it will show for a day at best, maybe two, but about the first time an airliner crashes, a hurricane develops, or some other more outstanding story, ours will hit the shelf and then we are exposed. No, we need another idea." "You're probably right," said Cam disgustedly. "I've considered contacting an animal rights group, but unfortunately many of them are looked at as being nut cases," he said with frustration. "Even if we would go that route, we would need someone that had a large enough of a name or presence that people would listen," said Doc. "I've also considered looking at approaching someone in Congress to bring into this, after all, they control the purse strings for all agencies," said Cam. "Yah, but who do you approach and how safe is that?" said Doc. "How do you know you can trust them?" "What would you think about a combined strike?" asked Cam. "What do you mean?" asked Doc. "Well, if we could get into a Congressman's office, we would bring the animal right people with some big names, a group of well-respected veterinarians and the media with us." "I don't know," said Doc. "The more people we bring into this, the more control we lose in this situation. I've gotta think about that one." "Well," said Cam, "one thing that I have been thinking about that I believe is crucial, is that we need to consider another possibility. No matter what we do, we are a risk to them and they know it. Right now things maybe have cooled down a bit with them thinking that they have all of our evidence, which is good. But I think we need to consider a protective strategy. I think that we need to be actively working on an antidote to Oboedīre. These guys play for keeps and if they even get a hint that we might be successful, I want us to have a means to protect ourselves," said Cam. "I've considered this as well," said Doc. "But it needs to be a fast acting agent of some sort, which is the problem." "Right," said Cam as he looked intently at his mentor. "Giving something IV or intracardiac are a couple of the fastest ways to do this as you know, but what I propose is that we look at developing an aerosolized agent that the cat would breathe in. This would lead to almost as fast of a response and is something we could all easily carry with us." "Hummm," started Doc as he leaned back a bit. "You're right by God. It could be something as simple as something like is used to keep hand sanitizer or glasses cleaner in and could be carried in a pocket or kept in the car. Great idea Cam!" said the vet as be smiled at the idea. "That's where you come in, Doc. I cannot even remotely think about doing any of this research at the lab. Your clinic is probably the best location to start this work," said Cam as he started to pace in the room. "We need to be very mindful of the need for ultimate secrecy. The fewer people that know about this the better, at least for their own safety.

I have started some research on my own. The computer that I am working on was purposely set up so that it did not have internet access to avoid being tracked. I keep it with me wherever I go. I've been visiting the local library and logging in under a generic access to do this research as well. So far, I have a couple of ideas which I hope are promising," said Cam as he looked at the window at a passing student. "Excellent," said Doc. "Do you have anything to show me?" "Not yet," said Cam. "I've just begun working on this angle so it may take a bit. Anything that I come up with, I will bring home with me. We'll meet at different locations to help make things more secure. After the two men had agreed on their next steps, they departed, Doc leaving about ten minutes ahead of Cam who left out of a difference exit in going to his car.

Susi had been at a luncheon with a few of her close friends from school; Susie, Jan, and Pam. They had known each other since elementary school. Susie was an elementary school teacher who was preparing to retire, Jan was a school librarian at a private school, and Pam had retired recently from a local factory. The girls tried to get together about once a month but that was not always possible. But today they had gathered at one of the local restaurants to catch up and just chit-chat. On this occasion,

Susi had another agenda for their meeting. They had shared information about their kids and grandkids and about work and for one, her impending retirement. They enjoyed their meal and after ordering their desert, Susi said to the group, "Girls, I think that I need your help with something. I can't go into any specifics at all, but I have become aware of something that needs to be brought to a halt. Again, I can't go into specifics, but need your help." "Sounds serious," said Jan. "Can you give us a vague idea of what it is about?" asked Susie. "Are you and Tom OK?" asked Pam. Looking at Pam, Susi said, "Oh yes. Tom and I are fine. This has nothing to do about us personally. Thanks for asking. I can't give any specifics about it, but we have come across something that is going on that needs exposed, something that most would find horrific, but are looking for a way to stop this that can be done discretely and safely. There are some pretty big-time players involved with this situation with some very significant connections that needs to be considered. Do you girls have any major contacts in the media or government that we've not ever talked about?" The group sat there and pondered for a little while. "Well," said Jan, "my brother's brother-in-law is a lawyer in Washington; don't know what he does there, but maybe he could help. Is that something that you think could help you?" "I don't know; probably not, but if you could find some more out about what he does and his contact information I'd appreciate it. Don't approach him though. Send his information to me in a letter; do not send an email, text, or phone call with this information. We believe that our computers and phones might be monitored. Any sharing of additional information could be done by arranging another lunch or dinner. There is a strong possibility that our activity is being monitored," said Susi. The other girls were taken aback by the serious tone and mysterious topic and did not have any options to share but would think about it and let Susi know if they could think of someone that might be of help. "Girls, I can't begin to tell you have important it is to keep this to yourselves. Even if you come up with someone; or Jan, if you speak with Mark or his brother-in-law, do not mention this to them. The people involved with this have far-reaching resources and we can't afford for any of this to be leaked to them," Susi said very seriously as she glanced at each of her friends. "Susi, your kind of scaring me. Are you in trouble?" asked Pam. "No, I'm not. But someone very close to Tom and I might be and we cannot afford to risk putting him at risk. Also, the other thing that I can say is that absolutely nothing illegal is involved in this by anyone on our side of the equation." All agreed to keep things quiet and that if anyone would come up with any ideas, they would get together again. The girls paid for their meals and left together; Susi's friends left worried about her.

Doc had agreed to take Dearfoot from Cam on the night Cam was returning to Louisville. Both had agreed that Dearfoot would be a great test subject for developing an antidote and they had made some Oboedīre for this purpose. Cam had already begun to consider the need and had shared with Doc the research he had performed to date. It was not much since he had just started. He had not proceeded far enough to even begin to consider any sort of testing as of yet, but was confident that would come soon. With Doc's experience with the drug, his willingness to help, and the need for Cam to work on this remotely, Doc's clinic was his best bet. They hoped this was something that they could develop quickly, because having such an agent would provide protection for them and also would add leverage in their battle against the adulterated use of the drug. Cam headed back to Louisville without incident and wanted to get in reasonably early. He could not afford to arouse any additional suspicion by not showing up to work and by being late either. Things needed to appear as normal as possible. His one new concern was for Doc. He was certain that his activities were being tracked and that they knew he had been in contact with Doc. He hoped that since he had worked with him over the years that he would not be considered as someone involved with this situation.

To all who brought animals for Doc to care for, Dearfoot was introduced as the new owner of the clinic. After all, anyone who knows or has a cat knows that we are allowed by them to share their space; at least from the cat's perspective. He has always been a good-mannered cat and gets along well with other animals. He had run of the clinic with the exception of the exam rooms when Doc was seeing a patient. Ali and Doc had a busy day at the clinic. Seven dogs, four cats, and an iguana and a parrot were seen. "Not bad for someone that was supposed to be slowing down," thought Doc as he was finishing up his paperwork. "Are you going to stick around much longer?" Ali asked her grandfather. "Yes, I think I'll stick around for a little while longer," said the Vet as he was updating a record on his computer. "What's with the safe?" she asked. While Ali was on vacation the previous week, Doc had built a safe into one of the clinic walls. It was about four foot tall and three feet wide. "With some of the work Cam and I are doing, I thought it best to have a more secure place to store our materials and research," he said. "Neither of us has any trust in those involved with this situation and I am taking nothing for granted with these guys." "You know, you're a pretty smart guy Grandpa," said Ali as she looked at the safe's location. "Using an electrical panel box cover to hide the safe was a brilliant idea," said the younger Hughes. Being a bit of a handyman, Doc had drawn up the plans for this and had completed the work himself. "Thanks Ali. Now run along, I've got some work to do," he said as he helped gently guide her toward the door. He locked the door and waved goodbye to her as she left. She was heading to his house to have dinner with Susi. As an extra precaution, he armed the alarm system, and although Cam might object, he had given Dearfoot a dose of Oboedīre as an added source of protection. He felt that considering the ruthlessness and disregard for the animals, these people would stop at nothing to serve their purpose, including silencing an old veterinarian.

Doc sat down and started going over some of the research that he had pulled from the internet while at the library. He was becoming a familiar face at the local college library. He and Cam agreed early on that using any of their personal or business computers for research would be foolish; too easily monitored. He centered his research on overdose treatment for patients receiving the component drugs in Oboedīre. It made perfect sense to start in this area since the goal in an overdose is to counteract or reverse the action of a particular medication or substance. He found that there is not a direct neutralizing agent for these medications, that primary treatment for these overdoses is supportive in nature. However, this was a starting point. Cam had also provided some of his research which not only was similar to the direction Doc had taken, but added research into general, generic overdose treatment. He also looked at potential herbal remedies toward this endeavor. Too many people in the medical world have forgotten that many of today's medicines began with the folk remedies of old so this angle could produce some possibilities. Cam seemed to have preponderance toward a more natural source of treatment or answer for aliments and clinic problems. After about being there an hour and a half after closing hours, the sun had gone down and it was dark outside. All of the sudden, Dearfoot rose up on all fours with his ears held high. He tensed as he listened intently to the surroundings. Doc noticed this quick change of demeanor and asked him, "What's wrong, boy?" Doc rose from his chair and started to look around, taking a look outside the clinic door. Dearfoot followed him; nothing to be seen. He walked around to the waiting room windows which had their blinds closed and raised the corner of one slat on the far side of the window, nothing there as well. Dearfoot jumped up next to him and watched. Dearfoot turned quickly toward the back of the clinic, raising his ears once again. Doc headed toward the back clinic door and heard a slight bump against the back door. He picked up the cordless phone and in the room next to him dialed 911. "911 dispatch. What is the nature of your emergency?" she asked. "Hello, this is Doctor Hughes at the Hughes Veterinary Clinic, 2005 S. Dixon Road. I believe that I have a prowler at the back door of my clinic. Could you please send an officer to check it out?" he said quickly and softly. "Are all of your doors locked and is anyone there with you?" she asked. "Yes, they are locked but I am alone other than the animals here," he said. "Stay where you are, I have an officer en route to your location. Do not open the door for anyone until the uniformed officer arrives. Do you understand?" she asked. "Yes, I understand," he said. "I will stay on the line with you until help arrives," she responded. In the distance after a couple of minutes, Doc began to hear the siren of the approaching police car. It took the officer about four minutes to arrive, his red and blue lights flashing against the office walls. After checking around the office, the officer came to the front door and knocked. "Doctor Hughes, I'm Officer Kelley with the Kokomo Police Department. It's OK for you to open the door." Doc turned off the alarm and came to the door and unlocked it and said, "Hello officer, thank you for coming. Did you find anything?" "Well I did not find anyone, but I did see some footprints at and around your back door," said the officer as he placed his flashlight back in the loop on his belt. As they were speaking, another police car arrived with his lights flashing. "You might have had a visitor, but he's nowhere to be seen," he continued. "Thank you for coming out and checking. Being here by myself, I felt too isolated and decided to have someone check," said Doc as he shook the young officer's hand. "I think I'll reset the alarm and call it a day and head home." The officers waited until Doc had closed up the clinic and was on his way home before they departed.

Doc decided to take Dearfoot home with him. He had grown fond of him and had become his shadow over time. Doc had locked up most of the information in the safe, but took a few things home to read later. He arrived home to find Ali still there. His dinner was waiting for him in the oven and Susi brought it from the oven and placed it in front of him at the dining room table. While eating, he shared the scare at the clinic with them both. "Grandpa, you're kidding? Right?" said Ali surprised. "No. Probably just a drunk," said Doc as he continued eating. "I think these late hours need to stop or you at least need to have someone else with you if you are going to be in the office late," said Susi fussily. "With everything that is going on with this drug thing, God knows who really was there tonight." "Well probably," said Doc. "You're right honey. I think that I'll start leaving before dusk as an extra safety measure. But you know; I did have someone with me. Right Dearfoot?" With that the cat jumped up on the table to Susi's dismay. With Doc's instruction, the cat jumped down to the floor. He remained there, following Doc's orders. "Well," said Susi. "I guess there is another great use for this drug! Keeping cats off of the dining room table." They all laughed.

Ali had gone home a little earlier and Doc and Susi after cleaning things up from dinner, they were preparing for bed. "Tom, you stayed late to work on this project for Cam, didn't you?" asked Susi. "Yes, that was part of the reason. I also had a couple of office things to take care of, but mostly it was the project. This is important; we need to find an answer right away," he said as he changed his clothes. "I know it is," said Susi, "but just please don't take any chances." Doc walked over to her and put his arm around her and gave her a kiss. "Don't worry; I won't," he said, giving her a hug. "I will start coming home earlier. Maybe I'll bring this work home and do the majority of the research here. I do have the gun safe that I can keep this information in. Sound good to you?" "Definitely!" said Susi as she gave him a kiss and a little pinch on the butt. "OK, then settled," he said. After their nightly getting ready for bedtime routine, they both retired to bed.

Dearfoot had become an adornment on the bed for the last week or so. It appeared that the cat had gained his place within their home. They had been asleep for about three hours when Doc felt the cat move quickly at his feet. All of the sudden, someone placed a hand over his mouth and at the same time placed something hard against his head. Susi awoke startled and screamed as she saw a dark figure next to Doc. "Shut up lady!" said the man. "Now y'all lay here right still and don't move," the man instructed Doc. "Lady, if un y'all don't want you man hurt, you'll do just as I say," said the man in the dark room. There was little moon that night, so the bedroom was quite dark. Even so, it appeared that the man's face was darkened by something. "Now Doctor, our little visit was interrupted earlier tonight by my stupidity. Ain't done that before, but no mind. We can git things done just fine if y'all listen up," the man said. "Now I'm gonna take my hand away from your mouth and my gun from your head; now don't do anything stupid now, y'all hear? Otherwise you might not be impressed with the outcome." Doc shook his head yes, still reeling from this spontaneous invasion. "Now, I need all of the information you've been working on; y'all know all of that stuff about the cats. I need you to git it purty quick for me, if y'all don't mind," said the intruder. "I'll, I'll get it for you," Doc said as he slowly pulled back the covers and started to stand up. "Now that's what I like; cooperation. Ain't it nice?" he said as he looked at Susi. She looked back at him, shaking from the shock. "Come on, honey; you gotta go with us," the intruder said as he motioned for her to get up with a flick of the hand holding the gun. Susi obeyed and walked over to her husband. They both started slowly out of the door, Doc placing Susi in front of him. They walked slowly down the stairs and on getting to the bottom, Dearfoot trotted in front of the group. Seeing him, Doc decided to take a chance. "Dearfoot, attack his face!" he yelled. With that, the cat immediately turned and pounced on the intruder with all claws distended, toward the face of the intruder. This sudden attack caught him off guard and he began to struggle with Dearfoot. "Yowww!" yelled the intruder as the cat's sharp claws began to rip at his face. He stumbled against the wall, dropping his gun with the unexpected attack and contact with the wall. The gun fell behind him as he continued to struggle. Doc pushed Susi toward the kitchen. "Call the police!" he barked. She ran toward the kitchen while the fight continued. The fury of the cat along with its quickness was overpowering to the intruder who continued to stumble around the foyer. He managed to fling off of him, but this was short-lived as Dearfoot continued his attack. As the intruder neared the door with Dearfoot tearing at his head, Doc saw his chance and he opened the door. When the intruder approached the door, Doc front kicked him in his exposed lower chest and the man and cat flew backwards from the doorway onto the front porch. This melee ended when the cat jumped to safety as the intruder tumbled down the front steps. Doc rushed over and grabbed the gun, returning to the doorway only to see the man had gotten to his feet and began to run from the house. He followed him outside onto the front porch; as the intruder ran, he blended into the night. Doc then heard the sirens in the distance, now realizing that help was on the way. He stayed there for a moment and then ran back into the house, with Dearfoot right on his heels, locking the front door. Susi peeked around the corner upon hearing the door close and saw Doc

standing in the foyer with the gun in his hand. Without
thinking she hung up the phone and came over to check on
him. Doc looked at her and said, "He's gone. Thank God."
Putting his arm around her, he said to Susi, "Everything
will be fine now. The police will be here in a minute. Now
when the police get here, we have to tell them this was an
attempted robbery. We woke up and found him in our
bedroom, startled him, he ran down the stairs and he
stepped on the cat's tail who then attacked him. We can't
say anything about the information he was after; we have to
keep it secret," he said strongly and toughly. "Ah, OK, I
understand," she said still shocked from the ordeal. "Just let
me do the talking, Hon," he said. Doc looked down at
Dearfoot who stood close by at his feet. "Thank you boy;
you really saved our lives!" as he looked at the cat, he said,
"Hey Susi, look. Along with the blood on his paw, there is
black." He bent down and on inspecting the cat's paw; he
rubbed off a blackened substance. "Face paint," he said
looking up at his wife. Within a couple of minutes the
police car pulled up in front and the officer jumped out and
looked around with his gun drawn. Doc opened the door
slowly and announced that everything was alright; the
intruder was gone. Doc handed the officer the gun and
began sharing what had happened as other police cars

began to arrive. Other cars began to arrive as well, one of them being the officer from earlier in the night. "Doctor Hughes, is that you?" asked the young officer. "Yes, it is," responded Doc. "Hey guys," the officer said, "I responded to a prowler call earlier tonight at his clinic. Doctor, it seems to me that these two incidents are probably connected." Doc looked at his wife and then back to the officer. "I suppose that maybe they are. I hadn't considered that," he said. "We need to get a detailed report of what just happened here. We'll contact the detectives who will look into this more. The gun this person had is a starting point. We need to cordon off the area and look for additional clues while we speak with you and your wife some more," said the officer. "One more thing," said Doc. "Our cat has some blood on his paws. You might be able to get a DNA sample from him." "Good. Where is the cat now?" responded the officer. "Dearfoot, come here," said Doc nonchalantly. Dearfoot trotted up to the group and looked up at them. "Being a vet, I supposed you've trained this guy," said the officer. "You could say that," said Doc with a small smile forming. The officers checked around the area and were unable to find anything suspicious. They obtained information from Doc and Susi on the break-in and would forward it on to the detectives and one of them would be contacting them in the next hour. Both were asked to not disturb anything while the crime scene crew gathering evidence.

20

TRIAL AND ERROR

Cam was more irate than ever when he heard about what had happened to Doc and Susi. Doc had called him on the pay as you go cell phone to let him know the details. "Doc," Cam said, "I really appreciate all that you have done with this and all of the help and support you guys have given me concerning this. But I can't allow you to put yourselves in further danger. I have a back-up plan and I will head that direction. You need to send me all, and I mean all of your material to the post office box I have. One of the guys I work with got it under his father's name for a little more protection," "Cam, I agree. Really didn't figure they would get this desperate, but it's out of control and I would never forgive myself if something happened to Susi," said Doc. "I've also contacted the alarm company that I work with at the office and they are coming over later today to install a system at the house." With this, Cam gave him the address and Doc said he would put it all in the mail in the morning. For this possibility, Greg had obtained a post office box at one of the local shipping stores. This helped give a little distance to Cam and the project. "Oh, and by the way Doc," said Cam, "I am assuming that you still have a good supply of our drug. "Yes, I still have a pretty decent amount," Doc responded. "Ok," said Cam, "first, you keep Dearfoot and for a while, keep giving him regular doses. It's obvious that he is a great guard for the two of you. Also, keep a small amount in your safe but keep the majority of it in plain sight, just make the bottle with a medication that you rarely use and just put it on your shelf. If someone comes looking for it, they will expect it to be hidden or locked away. If they do come and they find it in the safe, they'll think they found it all." "Good idea. Will do," said Doc. Each said their goodbyes and that they would hook up later when things died down. Cam returned to work after lunch and brought Greg up to speed about expecting a package in the next few days.

With the brazen encounter a Doc's home, Cam knew it was time to change the game up a bit. In the past, as a precautionary measure, he had sent a flash drive with some of the research and the video clip to his old friend, Andrew. Andrew had decided to open a practice in Ohio, close to his alma mater, Smith's State. He had been in practice now for a few years since he did not have an interest in being board certified as Cam had. He decided it was time to switch gears so he asked Greg to call his old friend Andrew and have him call him on his pay as you go phone. "Cam, how you doing buddy?" said Andrew. "Andrew! It's good to hear from you. How are you doing, my friend?" asked Cam. "I'm doing very well here," said Andrew. "Hey, what's with your friend calling me to ask me call you. What's up?" "We'll talk about that in a minute, what have you been up to?" asked Cam. After some additional personal reflections, Cam got down to business. "Andrew, you know that I sent you an envelope a while back that I asked you not to open," said Cam. "Yes, I remember it. I have it locked away. I've wondered what this is about," Andrew responded. "Well, I think it's time that we sit down and have a chat and for me to ask you a favor. Could we get together sometime real soon?" asked Cam. "Sure," responded Andrew quickly. "How about this coming Saturday?" he asked. "That would be great. We need to meet somewhere where we can talk privately, but that is frequented by a number of people as well. I have had a meeting like this at the university library at home. Do you think we might be able to do that at Smith's State?" asked Cam. "Sure, just tell me what time and I'll be there. Look forward to it!" said Andrew excitedly. "One other thing, Andrew, please do not share this meeting with anyone. I'll tell you more at that time. By the way, expect something else in the mail," said Cam. "OK, that's fine," said Andrew with a kind of quizzical response. "Also, Andrew, I need you to get a pay as you go phone so our conversations cannot be monitored," said Cam. "Wow, this sounds serious. You OK?" asked Andrew. "Yah, for now. Call me on your new phone when you get it so I have the number," said Cam. The two finished out the arrangements and Cam started to compile what he would need to take with him. To send this, and to do this without prying eyes knowing, Cam found a mailbox that was located under a bridge where it was isolated and he planned to send Andrew the additional material using it. If he sent it today, Andrew would probably have it by Saturday. Andrew called him the following day with his new phone number, still questioning what this was all about and Cam asked for his indulgence, that it was too complicated to share over the phone.

Saturday came and Cam had gotten up early to pick up his rental car. He never went back to the same company when renting as another way to help reduce the prying governmental eyes. He paid in cash as usual and made certain he had plenty of cash for the trip. It would take him about three to three and a half hours to drive to Columbus. Cam was purposely in the library about twenty minutes ahead of their scheduled meeting to scope out where they might be able to sit down and talk. He eventually found a room that was secluded enough as to provide the privacy he desired. Although not appreciated in a library, he made a call to Andrew in the room and let him know where he was at. Cam was trying to do everything he could for the two of them to not been seen together in public. Eventually Andrew showed up and the two old friends took a little time to catch up. After this, Cam started to share with Andrew the long and convoluted story about Oboedīre and the pleasures and challenges this discovery has caused. A little over an hour later, Cam had filled his friend in on the past highlights and then started on the future. "Andrew, now that you have an idea of what has occurred, the main reason I have sought you out is that I need your help in working on an antidote for Oboedīre. I know that I'm being watched, but I still can do research remotely at the college and library, but I have to be very careful in doing this. Would you be willing to help me?" Cam asked his old friend. "Let me get this straight," Andrew said. "The government is watching you, they have threatened you and you friends, and God knows how they are using the drug now, but it's a pretty simple answer to figure it's not good. Right?" Andrew asked. "Yep, that pretty much sums it up," said Cam. "Man, this is some kind of a story. This is amazing but I don't doubt for a minute the government has adulterated this if it does what you say." "Andrew, before you answer, take this a sprinkle about one gram of this on a cat's food. After a couple of minutes it should take effect. Then the cat will obey whatever you request, implicitly. Would it be possible for you to do this now?" asked Cam. "Ok, I'll do it," said Andrew. "Once you've done this, give me a call. I'll stick around here and I'll grab something to eat on campus. Give me a call and let me know what you think," said Cam. Andrew took the small vial from Cam and headed back to his clinic to try this mixture out. He said it shouldn't take him very long.

After about an hour and a half, Cam received a call from Andrew's new phone number. "Cam, this is Andrew," he said excitedly. "Oh, my Gosh!" Andrew said. "This stuff is amazing! I had the cat dancing! Actually dancing with me!" said Andrew. "Where are you? I'm back on campus." "I'll meet you in the library again, just in a different room. Look for me when you get there," said Cam. Cam hurried over to the library after he had grabbed a sandwich at the cantina. "Hopefully with Andrew this excited, he will be willing to help," Cam thought. Cam found an empty room and waited there for his friend. Once Andrew arrived, they talked about his experience and ultimately after a little discussion, Andrew agreed to help with Cam come up with an antidote. The two spent the next hour or so going over their thoughts and some of Cam's research to date. Andrew would get a post office box as Cam had suggested so that any sharing of electronic data or research would be done through the mail. They would keep touch with each other on their pay to as you go phones. Both men talked a little more as they left the small conference room and each looked forward to working together. They left at different times and from different doors. Cam was starting to get used to this clandestine life.

Susi came home one day from her lunch with her friends that day and called for Doc as she entered the door. "I'm in here," Doc shouted. "Tom, you remember that I told you a while back about me asking my friends to think of someone that we might ask for help on Cam's situation?" she asked excitedly. "Yes," said Doc. "Well, Pam just mentioned that her cousin was hired about a year ago as a policy advisor for Senator Earl Fryer. I believe that I've heard of this guy before," Susi said. "I'm going to do an internet search on him." "That's a good idea. Just remember, those bastards are probably monitoring our computer activity. Look up some general information about active bills, see what our Congressmen are doing and backing on the hill. Make it look like you are broadly searching Congress, not just this guy," said Doc as he continued to read his paper. After a number of key strokes and various link openings, Susi said, "Tom! You need to look at this. Senator Fryer is an animal rights activist! Could he be somebody that might be interested in our situation?" "Maybe," said Doc, putting his paper down to come over and look at the computer screen. He read the information and asked Susi to have Pam meet them at a local coffee shop to talk more about this development. "Don't stay on his page long. Start looking around like I mentioned," said Doc. As she started to do this, Susi said, "Hopefully this Congressman proves out to be someone we can work with. If so, maybe his clout can gain us access to the media." "Going to the media alone is too risky, but if we could find an advocate within the government to run with this, to attract more exposure and credibility, maybe we could get more traction; besides, maybe this will pull more of the media into the picture as well," said Doc.

Cam was confident that they were close to arriving at an antidote. About three and a half weeks later, and after many failed drug combinations, Andrew contacted him by phone. "Hey Cam, I wanted to touch bases with you. I think I might be on to something, but want your input." "Sure, how can I help?" asked Cam. "Your research and trials so far have helped. I think I may have something and want to get together with you to share. When can you come over?" asked Andrew. "Let's see. Today's Wednesday. I could meet you sometime Saturday morning. Would the library at the university work?" asked Cam. "No, not this time," said Andrew. "How about you us meeting at the Vet school at Smith's? I could show you what I have in one of the labs there. It's an interior room, so the prying eyes won't be a problem there either." "Us? Who's us?" asked Cam. "Well it's me and a short friend of mine, Felix the cat!" he responded with a little chuckle at the end. "Oh, I see. Sound good then. I'll see you and Felix on Saturday," said Cam. Andrew gave him he address, building number and room number at the Vet school. Cam was excited at the possibility that Andrew might have something; at least he was hoping he had made significant progress.

The remainder of the week was uneventful for Cam. His groups work on Uveitis had stalled and no significant progress was made. He personally had trouble maintaining a focus on the project; his heart was just not in it. Cam left CatGenus on Friday afternoon and went to his apartment. He called Ali since it had been a while since they had talked, to catch up and say hi. She was pleased that he had called and filled him in on what was going on at home. Ali had stopped by to see Cam's parents a couple of days ago and they were fine. "Man, I really need to call them. It's been way too long since I've touched bases with this," Cam thought to himself. They talked about when he might be able to come home to see everyone, but it probably wouldn't be able to be until next weekend at the earliest. Ali has arranged to meet a couple of her friends for dinner and she had just pulled up to the restaurant, so the two said their goodbyes and hung up. "Boy, I really miss that girl," he said to himself. He quickly packed a couple of things and headed out the door to get some dinner. He was going to head out early in the morning to meet with Andrew and wanted to get a good night's sleep, so an early dinner and early bedtime was on his agenda.

After his drive from Louisville, Cam pulled up in the parking lot closest to the building Andrew had indicated, parked his car and started walking to it. He was confident he had not been followed by anyone. He had trained himself to watch more closely for patterns and similarities since this has transpired. He called Andrew to let him know he was there and Andrew was already in the building. It would be more enjoyable to spend time with his friend openly, but he was being extra cautious, maybe a little paranoid that his activity was being tracked by drones or a satellite. The walk over from the parking lot was uneventful and it reminded Cam of some of his former college days. The ivy-covered buildings, the scurry of young people across the campus made him long for simpler times, even though it was not that long ago. Cameron liked the old building architecture and admired it as he walked toward the building where Andrew was. He had always been fascinated by the ornate carving and the fact that someone was able to make such beautiful pieces with hand tools in experienced hands. One day he hoped to be able to watch someone replicate this work. He came back to reality as he walked up the steps to the building where he was to meet Andrew, then opened the door and walked in.

On finding the lab, Cam walked in to see his friend playing with a cat; they were the only ones present. Andrew spotted him and waved. He looked at the cat and said, "Felix, go jump in his arms," pointing toward Cam. The cat turned to look at Cam and trotted over there, hopping from one bench to the next until reaching him. Once there, the cat gently leapt into Cam's arms. "Well I see the drug still works well," Cam said as he started to pet the cat. After verifying that the drug was effective with a few other tests, Andrew said, "Cam, I think I have something, but you'll see my problem shortly." He produced a simple misting bottle and then asked Felix to ring the bell that was attached to a string until being told to stop. The cat complied and began ringing the bell by hitting it with his paw. "Ring it faster," Andrew told the cat. The cat responded by ringing it faster. After a few moments of this, Andrew pointed the misting bottle at the cat and misted twice at the cat. The cat stopped hitting the bell and began to sniff around the area. In about thirty to forty seconds later, the cat walked over to Andrew and sat in front of him. "Felix, go over and ring the bell again." The cat responded and began ringing the bell. "Ring it faster," Andrew told the cat again; the cat responded. He misted the cat again and he stopped following commands again. "See my problem," asked Andrew. "I have developed a formula, but it is short-acting." Cam was excited. "Andrew, you're close; you're real close! Great job!" said Cam to his friend. Cam patted him on the shoulder and then asked Andrew about his discovery. "I combined glycopyrrolate and physostigmine in varying amounts until I observed this situation. As you probably know, these are two substances used to help address an overdose with a couple of the drugs in Oboedīre. My problem is that I can't neutralize the drug without there been an almost constant delivery of this mixture," he said with frustration. "Hummm," said Cam.

"Let me think about this for a minute." There was a pause for about a minute and then he said, "Andrew, do you have computer access here?" "Sure do! It's one of the perks from being a grad from here. I'm also an adjunct faculty member with the Vet school, so that gives me even more access." With that, Andrew logged into a computer and Cam seated himself in front of it. He began searching. His fingers moved quickly over the keyboard as he searched and read the various sites. After about forty-five minutes, Cam stopped pecking and was scrolling down a particular document. "Find something, old buddy?" asked Andrew. "Don't know for sure. Time and trials will tell. What I would suggest is that we focus in on a mood stabilizing agent such as those given for Alzheimer's or dementia. These meds are given to affect impulsive behavior and disinhibition. There are a number of meds that fall in this category, but I wonder if one or some of these will help lengthen the neutralization time," said Cam. "Andrew, you really have done well with this. I can't begin to tell you how much this means to me. I'll keep doing the research; you keep compounding and trialing your mixtures. You are very close my friend!" Both talked more at length regarding Cam's suggestion and the issues that they faced with this. Not all of the medications within this classification were used in Veterinary medicine and would not be available to them. "Don't worry," said Cam. "We will figure something out if we need to." They both played with Felix for a few more minutes, enjoying the entertainment that he provided. Cam thought for a second, realizing that it had been quite some time since he really had had a good laugh. He really needed this and appreciated their time together. Once finished, to help maintain their anonymity, the two left the building separately. Cam jumped back in his rented car and started back to Louisville after stopping for a bite to eat.

21

SOLUTION

"Cam," Doc said, "I think we may have an ear in Washington." "What do you mean," asked Cam slightly confused as they shared a cup of coffee at the Cam's favorite hometown restaurant, Louie's. Doc went further into what had transpired about the cousin of one of Susi's friends and his connection to a Senator. From what research we've done, this Senator is a guy that when he takes on a topic, he's like a pit bull and won't let go. Oh yah, to top it off, he's solidly involved in animal rights. He has a long documented history." "He's involved with animal rights?" asked Cam enthusiastically, not believing what he just heard. "Yep," said Doc. "We have verified it through this gal's cousin. Her cousin's name is Howard Talbert and is this guy's Policy Advisor. We did not give him specifics, but he said that the Senator will almost clear his calendar if there is a significant event occurring that involves animal cruelty. He has a strong track record for backing any legislation on all levels and even has a hotline for his constituents to call with their concerns." Cam was taken aback by this new development and he was thinking through the possibilities. "If we could get this guy's attention, then maybe there might be some press coverage to bring it further into the open. I'm concerned about governmental involvement without a public mouthpiece being involved. Both combined will help in making this reporting safer for us all. God knows there has been some pretty daunting and dangerous history to this situation. Whatever we do, we must ensure everyone's safety. Doc, two other things are out here to mention as well. One, I've got a little over a week left in my internship at CatGenus for my potential to become eligible for board certification although that is a small part in this; it's worth mentioning. The other thing is that I have to share is that someone else I know has been doing some research and trials on a reversal agent and he is very close to having an effective one. Whatever we do, I believe that we need to time our sharing of this information with anyone until after the reversal agent has been developed and proven effective. Having this will send a loud message to anyone that might again consider sending someone one of their feline friends to take care of us. I think this is a critical point. He has something now but it is too short-acting to be completely effective," said Cam. "I agree," said Doc. "We need that solid before speaking out. Each of us should carry it for some time afterwards. His development; did he use the aerosolized route as you suggested?" asked Doc. "Yes, and it allows for a fast response." "Great!" said Doc. "Maybe one day I'll get to meet this other Pasteur like you." "Sure, I'll be glad to arrange that!" said Cam blushing from the compliment.

The two gentlemen finished their meals and talked about other issues. "It's been some time since I've seen Ali," said Cam. "How is she? Is she seeing anyone?" "She's fine, Cam. And no, she isn't seeing anyone. As a matter of a fact, she asked about you the other day. The two of you kids really need to get together. When you're around; well let's just say she comes alive." "I noticed she's very happy when I come home. I feel kind of the same way." said Cam. "But until this is over, I won't take the chance of putting her at risk. God knows I've pulled you too far into this as well." "Don't you even think about worrying about me," said Doc. "I jumped into the aware there would be some challenges; maybe not to this level, but I'm a big boy and can handle my side of the game." They talked and enjoyed each other's company for the next twenty minutes or so. As they were sitting there, Doc looked out the window and said, "Cam, there has been a guy sitting in a white car across the street the entire time we've been here. Think it's anything?" "Could be," said Cam, "before you go home from here, drive around an obscure way home to make sure you're not being followed. I'll do the same. If someone is tailing you, give me a call and we'll talk about it. My bet is that they are just keeping tabs on us." "You're probably right, but after the invasion of our home, I now have a concealed carry permit and carry a weapon with me most of the time now," said Doc. "How's Susi with that?" Cam asked. "There was a time that she would have had a problem with it; but not now," Doc replied. "Well, you stay safe and let me know if anything difference comes up."

Cam continued to be careful at his actions during his last week at CatGenus. As the week progressed, he coordinated his activities with Scott to make certain that his work was passed on to the remainder of the team. As he finished out his final day at CatGenus, everyone stopped at his celebration party they had put together for him. "Well, what are you plans now, old man?" asked Scott. "Scott, I think that I'm going to take some time off and relax a bit. I have appreciated working with you and the others, but I have not taken much time away and a little R&R is welcomed," said Cam as he shook Scott's hand. "Good luck to you Cam," Scott said as he was leaving. Everyone pretty much had gone with the exception of Mark and Greg. Each of them was giving him a hand at packing up his books and paraphernalia. "Cam, I wish you the best," said Mark. "If there is ever anything that I can do for you, please let me know." "Thanks Mark," said Cam. "I will do that." "Cam, best of luck to you with the upcoming certification test. I'm certain you'll do well and pass it with flying colors," said Greg as he extended his hand to shake. "Good luck to you my friend." "Thanks Greg. I'll keep in touch," said Cam as he reached out to return the gesture. "Since you passed your certification test a while back, I'll touch bases with you soon after I take some time off to pick you brain about the test. I hope your decision to stay on at CatGenus works out for you and your family," said Cam. "Thanks Buddy; I'm looking forward to your call. Yah, the job they offered me here was sweet and I couldn't pass it up and I couldn't see uprooting the family, so staying here works for now," said Greg as he put a few more things in a box. Cam stopped for a minute and looked around. The lab wasn't as big as it was when he first arrived. He had learned a great deal while here, some good, some not so good. However, he was moving on in his career and he looked forward to becoming board certified; to correcting what the leadership at CatGenus had started, and to getting on with his life. "Cam, is there a girl in your life?" asked Greg as he walked toward Cam's car. "Yes, there is one in particular." "Good," Greg said. "I hope things work out for you and her. I want you to know that if there is ever anything I can do for you or help on any projects, just let me know." "Will do Greg. I will hook up with you down the road about collecting the information sent to the post office box. Thanks for everything." They deposited his things in Cam's car and they said their final goodbyes as he prepared to head for Kokomo. His belongings at the apartment had been boxed up and the moving company who should have delivered them by now to his new apartment in town. His mother and father were orchestrating the move on their end so when he arrived, most everything would be fairly well set up. He looked forward to spending time with them. With the upcoming freedom, he should have more time to do this.

Cam stopped and looked up at the CatGenus building. He had come here with high hopes and had definitely grown as a professional and person, but also as an adult to the ways of business and had a better understanding of the web of our society. He looked up at the impressive building and saw a man up in one of the higher floors looking out of the window. It was too high to discern who it was, but Cam had an idea of whom it might be. He got in his car and zoomed off to his next step in life.

A little R&R and then prep for the certification exam; something he was not really looking forward to. As he drove down the road, he began to consider his new found freedom and the realization that he might have time to spend with Ali and begin reconnecting. His plans however were interrupted by the ringing of his phone. "Hello," he said after bringing the phone to his ear. "Cam!" shouted the person on the phone. "It's Andrew. I got it! I got it!" he shouted. "You mean you worked out the antidote and it's effective?" said Cam enthusiastically. "Yes!" Andrew shouted. "Not only does it work, but once administered, the effects of Oboedīre any totally gone! Isn't it great?" Andrew said. "Wow! I can't believe it!" cried Cam. "Andrew, you are a genius!" "It is a combination of medications and you were right about that one drug category. With some tweaking, I figured it out. Can we get together sometime soon?" Andrew asked. "Andrew, your timing couldn't be more perfect. I just had my last day at CatGenus, so it's more up to you when we can get together. I don't have a schedule to follow anymore; at least for the time being," said Cam proudly. "Great!" said Andrew. "How about coming over this Tuesday or Wednesday? My day's light and so we could meet in the afternoon. I'm sure we can use the lab. Also, considering the weight of this, it might be better for us to not be on a deserted campus, if you know what I mean. How about Tuesday?" "I'd like to bring someone with me if you don't mind. He's been involved in the past with this and I think he would appreciate seeing this," said Cam. "Tuesday's fine with me. As far as your friend is concerned, as long as you are OK with him being there, I have no problem with it!" said Andrew. "Two o'clock work for you Cam?" "Two o'clock will be fine with me. See you then buddy!" said Cam. Cam hung up the phone and was ecstatic. "Finally!" He thought. "Now we have a fighting chance." Thoughts raced through his head as he continued on the long drive back to Kokomo; finally things were turning in their favor.

Cam arrived back in Kokomo about seven-thirty that evening. He had called his parents while on his way and his things had been moved in, most of the boxes remained unopened but his furniture was placed. Cam was glad that had been done. He was tired but looking forward to seeing everyone. As he pulled into his apartment complex, he was greeted by his family and Ali. Cam had called her too on the way home and she was excited to see him. "Cam!" said Ali as she came running over to his car giving him a great big hug once out. "Hi Ali," said Cam as he more than willingly returned the hug. His family had walked over, all saying hello and hugging him too. "Glad to see you home son!" said Orville. "It's good to be home Dad," said Cam in return. "Oh my yes," said Marjorie. "I can't tell you how great it is to be home," said Cam as he hugged them both. The smiles and the animations of the group would make apparent to anyone watching that this was a joyous time. Some tears of joy were shed that evening. They all made it up the stairs to his apartment and Cam looked around to see how they had laid things out. "Pretty good," said Cam. "Thanks for getting this done for me." "No problem," said he father. "Cam, where are your sheets? I'll make the bed for you." "Mom, don't worry…" Orville placed his hand on his son's arm. "Just let her so this son. She's been waiting for your return. She needs to do this for you." "OK," said Cam. "They are in the box marked bedroom stuff." With this his mother quickly surveyed the room, found the box and had retrieved the bed linen. She was off to perform her task. Many things had transpired since the two Robert men had been able to sit down. Orville, Ali, and Cam sat down at the dining room table for Cam to bring his father up to speed. Due to the length of this information, Marjorie was able to join them shortly after making Cam's bed. His parents were dumbfounded by what Cameron shared with them. "Cam, we believed that some things were going on; I never dreamed that it would have been this dangerous. Thank goodness someone was looking out over you," said his father with a concerned look on his face. "I know Dad," said Cam. I did not want to share this with you; the less that knew about it, the safer they were." Cam mentioned that he had an appointment in a couple of days to go over some new developments, so he would be leaving Tuesday morning after be picked up the rental car he needed. He used these couple of days to get his apartment in order and to take some time to spend with them and Ali. It had been way too long since he had spent some time on himself, and Cam enjoyed the freedom he was experiencing.

Cam and Doc arrived at Smith's State around one-thirty after an uneventful drive from Kokomo. After hearing what Cam had to share concerning the possibility of an antidote, Doc cleared his calendar to attend. The time driving over seemed faster than anticipated to Cam; probably because he and Doc conversed the whole way over; about the situation, about individual concerns about the safety for everyone involved, and about Ali. Cam really missed her and looked forward to a time when all of this intrigue and concern would be a thing of the past. The Smith's State campus was alive with activity since classes were in session. Due to this they had trouble finding a parking space and one that they would not have to worry about getting a parking ticket. Students were migrating between buildings with their load of books, some sitting on benches or at tables studying due to thee nice weather. Most had their heads down, lost in either their smartphone or tablet land. As they were heading to the lab, Cam commented, "Doc, I know that I'm not that old, but these guys look like we ought to be on a high school campus. It's hard to believe that I once looked that young." "If that's how you feel, how do you think I feel?" said Doc incredulously. Both men laughed and continued on their way. It wasn't a far walk and they arrived shortly at the building where Andrew had directed them to. "Andrew said he would be in room 163," as they walked down the hall. Turning right, they found their room, four doors down from the corner. As they entered the room, there was a commotion toward the back. As Cam and Doc approached, they could hear laughter and a slight commotion. Peeking around one of the students, Cam could see a cat; the cat was playing a memory matching game, with Andrew sitting on the floor holding the device. The students surrounding the scene were astounded by the cat's accuracy and its willingness to maintain his focus on the task. Andrew looked up and on seeing Cam he waved and told the group, "Alright everyone, show's over. I have some things to do. Have a great day." Andrew turned off the game and he told the cat to jump up on the countertop. The students slowly dispersed, many taking a moment to pet the talented feline before leaving. After a couple of moments, Cam and Doc were able to connect with Andrew. "Andrew, you remember Doc Hughes, don't you?" said Cam. "Of course I do! How have you been Doc. Long time, no see," said the young Vet. "It has been a long time Andrew," said Doc. "So, you're a Vet now. How wonderful!" After a short period of the two catching up, Andrew directed them over to the countertop where Shadow was. The last student had finally left the room so it was time for Andrew to demonstrate his mixture. Andrew named him Shadow due to cat's habit of always staying with him all of the time. The gray cat sat patiently on the side of the counter looking at the three men as though he were wanted to be included in the conversation. On coming up to him, Doc reached out and petted the cat, who continued to sit motionless on the counter.

"You know, something came to me the other night," Andrew said as Doc continued to pet Shadow. "You remember those two guys in Vegas with the trained tiger act? Remember one of them got pretty chewed up by one of the tigers?" "Yes, I remember them," said Doc. "I bet the one guy really would have liked to have had this drug before that!" said Andrew slightly chuckling. "Any way, you didn't come here for my bad sense of humor. Shadow received a dose of Oboedīre a couple of hours ago and with what you just viewed, it is obviously still effective. Now, watch," he said. Picking up a misting bottle from his bag, he pointed the bottle at Shadow and sprayed him a two times. The cat did not flinch. "Within five seconds, Shadow will no longer listen to my commands." After that time, Andrew gave a number of commands at which the cat ignored. "I've tested this over the past number of days and the effects neutralize the drug entirely. I speculate that along with the inhalation of the new agent and that through any absorption that is probably occurring in the cat's mouth, both of these situations are responsible for the fast action of this agent. We've got it by Jove!" said Andrew proudly, beaming a big smile at the two Veterinarians. "This is wonderful," said Cam. "This is so great! With this, we now can relax a bit. Everyone's safer now and we now have something to finally use in our favor. Now we can look toward proceeding with combating this predicament through other means." "Thank God!" said Doc. "This whole thing has turned into some kind of a nightmare and I'm glad we're starting to wake up from it."

The three continued to discuss Andrew's work and the composition of the agent he developed. He had brought his personal laptop with him; the wireless connection had been turned off for safety. He provided a detailed explanation of his steps in developing this new agent and its chemical composition. Due to the steps these people have taken, Cam made it very clear that everyone associated with this situation must have a supply of this antidote and carry it with them at all times. The people associated with this illicit use have shown their ruthlessness and will stop at nothing to keep them from succeeding at squelching their efforts toward eliminating the use of Oboedīre for perverse reasons under the guise of national security. Andrew took a plastic bag from his shoulder bag and handed them eight pocket-sized spray bottles. "Here you go fellas. I thought that you might appreciate getting these as soon as possible, so I put a few together. Get them to everyone involved for their safety. Cam, here's a copy of the formula for you to replicate as needed," said Andrew as he handed him a flash drive. "Andrew, you are more than amazing. We will get these distributed to everyone right away. There's one other step I'd like you to do, if you don't mind. Would you mail a copy of the formula and your work to the address." Cam wrote down the address and handed it to Andrew. "On the envelope, write the word "freedom." The person receiving it will know that it is associated with this situation and will keep it in a secure place unopened. We still need to maintain a high level of secrecy about this and we have an alternate source of data storage. He has been instructed that something happens to any of us, that he is to mail all of this to a major news organization to blow the top off of this." Cam and Doc talked about the Andrew's work and particularly the safety aspect this new agent provides. Doc pulled the small spray bottle from his pocket. He looked at the unmarked bottle and said, "Cam, hope we don't need this, but glad to have it." "Amen!" said Cam. After a little more discussion and accolades to Andrew, the three decided it was time for Cam and Doc to head home. Both men exited as Andrew stayed behind for a while to avoid detection. Cam sighed as he continued toward home. "We're getting close, real close." The two men continued to chat on their way home about angles and possibilities toward this new development and how to proceed.

Murphy had been sitting in the situation room watching the two from the satellite feed of the drone's camera as the two men walked on campus, away from the building they had just left. This activity had sparked the interest of the senior advisor for the Navy and he was ordered to follow up. It is typically unlawful for the CIA to spy on US citizens, and the military hardly ever does, but when the topic of national security comes into question, the rules get bent. Cam's more frequent visits to Smith's State had aroused their suspicion, requiring a more in-depth assessment. "Keep digging into Robert's background. There has to be a connection to this person or persons he knows at Smith's State," he said disgustedly, speaking to one of the analysts next to him. Unbeknownst to the principle players involved in this, their homes and other frequented locations, specifically Doc's clinic, has had visitors recently. Nothing had turned up in these clandestine efforts, so Cam's movements required a higher level of review. With the principle players being closely watched, something eventually will turn. Even as the two men traveled back to Kokomo, they were under constant surveillance by the satellite high above them. Their conversation back to Kokomo was lively and upbeat, feeling a sense of relief with this new development available. Upon their return to Kokomo, everyone involved with this situation each received the small spray bottle that

Andrew had prepared for them. Each received instructions about the use and speed of action. They all were relieved to have this in their possession and would keep it with them at all times.

22

HELP

Pam called her cousin, Howard Talbert, to say hello and to re-connect. It had been a few years since they had seen each other; their family is not much different than most others. Time goes by all too quick and everyone gets too spread out today to be able to maintain contact as in days gone by. Even with the technology of today, it still takes the time and effort to stop long enough to connect with family and friends; something which is on the decline in our society unfortunately. "Howard, how have you been?" said Pam. "I've been doing great, Pam. It's great to hear from you. How are you doing?" he responded. "We have all been doing well. It has been way too long since we've talked. Are you still single?" she asked, but she knew the answer. "Yes, I am. My life is too hectic and crazy to really be able to meet and build a relationship with anyone." "I understand," said Pam. After they had taken some time to catch up on their respective families, where they were and what they were doing, Pam finally broached the subject. "Howard, are you still involved with animal rights?" "Well, yes I am; probably more than ever. Why do you ask?" "Well I can't go into any specifics, because I really don't have them, but I know some very good and trustworthy people who may benefit from your boss' help." "Senator Fryer?" he asked a little confused. "Yes, Senator Fryer. My friend knows someone that is a veterinarian and has gained knowledge of something that is involving animals being wrongfully used. He also has done research on Senator Fryer and knows he is an animal rights advocate as well." There was a pause on the phone while Howard was processing this. "You don't have any specifics?" asked Howard. "No I don't. But I have known most of these people for a long time, and one in particular all of my life, and they need someone pretty high up in the world to help them with this." "I see," said Howard. "How can I help?" he asked. "Howard, this veterinarian has just moved back to Kokomo and would like to meet with you if at all possible. Do you have any time in the near future where the two of you could meet? He's willing to meet you wherever it is convenient for you." "Well as a matter of fact, I have a meeting in a couple of weeks in Indianapolis. I think that I could work something out then if this works for your party. Hang on for a second. Let me check the dates. I'll be right back." Howard placed the phone down while he went to check his calendar, returning shortly. "Pam, I will be there on Wednesday the eighteenth and Thursday the nineteenth of this month. I could meet with him after eight PM on the eighteenth or sometime after six PM on the nineteenth. That's about the best I can do. I'm flying out early on the twentieth. I'll be willing to listen to his story, but I can't guarantee anything." "There's no doubt in my mind that he will make one of these times to meet with you. I'll call you back as soon as I speak with the parties on my end. Thanks so much Howard. From what I gather, these folks on my end have been dealing with a pretty tough ordeal," Pam said. The two continued their call for a few more minutes before hanging up. As soon as Pam hung up from speaking with Howard, she then contacted Susi with her news and asked to speak with her friend and let her know what would work out so she could inform Howard.

With their meeting having been arranged with Mr. Talbert by Pam, Susi's friend, Cam was excited but didn't want to get his hopes up too much. They had decided to meet at an oriental restaurant on the north side of Indianapolis, a place that Cam had eaten at before. Their meeting was set for eight-thirty on the night of the eighteenth. Mr. Talbert had come to Indianapolis to meet with representatives of the local universities to discuss funding challenges in education which facilitated their connecting. The restaurant Cam had chosen offered a quiet atmosphere and by virtue of advanced planning, allowed him to reserve a private room for the meeting. Pam had provided Susi with a picture of Howard to make it easier for Cam to recognize him. On Howard's entrance to the restaurant, Cam approached him and introduced himself. "Mr. Talbert?" Yes, I'm Howard," the gentleman responded. "Mr. Talbert, I'm Dr. Cameron Robert. It's a pleasure to meet you, sir," said Cam as he extended his hand to shake. Mr. Talbert returned the gesture. "Mr. Talbert, I have reserved a room toward the back for us to sit down and talk about this issue. Shall we head back there?" said Cam. "Certainly," said Mr. Talbert. "Please, call me Howard." "Alright, Howard, thank you. Please call me Cam." The two walked back to the reserved private room and had a seat. The waiter came into the room and after the two gentlemen had made their selection, he exited. "Dr. Robert, in the initial discussion that I had with my cousin Pam, she couldn't give me any specifics, but she said this issue has something to do with mistreatment of animals; am I correct?" "Yes, to an extent, but also a misuse of animals," "Misuse?" asked Mr. Talbert curiously. "Howard, what I am going to share with you is very risky for me and those associated with me. How do I know that I can trust you on this?" asked Cam. "Cam, animal rights is a subject which is near and dear to my heart just as it is to Senator Fryer's." He pulls his tablet from his valise and begins typing. "I also am involved with PETA and my local ASPCA. My desire to help animals is well noted as you can see here," Howard noted as he handed his tablet to Cam. On the tablet, Cam viewed a variety of pictures. "Those first pictures were of me helping rescue animals in the Gulf oil spill. The next shots are animals that I helped rescue from a farm close to my home that had allowed their animals to nearly starve to death. If you would like, I can pull up additional information from the agencies that I am affiliated with if you need additional proof of my sincerity." "No, that won't be necessary, Howard. I've seen enough," said Cam as he handed the tablet back to him. With this development, Cam then went through a lengthy sharing of the events that transpired over past. They continued to talk, and even though their food had arrived, the two men focused their attention toward the story Cam was unfolding and the ensuing questions concerning the past events. "Cam, I hate to say this, but sometimes some of people on our government get out of control or become too fanatical about their jobs and do things that most of us would find as appalling. Don't get me wrong, I appreciate their attempts to keep us safe, but there are ethical and moral boundaries in everything we do," said Howard. "Cam, this sounds like something that Senator Fryer would without a doubt sink his teeth into for a number of reasons. However, knowing Washington and the press as they are, other than you and the personal reporting of those close to you, you said you have something that provides definitive proof that this is drug is being used inappropriately? Without this, no one of the Hill will come within a mile of touching it." "I do. I saved this as a last item to share. You don't show all of you cards in poker until the end, and I'd say this is about the time," said Cam. He then produced his laptop and after it came to life, he plugged a flash drive into the USB port. When he accessed the video file, he turned the laptop toward Howard who then sat and viewed the horrific recording. He gasped in horror as the recording unfolded. "Oh my stars!" shouted Howard as he watched the gruesome example of the adulteration of the drug. "That's horrible," said Howard, shocked from the graphicness of the video. "How or why in the world would anyone even consider such a heinous use of an animal in this manner. Do you have any idea of who group may be involved in this activity?" asked Howard as he slid the laptop back toward Cam. "Well, I know that the CEO of the company where I completed my internship was a former Navy Seal and that a co-worker and I met with scientists from Homeland Security. Past that I can only speculate. But, why perform a test such as this unless you either were investigating the possibility or plan to use it to kill people," said Cam. Howard on hearing this said, "There is absolutely no doubt in my mind that Senator Fryer will respond to this. I will bring him up to speed on this issue at the earliest possible moment. This must stop!" Cam smiled and sighed in relief, then looked down at his cold dinner. He wasn't a bit hungry. Each man was distressed by the revealing of this material. However, Cam then did begin to come around and realize that for the first time since this situation had surfaced; that now there maybe was light at the end of the tunnel. "Give me your contact information and I will get back with you after I have had an opportunity to share this with Senator Fryer. It might take some time, so please be patient," said Howard. "That's fine. I appreciate your willingness to help with this and look more than forward to your call," said Cam excitedly. The two left the restaurant, shook hands and went their separate ways. Cam purposely left about ten minutes after Howard.

Cam left the meeting more optimistic than he had ever been. Getting this stopped for the benefit of the animals was important, but equally important to him was the safety of those he loved and cared about. His lack of dinner was catching up to him as he drove home, so he stopped and grabbed a sandwich at a fast-food restaurant. As he wolfed down the sandwich, he headed back to Kokomo, a route he could almost drive in his sleep. He knew the way like the back of his hand. He decided that seeing how it was ten-twenty, that it was too late to stop by to see his parents; he'd see them tomorrow. As he continued down the road, the traffic thinned out the closer he got to Kokomo. He thought about the night's event and how he hoped things would progress quickly. He looked in his rear view mirror and noticed a single car probably about one-quarter of a mile behind him. "I think that car has been there for a while; most of the traffic peeled off some time back," he thought to himself. "The Tipton turn off is coming up here soon, let's see." Around a mile later, Cam turned east onto the road to Tipton and watched. Shortly after he was down the road a bit, the car turned in his direction. "Maybe I'm more paranoid than I should be," thought Cam as he continued on. On getting into Tipton, he stopped at a Quick-Mart and went in, looking to see if a car passed. It didn't. So, he purchased a candy bar and pulled out again. "I'll take the state road that runs through Tipton part of the way back to Kokomo and just keep an eye out," thought Cam. Coming onto the intersection, he turned north and after a little while, another car turned his direction, about the same distance behind as previously noted. He continued on and once at Division road, he looked; the car was still there. He turned west and headed down the road, going back to the main highway. The car turned west as well. Cam decided to make sure that he was caught by the light at the highway; his plan was to see if the car pulled up behind him. The car turned off north at a crossroad behind him. Cam took a sigh of relief, but to be sure, he decided to continue on through the intersection and to turn on the next county road, which would eventually become Park road in Howard County. After being through the intersection for about three hundred yards, lights again appeared behind him. Now he was getting concerned. Not much traffic, but a car continues to be behind him. "I'll turn here on Park road and just watch," he continued thinking. The following car went through the intersection as Cam turned north again. As he proceeded north, the car turned north behind him again. "This has to be more than a coincidence. I'm being followed," he thought. He sped up to put more distance between him and the trailing car. The distance grew and as Cam passed through another intersection, the lights behind him vanished. "Whew," thought Cam. "I am being paranoid. But you know, we're too close to seeing an end to this mess, I'm going to stop by the clinic. I think that I would feel more comfortable tonight with a friend." He drove to Doc's clinic and picked up one of the cats that had become one of the clinic cats. He also grabbed a can of moist cat food as he and headed out the door. He re-set the alarm, locked the door and returned to the rental car and pulled a small bag from this wallet and opened the food for the cat. Sprinkling the sample of drug he kept with him onto the food, he subsequently placed it on the floor of the car for the cat to begin eating. The cat rested low on his feet to stabilize himself and scarfed up the food and drug quickly. Cam now had a watch cat for himself. "Smitty, jump up on the seat and lie down for me," he requested. The cat complied with his request. Cam and his friend arrived at his apartment shortly after this and found everything in order; no visitors were evident. He then checked to make sure everything was locked up.

Felling confident that his home phone was being monitored, he called Doc, although somewhat late. "Hey Doc, this is Cam, sorry to call so late," speaking to his mentor. "You OK Cam?" asked his friend. "Yes, I'm fine. Hey, I just wanted you to know that I have Smitty from the clinic with me tonight. Thought it was not a bad idea to have a little extra security tonight." "Good. We have our friend with us as well. Keep him as long as you need," said Doc. "Besides, I'm sure the apartment is lonely anyway." Their conversation was brief due to the time of night. Cam was sure that Doc had been in bed. His call was primarily for another reason. He figured that Doc's line was being monitored as well and by calling him, those listening might think twice now about visiting him through the night.

23

SHARING

Murphy had made certain that the information regarding this drug was provided to the Director of the FBI, Kels Hollingsworth. Kels Hollingsworth was the first female Director of the FBI. She had developed a reputation of being aggressive and committed to her role and was of the highest moral character which was well-known and assisted her in making difficult decisions. She instructed the agency's legal and ethics departments to review this information and to evaluate its potential use with the agency. Finally, after about three months of the legal and ethics department's review of the material on this drug and its proposed use, their reports made it to her desk. Kels asked to not be interrupted as she studied the reports carefully. She felt that this decision was a critical one for her agency and wanted to read it from front to back in one setting. Even though the reports were somewhat lengthy, she would have this review completed faster than most.

After fully reviewing this information, she made a call to Murphy who had contacted her a number of times in the recent past to offer any assistance she might need. This irritated the Director a bit, but she held her ground on making a decision until the reports were available. "Mr. Murphy, this is Director Hollingsworth. Hope everything is well with you today." "Yes, I am fine. Thank you for asking," he responded. "Mr. Murphy, I have finally received the reports I requested from out legal and ethics departments on this use of this drug within our agency. From what they have provided me, I must report to you that our agency will not be using this drug in our efforts to curb crime." "Director Hollingsworth, I am distressed to hear this news, for I believe that the benefits of use outweigh the risks when one considers the outcome," he said somewhat scornfully. "Mr. Murphy, I have made it my life's journey to work within the law to bring criminals to justice and that has always worked well for me and I expect to continue to follow this practice throughout the remainder of my career. While I can see some benefits with the use of this drug, our departments believe its use is borderline legal, even with a court order, and definitely unethical from an animal rights perspective. Again, its potential benefits are without question. Its use is not the same, so our agency will not use it," she said confidently and coolly to the gentleman on the other end of the phone. "Director Hollingsworth, I am sorry to hear this decision. Would any of the reviews from our sister agencies be worth your consideration toward altering your direction?" he asked. "No, thank you. I believe it is the best interest of our agency to continue with the course chosen." "I see," said Murphy disheartened. "Good day to you Director." With this they both ended the conversation. Upon hanging up the phone, Murphy looked at his assistant, Dale Thomas and said, "The FBI is not going to use the drug; their loss. I question whether it is time for Director Hollingsworth to find another position."

Since England was such a close ally to the US, consideration was given to share this development with the Brits. There was a definite reluctance in the mind of many that sharing this information with others would compromise the secrecy of the drug and project. After a number of lengthy debates, it was finally approved to shar with their closest ally. The CIA Director made a personal visit to the MI6 Chief with the information on this new drug. After their lengthy conversation and review of the data, it was decided that MI6 would research the topic closer. Their review of the material provided was considered promising by many. However, it had been decided to not provide the drug at this time, until an assessment by their government was completed and a definite interest was expressed. Once this assessment was

completed and sharing with leadership at a higher level,
senior leadership within the British government found the
prospect of using an animal in this manner and under the
influence of a medication would be a violation of their
laws. With that, the MI6 Chief expressed his appreciation
of the offer, but informed them of their government's
decision to not use this agent. The CIA Director shared this
information with his team. Word eventually filtered down
to Murphy who was stunned with this news.

24

END GAME

The following Monday was Cam's first official day from his perspective since he had finally become a Veterinarian. Cam had fully intended to share this information as soon as they all had come in at the clinic, but the morning was stacked up with patients and there really was no way for him to pull them off to the side and give the subject the attention that it needed. As they all finally had taken a break for lunch, Cam described to Doc and Ali about the previous night's meeting with Mr. Talbert. They had decided to go to one of the local drive-in type, home town hot dog stands where they could sit outside and share the news in Cam's rented car that he rented specifically for this occasion. "Doc, I know that this was the first meeting with Howard, but he was able to convince me of his sincerity and interest in animal rights. He was genuinely concerned and shocked at what I shared with him. It clearly angered him, especially when I showed him the video," said Cam. "I would hope so," said Doc. "How about the Senator? What does he say about his stand on this?" "He was absolutely certain that the Senator would be as outraged as us about this, but he did state that he was not able to speak for him; that he would have to share it with him as soon as possible for him to decide if he wants to act on it or not. He also stated that he could not guarantee anything, but he did say he felt quite confident that the Senator would be as horrified as us," explained Cam. "The one thing that I did was to give him a copy of the video." "Cam..." started Doc. "I know. I know, what you're probably going to say Doc, but it felt right. He said that no one on Capitol Hill will move on much of anything without proof, so I took a chance," said the young Vet as he shrugged his shoulders. "I suppose you're right Cam, but damn, what a big risk!" said his friend. "Howard said he would get back with me once he had a chance to talk with the Senator; he just didn't know what that might be," said Cam as he took a bite of his Coney dog. Ali stayed quiet through the conversation, soaking in what was being said. But down deep, she was more than worried about this young man that she has decided was the one for her. While they were talking a lone man had taken a seat a few tables away from them with his back to them and was devouring his lunch without fanfare or notice. Once the three had left to head back to the clinic, he finally left as well.

Cam began to help Doc around the clinic; it was almost like he had not left. Ali was bubbly and hummed around the clinic, a clear sign she was happy to see him back. Without a doubt, Doc appreciated his return. For a man that was supposed to cut back on hours, it had just not been possible. There had been this problem with the Huffman's horses that seemed to pass from one horse to the other that he needed to treat. He had also needed to assist Orville with the birth of a couple of calves recently. The small animal business had been busier than it had been in a number of years and so his ability to cut back was just not there. "Cam, I can't tell you how happy that I am that you are back. Susi has been bugging me for the longest time to tell people no, but I just can't bring myself to do this." The experienced Vet said. "There is no doubt that you can step into this practice and begin you career without looking elsewhere." "Well Doc, I am looking forward to being a real Veterinarian, not a lab rat as I have been for the past few years. I'll be very happy to help you here; the only thing that I ask is that I will need some time to prepare for my boards. I plan on attending a board exam preparation course sometime within the next month or two, but other than that, I'm yours! Thank you for your trust in me and your interest in my working with you. I'm honored." said Cam happily. "Yah, Yah, Yah. Just get to work!" said Doc with a little grin. Ali stood in the background listening to their conversation smiling. She had waited for this day for quite some time. Cam jumped right in and quickly became a member of their team again, very similar in some ways to the time he had worked there before, but now he was Doctor Robert and was able to offer more to everyone.

About two weeks or so after the meeting with Howard, Ali, Doc, and Cam were working on catching up on some paperwork the office at the clinic. He and Ali had reconnected over during this period and were becoming more of an item, as was noticed by Doc. "Cam, I'm glad to see the two of you kids finally being able to spend some time together. It's been kind of somber around here if you know what I mean and it's nice to see my granddaughter coming back to life." "I know," said Cam. "I really missed her, but did not feel comfortable putting her more at risk. Things are a little safer now with the antidote, but also because we have someone at a high level that is becoming aware of what in the hell's been going on," said the young man looking at the man he considers as a second father. Both smiled at each other and then they turned their concentration to the afternoon's packed schedule. Now that Cam was back, Doc now felt comfortable with taking a day off through the week and typically would take every Friday off to spend the day with Susi.

As few days later, the day had come to an end and the three were working on getting things everything recorded concerning the day's activities and restocking each of the exam rooms. All of the appointments for the day were done and they were close to going home. Ali was working on preparing bills to send out, Cam was straightening up the waiting room after he had restocked the rooms, and Doc was making some last notations in a couple of patient charts. Once they got this all done, they had all planned to get together for dinner; Cam was making barbeque ribs for the bunch. Once finished, they all were talking over the schedule for the coming day when the door opens. In walks a man who had three large cats following him in through the door. "How y'all doin'," says the man as he steps further in, rubbing his face. Ali turns to address the person that had entered. The man notes in his southern drawl that it has been a while since his cats have had a visit to the vet and thought he might bring them in for a check-up as Ali listens to him. Cam and Doc had their backs to the man, but heard the conversation developing in the background. The more the man talked, something begins to catch Cam's attention. Chills start running down his back. "I've heard that voice before," he thinks. His heart begins to pound hard. At about the same time, Doc stops as well, almost like telepathy, he sensed something is wrong. Not saying anything, the man steps back and then he turned his back to the group and flipped the sign from open to closed. "I'm sure y'all are ready to head home," says the man to Ali.Cam and Doc turn and begin to come closer to the waiting area and stop at the counter. As the man turns, Doc gets a look at his face and he sees faint multiple straight scars across his face. His heart is pounding hard as well by now. Without a word from the man, the three cats separate and each one comes somewhat closer to each of them. Both men know that this is not a visit for services; they both have met this man before. "Now I will understand if y'all can't see them now, but it's kind of important for y'all to see them; at least personally to me," he said in his slow southern drawl. "I see sir," said Cam. "We usually do set appointments, but there have been times where we have made exceptions. Haven't we met before?" "Could be," said the lanky man. "Maybe you had a tire problem?" "And if I'm not mistaken," said Doc wryly, "Weren't you a visitor at my house little while back?" "I think that's a definite possibility," said the man as he trained his eyes directly at Doc, a smirky grin starting in the corner of his mouth, staring almost like he was staring through him. Until this, Ali had not picked up on anything, but with

Doc's and the man's comments and tone, a light bulb went off in her head. Her heart begins to race as well as she looked at Doc and Cam. She remained silent, realizing, "This was the guy who attacked my grandparents!" "I think, considerin' all of the time and trouble that has been wasted on y'all, it's time to bring this game to an end. There's a lot of people concerned about who y'all being talkin' with and frankly, they think it has to stop," said the man coldly. Cam looks over at one of the hanging plants at the end of the counter somewhat close to him and reaches over slowly and as he does, the man watches him closely. "I'm sorry, I don't think that I get what you mean," said Cam. He looks over at a plant and grasps a small spray bottle and after he brushes off a few leaves, he then sprays the plant with the mixture. Some of this spray falls over toward the cat closest to him. Cam releases another spray as he lowers the bottle which hits the cat more in the face. Doc, seeing Cam is doing, agrees with him said that they almost forgot the nightly ritual which is to care for their plants before leaving. "I'm assuming that we might be staying a little late tonight," said Doc as he slowly grabs another bottle and walks around toward the plant in the window on the wall opposite from the front door. One cat follows him and as he arrives near it, he sprays the plant and then looks over at the cat and sprays it above the cat. "You know, some cats are good with doing this, most aren't," said Doc. "Sometimes doing this gives me an idea of the cat's temperament before treating, spraying at him again. Ali realizes what the other two are doing and follows their lead, spraying another plant a couple of times close to her on the counter which also falls upon the cat closest to her. "Y'all are kind of squirrely ain't ya?" said the man. "No matter, I think we've all danced long enough and it's time for the music to stop," he says sternly. Ali sprays toward the cat closest to her and the man yells, "Hey, y'all need to learn somethin'. It's because of y'all that my face is like this and it's time for payback!" He stops and paces over to the side of the room, obviously angry and then looks at one of the cats and yells, "Aggro!" Nothing happens. "I said Aggro!" repeated the man louder. The cats act disinterested and begin to wander around, sniffing the area, ignoring his command. He then looked at all three of them and then says, "Oh, I git it. You guys have figured out how to reverse this stuff. Well you sons-a-bitches! Y'all make it hard for a guy to learn a livin' don't ya?" Then he reached behind his back with his right hand saying, "Well, I guess we gotta do this the old fashion way," as he grasped his gun and started to move his right hand forward.

The next thing they all hear is what sounds like a number of vehicles pulling into the parking lot. The commotion distracted the three victims and the man and he moves quickly over toward the door, looking out. "What the hell's goin' on?" he snapped. "Don't have a clue," said Cam as he looked through the door relieved. "Whoever it is, git rid of them!" the lanky man orders. In a moment, people were jumping out of their cars and began pouring in through the clinic door, some in suits, some now coming in with shoulder TV cameras. The first one through the door says, "We're here for the Senator Fryer interview. When is he projected to be arriving?" The three each look at each other dumbfounded. Cam pulls himself together and says, "We had no idea anyone was coming here. What are you talking about?" More people push their way into the clinic, various other reporters and cameramen start pouring in. "We received notification from his office that he was slated to be here around five-thirty this afternoon for a press conference. Where should we set up?" asked one of the news crew members. As this scene continued to unfold, the lanky man drifted slowly toward the back of the waiting room edging himself closer to the door as he pulled the back of his shirt down. "Come on, boys," he said somewhat loudly, expecting his cats to follow his command. They ignored him. To the people that had just come into the clinic, this man was a non-existent entity. They were concentrating on their duties and on vying for the best spot. The lanky man then looked at Cam and stared coldly at him. Cam could see the disgust in his eyes, the tightness of his face straining against the number of scars on his face. The man raised his hand and made a V with his index and second finger. He then pointed these fingers toward his eyes and then with his hand he closed his hand he then extended his index finger and raised his thumb to give the appearance of a gun and then pointed his hand at Cam. He then quickly moved his thumb forward to imitate the hammer of the gun striking the cartridge. Next he slowly worked his way out of the door, the three cats left wandering in the waiting room that began scurrying, looking for a way to escape the growing crowd.

The three looked at each other and all gathered close and hugged each other, oblivious to the noisy crowd. Thank goodness that antidote worked and worked as quickly as in the tests. About ten minutes later, another horde of people began to pull up into the parking lot. It was Senator Fryer's advance team who forced their way into the clinic and insisted that some move out. His public affairs coordinator surfaced and began to brief Cam, Doc, and Ali on what to expect with upon his arrival. He then focused his attention at the crowd of reporters and gave them a quick synopsis and his expectations. This was projected to be a live broadcast from the clinic, so everyone did their best to look presentable. Senator Fryer was slated to arrive in about fifteen minutes. The security personnel roamed through the entire clinic and established it was clear of any concerns. This invasion of personnel was surprising to say the least to the group of three who were still trying to process what had just happened with the lanky man. Cameras and lights were strategically placed and the press was further instructed to refrain from any questions until the Senator had met the three and had made his statement.

The time passed quickly and Senator Fryer and his entourage walked through the clinic door. He smiled, waved and nodded his head at the media personnel as he entered. Howard Talbert was directly behind him and moved up to introduce Cam to him. Cam in turn introduced Doc and Ali as well. The public affairs coordinator gave some last minute suggestions and comments to the Senator and his group and then the press conference began.

With the cameras flashing, lights glowing, and the microphones thrust toward the Senator, he began, "Good afternoon, everyone. I am Senator Earl Fryer and I am here today to share with you a deplorable act that has been going on within certain governmental agencies that are using animals, cats specifically, for unimaginable purposes. You all know my stance on animal rights which is why I have asked you here today. These fine folks here, Cameron, come up here if you would; this young doctor discovered their actions innocently. This brilliant young Veterinarian discovered a new drug while working on developing a drug to combat Feline Cognitive Dysfunction. However as a result of that research, he inadvertently developed a drug that will allow humans to control cats. After taking this drug, cats will obey all commands given to them without question. That is where the problem lies. Elements within our own government have taken this drug and based upon the information that I have received, from a video that I have viewed, have utilized this drug for untold horrific uses, the likes that most of us could not imagine, all under the guise of national security. Let it be known, I am an American through and through and believe that we live in the greatest country in the world and that we must combat evil and the inequities of the world, but this situation is way beyond acceptable limits. The flagrant use of this drug for these purposes boldly under minds the values of our society and the rational thoughts and actions of the common man and must be stopped immediately.

These fine folks have gone through quite an ordeal at the hands of some of those in our government that work in the shadows. Although these people in our government believe that what they are doing is in defense of our country and our way of life, they have adulterated these beliefs to fit their goals. Let it be known wide and clear, that this subversive activity against our citizens will end as will the unheard of use of these animals and hear this loud and clear, to those that are involved, that if anything even remotely bad, unexpected or questionable happens to any of the people here or that have assisted in combating this effort, you are fairly warned that no stone will be unturned, no haven safe enough for you to hide in. We will find you and we will bring you to justice wherever or whoever you are. I will call for the convening of a special committee to look into this unimaginable situation and to date I have seven other senators that support this action, based upon the limited information we have at this time. To all of those involved, move on, cease and desist or we will impart the full force and drive of this great body to suppress your actions, wherever you are. Now ladies and gentlemen, I will take your questions," said the Senator standing erect in front of the group, Ali, Doc, and Cam standing all around him. A variety of questions surfaced from the media crowd, most directed toward the Senator and some directed toward Cam. The suddenness and lack of experience with this type of occurrence left the three shocked caregivers a little limited in their responses, primarily due to not having much time to process what was occurring. Cam answered their questions without specifics, but he did acknowledge that he believed multiple US agencies were involved. He too agreed that we must fight terrorism and illegal activities, but this can occur in a much more civilized manner than this is now being done as the result of the use of this drug. The press conference lasted for another twenty minutes.

After the Senator and the three had taken a number of questions, The Senator's press secretary stepped in to help end the press conference by saying, "Ladies and gentlemen, thank you for coming. In short order our office will be providing you with a prepared statement regarding this conference and its content. Please channel any questions that you might have to my office and we will respond back to you as quickly as possible. Right now, the press conference is over. The Senator would like to speak privately to these fine folks, so if you don't mind, please begin to gather your materials and work your way out into the parking lot. Again thank you all for coming." With that, the reporters and cameramen began to work toward meeting his request, a few tried to get a couple more questions answered, but they all eventually moved outside to prepare the remainder of their reports for the coming evening news broadcast. A number remained in the parking lot for approximately the next hour.

"Cam," said Senator Fryer, "I am so glad that we have become aware of this situation and I am more than glad to do whatever I can to bring this use to an end. You and your friends are a very brave group of people and I admire what you have done." "Thank you sir," said Cam. "There are a number of other people behind the scenes as well that deserve credit as well. I will share your comments with them as well." "You do that son," said the Senator. "I assure you that I will do everything in my power to bring this to a halt. The attacks and invasions of privacy, the hideous use of animals for God know what, and the blatant disregard for our laws requires this be dealt with swiftly." Handshakes and thanks continued for the next few minutes prior to the Senator leaving. His press secretary provided the group with direct contact information and instructions on how to contact the Senator in the event of an emergency. "I must say," said the press secretary, "It has been quite some time since I have seen him this fired up. Rest assured, this will be addressed."

All of the fanfare had died down and the three collaborators were sitting back, trying to allow the strange course of events that had just occurred soak in. Susi and Cam's parents had shown up just a little before; all were beaming about the press conference and the notoriety their family members had just received. Smiles were across the faces of most. Cam, Doc, and Ali all realized how closely they had come to death; something that would be shared with their family later. They all did appreciate the moment and the new found status and from the notoriety and help toward correcting this disturbing situation. "Doc," said Cam. "Yes my boy?" responded to aged Vet. "I think that we need to drive over to Ohio and buy Andrew the biggest and juiciest steak possible!" "Agreed!" said Doc as the two smiled at each other.

Everyone had decided to head over to the Robert's farm for a celebratory dinner. Everyone had left except for Cam and Ali who took some time to be alone. Cam walked over to Ali and taking her in his arms, he passionately kissed her, as she did in return. They looked into each other's eyes with the fixed look of love; Cam now felt as though he could continue with their relationship, something that he wanted to do for quite some time, but it was not safe, and he was excited to be finally able to spend time with her. They walked over to the car and began to get in, when Cam noticed something under the windshield wiper. He stopped and reached over to grasp the paper. He read it and it said, "You may have won this one, but we'll meet again. You betcha!" Cam looked at the piece of paper for a moment and then tossed it away. "What's that?" asked Ali. "Oh, nothing much. Just a mistake on someone else's part." He smiled knowing that they had finally won this war against the powerful machine they had challenged. They jumped in Cam's car and headed toward their future.

www.ingramcontent.com/pod-product-compliance
Lightning Source LLC
Chambersburg PA
CBHW071205250626
47159CB00001B/204